The
CUTTING
EDGE

Center Point
Large Print

Also by Ace Collins and available from
Center Point Large Print:

The Yellow Packard
Darkness Before Dawn

**This Large Print Book carries the
Seal of Approval of N.A.V.H.**

The
CUTTING
EDGE

ACE
COLLINS

CENTER POINT LARGE PRINT
THORNDIKE, MAINE

This Center Point Large Print edition is published
in the year 2014 by arrangement with Abingdon Press.

The text of this Large Print edition is unabridged.
In other aspects, this book may vary
from the original edition.
Printed in the United States of America
on permanent paper.
Set in 16-point Times New Roman type.

ISBN: 978-1-62899-120-8

Library of Congress Cataloging-in-Publication Data

Collins, Ace.
The cutting edge / Ace Collins. — Center Point Large Print edition.
pages ; cm
Summary: "On the verge of becoming a supermodel, Leslie Rhoads is
assaulted by a drug gang and disfigured with a broken bottle. Without
her perfect face, Leslie encounters more trouble as she seeks to rebuild
her life: unrequited love, thoughts of suicide, and her assailant out to
finish the job"—Provided by publisher.
ISBN 978-1-62899-120-8 (library binding : alk. paper)
1. Assault and battery—Fiction.
    2. Displacement (Psychology)—Fiction.
    3. Life change events—Fiction. 4. Self-acceptance—Fiction.
    5. Large type books. I. Title.
PS3553.O47475C88 2014
813'.54—dc23
                                                        2014007840

To Edith

The
CUTTING
EDGE

1

"Unbelievable," Leslie Rhoads sighed.

"Well, it shouldn't be," Carlee Middleton shot back, "you've worked long enough to get it."

"Still."

As Carlee smiled, the younger woman picked a magazine off the desk and walked over to the office's large window. As the sunlight hit the cover, she once again shook her head. Spotlighted in the golden haze of a New York afternoon, staring back at her from the cover was the vision of female perfection—natural honey blonde hair, a seductive smile framed with sensuous lips, a perfectly turned-up nose, deep, passionate blue eyes, and straight white teeth. The woman in the photograph was the definition of iconic beauty. She had the face women craved, men wanted, and cosmetic surgeons tried to duplicate. She was perfect—well, as perfect as anyone could be.

"I still can't believe it's me," Leslie exclaimed, the sun catching the excited sparkle in her eyes. Glancing across the city spread out below her agent's fifty-seventh floor office balcony she laughed, "Well, New York, this country girl has finally arrived!"

Carlee laughed with her, letting the twenty-four-year-old model soak in the excitement for a few moments and then, even while her visitor's heart was racing, she broke in, "A first-time national cover is always so exhilarating. I remember my first one. What a day that was!"

The older woman's words apparently landed on deaf ears. Leslie seemed far too consumed by the image staring back at her to even realize the agent had spoken. In fact, the world had stopped moving and time was standing still. Carlee knew the feeling; it was as if the best of every Christmas and birthday had all landed in one place at the same instant. And it was all because of one simple photograph.

She'd been one of a dozen models chosen to compete for this cover. None of them knew if they had the right look to get it. It was all in the hands of the CEO. The shoot had been three months ago, and when Leslie hadn't heard anything the model must have figured she hadn't made the grade. But now Carlee was giving her the proof that she was in the same league as the models she had idolized all her life!

Getting up from her desk, Carlee caught Leslie's eye. "Come on back down to earth, we have some new business to talk about." Motioning to a table in the corner of the huge office, she led her client over to a mass of clippings. Even as Leslie sat down, her eyes remained glued to the latest issue of *Fashion and Style.*

"I just didn't realize how good it would feel," Leslie cooed. "I mean this is me! Carlee, I owe you so much for getting me this."

"Well, kid," Carlee's voice was now dry, but the smile still showed on her face, "it is a start. Tonight and tomorrow you'll be on newsstands coast to coast. Your face will be on street corners and in airports. Millions who didn't know you existed will now memorize this image. Women will try to duplicate your look and men will long to find you. That's the way this crazy business works. But it only works that way if we keep working. So now we need to move onto more important things. I've got something here that's much bigger than a single magazine cover."

Leslie stopped staring at her picture and studied her agent. "What could be bigger than this?"

Carlee didn't keep her waiting for long. "Les, I've shown the folks over at Drum Media some of your work and portfolio. They loved what they saw and they've convinced one of their clients that you might just make the perfect girl for their next national ad campaign. In fact, after talking to them this morning, I know I can get it for you. It could *make* your career! We're talking numbers in the six and seven figures. It could be bigger than a dozen magazine covers."

Carlee stopped for a moment to allow the young woman to grasp the magnitude of what she had just said. As she did, she looked down into a trusting face that still harbored a great deal of innocence. No artist could have created this woman. She was simply one of the most beautiful creatures she had ever seen. In a world full of plastic, she was the real thing, a vision of what every person thought the girl next door should look like. Carlee had a hundred different models, and most of them were incredibly attractive, but none of them had what this girl did. Leslie was touchable, a bit more human than all the others. There was something about her that indicated she was more than just a commodity. In four years of working in New York, she still came across as fresh, not cynical. This business hadn't hardened her.

Just three decades before, Carlee had been considered just as perfect. She was the hot model, the one that all the men were hung up on and the girl who made millions for the agency. But the business of surviving on looks and nothing else had broken her small town naïveté in a hurry. She quickly discovered her face and body were nothing more than a product without a soul. It was time to drive that lesson home to this girl as well.

"Your look is perfect right now," Carlee explained. "I know what it's like to have that moment. I had and held onto it for five years starting when I was your age. So while you might want to bathe in the spotlight right now, Leslie, you can't. You have to be cold and calculating to make it in this world. That's what I learned as a model and that's why I'm so good at peddling what you have right now. It might sound harsh but you are a piece of meat to me."

Leslie's eyes jumped from the cover to the woman. The model knew time was limited. After all, Carlee had been on scores of magazine covers. She'd been the toast of New York and Paris. But now, despite a couple of facelifts, the years of living hard and on the edge showed. Her eyes didn't glow, not even now when she was about to have one of her models hit the real big time. Yet, it might have been more than the years, it might have been all the sadness in her life.

Carlee had been married four times, all ending in bitter divorces. In between the marriages had been numerous affairs, so many that she had once told Leslie she didn't remember all the men and all the lines. There had been pills and booze, not to mention countless packs of cigarettes. And yet, she still boasted she was one of the lucky ones. She had survived.

Moving to an end table beside a leather couch, Carlee picked up a thirty-year-old fashion magazine. She briefly studied it before handing it to Leslie.

"You know who that is?" Carlee asked.

Leslie took the publication, studied the cover

model's high cheekbones and deep eyes before shaking her head.

"That was Connie Creast," the agent explained. "We started together and for a while she made the big bucks. So did others who shared the stable with me way back then. How well I remember the names—Melody Reason, Fawn Telch, and Becca Woodcastle. Yet none of these girls are left in this business. When their looks played out, when age caught up with their bodies and faces, they were forced to look elsewhere. They were like you. This was their whole life and none of them ever went after higher educations. So all they had was a face and a body. The alternatives left to them when the camera saw their age were so degrading, they were rarely mentioned or seen in places other than cheap bars or motels. You need to know that, Leslie. You need to understand that you have to make it while you can and invest it. Even as we speak, the clock is ticking."

Carlee stared at the young woman whose career she guided. "You're different than I was when I was your age. You don't yet realize that in this business, you are not a person—you're a commodity. You have to grasp onto that fact! You have to understand that the person on that cover is not you, but rather it is just an image! It is nothing more! As long as you can separate what you sell from who you are, you will be fine."

Leslie nodded. "Does this have something to do with Drum Media?"

"This offer we just received," Carlee continued, "I can't begin to explain what it means to me to get this for you."

The agent sat down beside Leslie, grabbed the model's hands, and looked her squarely in the eyes. "For years, I've dreamed of landing a big-time gig. I wanted to place someone in a campaign that could and would catch the public's imagination—something that everyone would be talking about. This is it! Leslie, they want you!"

Carlee smiled. "This is going to be amazing! Mike Thomas over at Drum has convinced the marketing directors at H & B to use you as the central girl in the Passion Nights perfume ads. It means great big bucks and a huge amount of exposure. Probably every morning talk show in the country will want you, as will magazines and newspapers. You'll be all over the Internet. You'll be the biggest face in the business.

"Consider this. These people have been looking all over the world for over a year now, everybody has been after this job, everyone has been wondering which of the big names would get it, and they want you. You are going to get to replace Erica Budig."

If Carlee had expected to be greeted with a hug and a shout, she was disappointed. All she received was a blank, stunned stare. Rather than respond, Leslie slowly got up from the table and once again looked out into the New York afternoon. The room was deathly still as one woman buried herself in her thoughts and the other waited for an answer that she knew must come.

Carlee knew that for four long years, Leslie had struggled just to make ends meet. She had eaten cheaply, worked hard, lived in run-down apartments and almost given up a hundred times, and then, just in the last few months, things had begun to click. First, she had gotten a spot as the girl on the Buffalo Scotch ads and then the cover of *Fashion and Style*. The first two she had taken, one with some reservations just to get a shot at something big and the other as a way of living a dream. Now that it had happened, one of the biggest companies in the industry wanted her, she acted as if she didn't know if she really wanted it. Why she was so troubled by what looked like the biggest break of her life?

2

Not looking at Carlee, but rather continuing to stare at the New York skyline and harbor, Leslie asked, "Are you sure they want me?"

"No one else but," Carlee replied excitedly.

Still studying the city, Leslie questioned, "Passion Nights always uses the ads with a woman in a very sexy situation. Isn't that right?"

She turned so her agent's eyes would be forced to meet hers when she answered.

Nodding her head, Carlee waited a moment and then replied. "That's part of it. That's what has made this such a big deal and the product so hot. That's why everybody is talking about it. It's controversial, but that sells. Still, it is really all hype, no big deal. Besides, you have a great body, one of the best. You'll look super and we're talking about a huge amount of money for just a few days work. There are no real options here. This is the best thing that could happen to a model's career."

Shaking her head, Leslie quietly stated, "I've never done anything like this. I mean they wear practically nothing." In truth, they wore less than nothing.

Immediately jumping to her feet, Carlee gently put her arm around Leslie and sincerely explained, "But, Honey, nothing like this has ever happened before. This is once in a lifetime. I've been trying to get one of my girls hooked up with this company for years. This is a big shot for all of us. It is not like being in a porn magazine. It's a commercial. It's no big deal. You're a model. Your looks—your body—that's what we sell. It's all you've got. Without it, you're nothing. You have to separate the image from the real you. You have to think of yourself as the commodity. Remember, the clock is ticking!"

Leslie might have pretended she was unaware of what was being asked, but in truth she had been fretting about this for a long time. It had to come and here it was, the moment she both yearned for and dreaded. She once again picked up the issue of *Fashion and Style* featuring her image on the cover. Slowly she leafed through the pages, finally stopping and staring at a perfume ad. Handing the magazine to the agent, she shook her head. There was a model barely wrapped in a towel talking to a man. The man's face wasn't shown, but the broadly smiling woman was fully identifiable. So was almost every mole on her body. One sentence accompanied the photo and it boldly stated, *This is what my Passion Nights are all about.*

"Listen, Leslie," Carlee words were now soft and soothing, "it might be hard for you to picture yourself like this, but it's not that bad. It is just work. After a few minutes, you'll forget you're naked and it'll be easy. Just like any other shoot. I remember my first gig like this one. I was nervous, but after that, everything else I did was easy. Hey, now I can joke about it. So, don't blow this, Honey. This is a once-in-a-lifetime chance. Remember, this isn't you, it's the product you are selling."

Leslie turned and stared at the city skyline through the window. Her blue eyes were now troubled as she wrestled with her thoughts. A battle was being waged in her head and her soul. With each passing moment, it seemed that her mind was getting stronger and her heart weaker. Finally, after long moments of pained silence, she collected herself and returned to the table. When she and Carlee again sat down, she tried to explain just what she was feeling.

"Carlee, I know that every other girl in the agency would kill for this. For them there would be no hesitation. But you've got to understand, there are people back home that would—well, they would . . ." Leslie paused for a moment, struggling to find the right words. She was weakening and she knew it. Still, she had to make Carlee understand why she couldn't just jump at this chance.

"When I took the job as the girl in the whiskey ad," Leslie's voice quivered as she remembered the time, "some people in my hometown came unglued. You remember I told you that my cousin's husband was killed in a car accident and the kid that had been driving the other vehicle was drinking Buffalo Scotch. I knew that and I took the job anyway. I convinced myself, and you convinced me, too, that Steve's death and my cousin's loss really didn't have anything to do with me. It was just a job. The fact that I don't drink didn't even enter into it either. I remember you told me that I didn't have to like the stuff, only look like I did. Well, I rationalized that, and I did it.

"Now, if I take this job, I know that some members of my family and friends would be so embarrassed. I'm thinking of my dad right now. Seeing me in this state of undress would be bad enough, but with a man! And within days, the shots would be all over the Internet. I don't think there's any way I could rationalize that. I'm not perfect, Carlee. I've never considered myself a saint, but I don't think they could handle it. Back home, I'm still pure and chaste. I'm still that cheerleader from Springfield High. My dad would probably die if I modeled bras for Victoria's Secret. I just don't think I could do this to him."

Throwing up her hands, Carlee shook her head, smiled, and then in her best big sister voice announced, "Leslie, you're twenty-four years old. You haven't lived at home since you were eighteen. You're a grown woman. Mommy and Daddy don't run your life anymore. What anyone thinks back home is not important. It's you that you've got to think of first. Nobody else. Don't you know that?"

Leslie nodded her head unconvincingly. "But it's more than me."

"If you turn this down," Carlee continued, her

worried expression revealing what this opportunity could mean to her as well, "you'll spend the rest of your life as a nobody. You will be just another model who almost made it. You'll never amount to anything and never know what you could have done. But, if you take it, you'll have a chance to be a star. I never got an opportunity this big, but if I would have, I'd have grabbed it in a minute. Don't be stupid! Playing a wild woman in ads doesn't make you one in real life. People in today's world know that. The image is just the commodity you are selling. It's not you!"

Leslie looked back at the cover of *Fashion and Style*. In her mind, she knew that as a model the decision she had to make was to do the ad. She'd been looking for a career maker like this. But she could still see her Dad's face, as well as the faces of everyone she knew in Springfield, and the thoughts of all of those people looking at her *that way* caused her to hesitate.

Carlee's voice interrupted her thoughts. "Leslie, consider this. If your parents weren't around and if there wasn't anyone else but you, would you do it?"

Opening the magazine back to the perfume ad, Leslie tried to block out all thoughts except those that dealt with her career. She imagined all the things she could do with the money. She pictured the new apartment, the new clothes, and all the important people she would meet. She also imagined all the offers that would come her way. Somehow, she began to believe that if she were alone—if there weren't anyone else—she'd take this job in a minute. In fact, she knew she would.

Still, life wasn't that simple. The fact was, she wasn't alone. And while it might be easier to compromise her own inhibitions for a lot of money, there were other people who would feel the full force of this decision, too. Like it or not, she had to think of them.

Getting up from the table and walking back to her desk, Carlee pulled a contract out of the top drawer. She traced her steps back to the table and tossed the document in front of her client.

"It is yours," she explained, "all yours. Every dream you've ever dreamed, a bucketful of fun times and happiness is yours when you sign the contract. The money is all up front. It is easy, legal, and clean. Just sign. That's all you've got to do."

Picking up a pen, Leslie looked at the empty line that was waiting for her signature. Then, glancing back at the magazine ad, she put the pen down. Still staring at the ad she asked, "Carlee, how long to I have to decide?"

"I could probably talk them into a week," Carlee answered. "After all, they want you pretty badly. They're not even considering anyone else at this time."

Handing the unsigned contract back to her

agent, Leslie got up from the table, picked up the advance, review issue of *Fashion and Style* from the table and walked across the room to once again look out the window. Looking far below her, she was seeing more people than lived in her hometown. Yet, at this instant, these millions who didn't care what she did didn't seem nearly as important as the few folks at home who did. As her eyes watched a jetliner cross the sky, Leslie caught her agent's reflection in the window.

"Carlee," she began. "I don't have any jobs coming up so I'm going to catch a flight home. It's been almost a year since I've been there, and I think that it's time I go back and see my folks. Besides, I can't hear myself think in the middle of the city. I'll get back with you just as soon as I know what I need to do."

"Which way are you leaning, Leslie?"

Leslie took a deep breath. "You have to grab a break when it comes your way, don't you?"

"Sure do. The clock is always ticking on beauty. You can only sell it for so long."

"Then you know the answer," Leslie whispered. "But I need to go home and at least find a way to tell my folks."

Sweeping her blonde hair off her shoulder, Leslie quickly hugged Carlee and with strong, long strides, hurriedly exited the office.

As the elevator sped down to the first floor, Leslie didn't see the other people riding with her.

As she exited the building onto the busy street, she didn't notice the clouds cover the sun or the shouting of street vendors trying to interest her in a great deal on a Rolex. She didn't even notice a city bus rolling by with her picture pasted on the side advertising Buffalo Scotch. Leslie was lost in thought, trying to justify what she was sure she would do. As she quickly walked to her apartment, one question kept creeping back into her thoughts.

"Is it worth breaking Daddy's heart?" After all, it was really him she was most worried about. Her mother always found a way to justify everything, as long as it meant Leslie was in the public eye.

Passing by a Passion Nights ad in the window of a department store, she paused and watched two businessmen pointing at the model in the photo. She could tell by their expressions that their minds were not on perfume. Shaking her head, she suddenly realized soon she would be the figure creating all the talk. Hurrying away, she wondered if she was in the middle of a dream or a nightmare.

3

The plane roared west into the night. After Leslie had fought off the advances of two different traveling businessmen intent on buying her a drink in the lounge and finally gotten a window seat with no one seated beside her, she once again thought about the offer that Carlee had presented. In a way, it was just too good to be true. But, of course, everything had a price and it was the price that bothered her most. It was even that price that had made her fly home to fully consider her options. Simply put, she had to confront her past before she could justify her future.

If she had stayed in New York, Carlee would have quickly worn her down. In a matter of days, maybe hours, the agent would have convinced her to go for it. But this was one of those decisions that only the person having to live with it should make. After all, they wanted Leslie Rhoads, or at least the skin, teeth, and hair that surrounded the real person. And that was what had always bothered Leslie about the business. No one ever seemed to get beneath the skin and find the real person. No one seemed to care where you were from or what you did, only that you didn't put on any weight, kept your hair in good shape, and never broke out in rashes. Perfection was a look and that was it. Of course, it was a look that Leslie had been born with. It was the main reason she'd won so many pageants and been so popular in high school. Her life had always been about the way she looked.

Over the last few years she had seen a host of other "beautiful" girls look in the mirror and suddenly become dissatisfied with the way they looked. Many began to dwell on one feature or another as the reason they hadn't become the cover girl for *SI* or *Cosmo*. The end result was an appointment with a cosmetic surgeon and an attempt to improve on what most people would have thought was perfection. Of course rarely did these fixes lead to big jobs, only bigger disappointments and lower self-esteem. The fact was, a "look" couldn't be manufactured; it had to be a gift of birth.

As she thought back over all the years of hard work, beginning with local modeling for department stores during high school and college, and finally dropping out of school and trying the streets of New York, Leslie couldn't remember all the times she had almost given up and returned home because the business had become too dehumanizing and lonely. Yet, after Carlee had latched onto her and convinced her that she had "the look," she had endured all the long hours and hot lights just to get that big break reserved for so very few. And all it had taken was one person believing in her.

Except for the liquor ad, her friends had supported what she had done. It seemed her mother actually lived through her work. But it was probably because of her dad's support she had tried to maintain a certain higher lifestyle. She'd never done drugs, turned to alcohol or smoked, and even though there had been men in her life, she had not indiscriminately jumped into bed with anyone. She wasn't pure in the sense of a high school girl who never missed Sunday school, but she was a long way removed from the lifestyle that most of her associates embraced.

Probably because of her record, and the depth of trust that her father had in her, Passion Nights' offer was so hard to accept. Not only would she be letting him down, but she would be allowing herself to be portrayed as something that she wasn't. But everyone who looked at the ads wouldn't know that. They would think she was just another cheap ride. On the other hand, the money, the chance at fame, the mere fact that it was a "big" job, made her feel she couldn't really turn it down. This opportunity was what she had worked toward for years. After all, it's not like she was doing a centerfold. Yet, deep down in her heart she knew that if she had problems distinguishing between a distinctive fashion statement and a straight pinup, there was no way anyone who knew her, as well as the millions who didn't know her, would be able to separate the two.

During the more than two hours she spent on the jet, and then another hour flying on a small commuter plane, she didn't come up with a single solution to her situation that offered her any peace. When she'd left, she'd thought she was making the trip to try to convince or at least explain to her dad why she was going to take the job. But how could she tell him she had to do the smart thing when he'd likely see it as the wrong thing? As the pilot informed his passengers to buckle up, she was more troubled than she had been in Carlee's office.

4

It was already past midnight when her flight arrived and the passengers departed at Springfield's small terminal. Only six other people got off with Leslie and within minutes they all disappeared into the night. Commuter flight 646 was the evening's last scheduled arrival, and although there were a few maintenance people, whom she could hear, but not see, the airport suddenly seemed completely deserted.

Picking up her bag, she pulled out her cell only to discover the battery was dead. As she glanced around, she located a pay phone. Walking over to the relic from another age, she dropped two quarters in the slot and began to call her folks' familiar number. She'd tried to reach them before leaving New York, but they had been out. Since they didn't even have an answering machine and rarely turned their cell phone on, they still didn't know she was coming. Now, halfway through dialing the seven digits, she stopped. No reason to wake them up and make them come down here at this time of night. She'd grab a cab and stay in a motel until tomorrow. After all, it'd be a whole lot better to discuss this on a good night's sleep. So she hung up the receiver and hit the coin return lever.

The sound of the quarters hitting the bottom of the coin return and bouncing out onto the tile floor echoed throughout the empty building. Leslie followed it as it rolled around a corner and then slid under an insurance machine.

"Great," she whispered.

Returning to her luggage, she slipped her purse in her suitcase and looked around to locate the nearest exit. As she slowly stepped across the large empty waiting room the sounds of her heels bounced off the walls, hovered around the old terminal, and lingered as if she were walking in an empty shower room. If she had been this alone in New York she would have been scared, but she knew that it was nothing to worry about in Springfield. In fact, the solitary night offered its own kind of peace. Smiling, the warmth of being home flooding her senses, Leslie charged out into the fall night.

When the automatic door ushered her into the night air she was greeted with a burst of cool September wind. Walking to the curb, she glanced one way and then the other for a cab. Seeing none, she sat her bags down and waited. The silence of her small town that had brought such comfort a few moments before now bothered her. It was like she had the whole world to herself. She wanted action, but instead she was given nothing but the chirping of crickets.

"Well, kid, what're you going to do now?"

Leslie was amused she had spoken those words out loud. But talking to herself was normal behavior. She'd been doing it since she was a child and it had grown even more common when she'd gotten an apartment by herself. "So, what am I going to do now?"

Taking inventory, she quickly realized that the only possibility besides waking her folks was going back in the terminal and calling a cab company. Deciding on that option, she retraced her steps, found another quarter, looked up the number of the Blue Cab Company, and dialed. It took five rings before someone answered.

"Blue Cab," said a woman who sounded sleepy and bored.

"Hello, I'm out at the airport and . . ." Leslie didn't get to finish before the woman cut back in.

"It'll take about fifteen minutes, maybe a little more. Buford's got another fare right now, but if you don't mind waiting, I'll send him out for you when he gets through."

"No, I don't mind waiting," Leslie quickly replied, "I'll meet him out on the curb in front of the terminal."

"Suit yourself. He'll get there as soon as he can," the lady still sounded only half awake and completely uninterested in what she was doing.

Nevertheless, Leslie offered a "Thank you," but the woman hung up before she could have heard the words.

Putting the receiver back in place, Leslie once again took a look around the old building. It'd been years since she had been here. The last time was in high school the summer she flew out to her Aunt Susan's. She was fifteen. The place seemed so much bigger then. As she observed the old chairs and worn carpet, home suddenly looked tacky and old. This airport was out of touch with the real world. Kind of like the town itself. That's why it was useless to explain why she had to do the ad. No one here was in touch enough with today's realities to see it was harmless. They were so far behind the times, everyone who lived outside the city limits still had dial-up, if they had Internet service at all. Coming upon a gum machine, she rummaged in her purse for a nickel. Finding one, she dropped it into the slot, pushed the lever, and waited. Nothing came out.

"Great," she muttered. It was obviously not her night.

Out of the corner of her eye she noted something she had not seen the first time she had walked through the terminal. In a closed lounge, now only lighted by flickering neon signs, hung a huge Buffalo Scotch poster displaying her smiling face. It was at least four times life-size. Setting her bag in a chair, she walked over to the lounge's window to take a closer look, but before she got there, another fresher image caught her eye. Stacked on an overflowing newsstand in another closed shop were a couple of dozen new copies of *Fashion and Style*.

5

"It's out," she whispered to no one. How did these people get it so fast? A small, hand-lettered sign was taped to the wall above the magazines. Moving closer, she read the words.

SPRINGFIELD'S OWN LESLIE RHOADS ON *FASHION AND STYLE*'S COVER. LIMIT TWO MAGAZINES PER CUSTOMER.

Smiling, she stood in front of the closed door for several minutes hoping that someone would walk into the building, look at the cover, and then her, and make the connection. It could be a janitor or maid, she didn't care, she just wanted to have somebody stop, notice, and recognize her. When no one came, she finally moved back to the place where she had dropped her bag. Taking a seat, she got out her own copy of the magazine and studied the picture that was evidently so important to this town. After a few minutes, a broad smile crossed her face, followed by a little giggle. The thought of being a celebrity in her hometown was one she enjoyed a great deal. If she did the perfume ad she would be a celebrity everywhere. That thought suddenly appealed to her even more. Fame and fortune were headed her way.

"This is so neat," she whispered, not just talking to herself again, but answering, too. "Come on, kid, there has to be a better word than that. I mean that sounds like something you would have said when you were thirteen."

Suddenly realizing she was again speaking aloud, Leslie glanced all around her to make sure she was alone. Satisfied she was, she dropped the magazine back into her bag and checked her watch. It had been ten minutes since she'd called.

Getting up and stretching, she once again picked up her bag and headed toward the exit. She was more than ready to find a motel and a bed. Once outside, she dropped the stuffed bag on the curb and looked toward town to see if any cars were lighting up the road. But as the minutes dragged by with still no cab, it began to appear that Buford was never going to get there. She'd almost given up and trudged back into the tiny terminal when she spied a set of lights leave the main road and turn into the airport parking lot.

"Finally," she breathed, picking up her bag.

The car that pulled up to the curb was white, had no light on the top, and had nothing written on its door. If this had been New York Leslie would have thought it strange and backed off, but in little Springfield it was probably what all the Blue Cabs looked like. The old sedan's windows were tinted, preventing her from being able to see in and probably Buford's way of beating the summer heat. Taking a step toward the curb, she reached for the back door handle, but before she could grab the handle, the door jerked open. In a split-second, a man jumped out of the back seat, grabbed her, and shoved her into the middle of the car. Before she could even look up, some-one got in beside her, slammed the door, and the car sped off.

"What the . . ." but before Leslie could finish her question, someone shined a flashlight directly into her face. The light made it impossible for her to see anything.

"OK, lady," the voice was that of a male on the passenger side of the front seat, "give me your purse."

"I don't know where it is," she gasped, her hands searching the seat beside her. As she felt the corner of her suitcase sitting on the floor-board, she hurriedly burst out, "It's in my bag!"

The reality of what was happening began to sink in. She was in trouble and there were no options.

A person sitting directly on her left pulled the bulging leather suitcase off the floor and opened it. Tossing a pile of clothes into Leslie's lap, he finally found her purse. Grabbing it, he pitched it to the person with the flashlight. Leslie could hear the man going through it as the car left the airport parking lot and headed for town.

"Is this all the money you got lady?" a voice asked after a quick search.

"How much is there?" the man on her left demanded of the first man.

"A couple of hundred and some credit cards. Not a real good haul. Did you find anything else in the bags?"

"Naw, just a bunch of clothes and stuff. Nothing worth pawning."

Keeping the light directly in her eyes, the man who had gone through her purse barked to the driver. "OK, when we get to a crossroads, stop. Just make sure no cars are coming. We can't afford to be seen.

"Now lady, when we let you out, you lie down in the ditch for five minutes. Then you can get up and flag somebody down. If you get up and try to see us—we'll shoot you. Do you understand?"

Leslie nodded.

"Hey, look at this," the one on her right hollered pulling the magazine off the top of the clothes that had been thrown in Leslie's lap. "It's her, isn't it?"

The flashlight man grabbed the magazine, shined the light on it and then Leslie, and uttered, "Well, we got ourselves a star here, boys. Jim, drive on into town and find a good quiet place. We'd better look this number over real close. She's bound to have some more stuff on her."

As the car sped into town the man who did all the talking looked through Leslie's purse again. After he'd finished, he began to question her.

"Where do you keep your drugs?"

"I don't use them," she quickly responded.

"Sure," the inflection in his voice told Leslie that he didn't believe her. "I'm not stupid. I've heard the stories. I know that all you models do junk. Now where did you hide yours?"

"Honest," Leslie angrily snapped back, "I don't do drugs. You can search all you want to, but you're not going to find any."

"Hey Jake," the driver informed the man obviously in charge. "The alley behind the old Wilburn Building is up ahead. No one is ever in there. How about parking there?"

"Yeah," Jake responded, "that'll work."

Up until the car turned into the alley, Leslie had managed to stay fairly calm. It had all happened so quickly and unexpectedly she hadn't felt any real panic or fear, only anger and impatience. But now, the reality of what was going on hit her like a ton of bricks. These four men were not only going to rob her, but if she didn't give them enough of what they wanted, they might rape her. At this moment, her magazine cover was actually making her appear to be something she wasn't—rich and worldly. She had to convince them that they had her all wrong.

6

"I don't know what you think," she began, her voice quavering, "but just because I'm on the cover of *Fashion and Style* doesn't mean I'm loaded. I barely had the money to fly home. I work hard and I use everything I pull down just to live on."

"Sure," Jake replied, "and I bet you eat on food stamps."

"Seriously," Leslie pleaded, "you've already got it all. So why don't you just let me go."

"Listen, lady. I decide when we've got everything we want. You have no power here, so you just shut that pretty little mouth of yours."

The car rolled to a stop in a dark alley where three buildings joined to make a dead end. Even before the motor had been killed, Leslie was pulled out of the vehicle and roughly tossed up against a dirty brick wall. Within seconds, the flashlight was again shining in her face. She had yet to see any of her captors' faces.

"OK, pretty baby," the man holding the light was once again doing the talking. "If you're on the cover of *Fashion and Style*, then no matter what you say you've got to be loaded. Where's the rest of it? You wouldn't travel with just pocket change like this."

Leslie, now beginning to feel real fear, just shook her head.

"Go through her bag again, Jim," someone growled, "and look everywhere, maybe she's hiding it in there."

As the two men who had been in the back seat with her looked through her things one item at a time, the other two stared at her in the light. Time crawled by as the search continued. Deep down she was praying that when they found nothing, they would just leave her alone, taking the money she had brought and running, but try as hard as she could, she couldn't convince herself that they'd be satisfied with that now that they had seen the cover.

"Nothing, just clothes and makeup," one of the searchers informed the flashlight man. Rather than give up, he offered another possibility. "Of course, she could be hiding something on her. I'll search her. I'll do a good job, too."

Leslie didn't give any of the men a chance to move any closer to her. Tears now beginning to stream down her face, she blurted out, "I don't have anything—nothing except that money and this watch!" She hurriedly pulled the small gold-chained timepiece from her arm. "Here, you can have it. It's bound to be worth something!"

Grabbing the watch from her hand, the leader

looked at it in the light, tossed it to one of the others before turning back to the woman. "Not good enough, Sugar, let's see the rest."

"I tell you," Leslie's words were now coming out in between small sobs, "I don't have anything. You've got it all."

For a few moments, no one moved or said anything. Pulling a bottle from his coat pocket, one of them took a long draw, and then passed it on to the one they called Jake. Taking the last swig in the fifth, he threw the empty at Leslie's feet. The bottom broke off as it smacked the wall, rebounding off the brick and hitting the side of her shoe. Glancing down, she could see it slowly spinning beside her foot. Even in the dim light, she recognized a buffalo on the label. So this is the customer she was selling to. Classy group!

"Well, baby," Jake was speaking for the group, "you'd better come up with a way to make this little job more profitable or we might have to do something that none of us want to do."

After taking a deep breath in an effort to steady herself, in as slow and calm a voice as she could manage, Leslie said, "I just don't have any more. Even the earrings I'm wearing are fake."

Jumping quickly forward, Jake shined the light directly into her eyes, and screamed, "You're on the cover of this flipping fashion magazine. You have to be making big money. Now, where is it?"

Leslie, once again sobbing, just shook her head.

As she pushed her back flatter against the dirty wall, the other men began to grumble. "Let's kill her," one offered.

"That's stupid, man," another cut in, "she hasn't seen us. She couldn't make a positive ID. Let's just let her go and get out of here."

"What?" said the driver. "You want to let a prime piece of meat like this go without trying it out. You're crazy! If she can't pay with money, then I'll take that body. Let's all take it! She's a model. She'd probably even enjoy it."

Rape? the thought scared Leslie to death. She could take the humiliation of being robbed and terrorized, but not raped. Anything but that! Coming completely unglued she jerked away from the wall and tried to make a break for the open end of the alley.

"Jake, she's trying to run!"

Her long legs carried her only twenty feet before she was caught and pushed to the ground. Grabbing her by the collar, someone dragged her back to the wall.

"Now, don't try anything else, or we'll kill you," Jake warned as he put the light back in her face.

"She's a looker, isn't she?" one of the men laughed.

"And she's got some spunk," another offered.

"Yeah," Jake barked as he backed off and let the light play down her body. "This'll be worth a lot more than the few bucks we picked up."

Shining the light back in her face, he asked Leslie, "You *will* make it worth our while, won't you?"

A voice inside Leslie was now telling her to fight, to go down with all the honor and respect she could muster. She figured that when they were through with her they would kill her anyway, so why make it easy for them? She'd scratch and claw for as long as she could.

"You're first, that is if you can handle her," Jake said to the driver. "I'll hold the light, but first I want a show. OK, cover girl, take off your clothes."

Leslie didn't move.

"Come on, get it in gear. You heard what I said. You models parade around naked all the time. Take 'em off, real slow."

Biting her bottom lip, she stood silent, ignoring Jake's request.

"Hey, chick, this is your last chance. If you don't pull off those clothes now, I'll cut 'em off. It's your choice. But you sell your body all the time, so this should be an easy gig for you. You're getting off cheap."

Looking back at the four shadowy figures waiting on the other side of the light, Leslie just shook her head and whispered, "Not for you or any amount of money."

"Hold the flashlight," Jake ordered. Moving in front of her, he grabbed the neck of her silk blouse and in one swift move tore it clear to the waist. But before he could even look at what he had unveiled Leslie raised her knee and with a quick kick sent him to the ground.

Stepping forward, the driver struck her with a raised fist, the blow glancing off her right cheek-bone and forcing the back of her head to ricochet off the wall. Bouncing up, Jake stopped the slugger before he struck her the second time. "I'll take care of this," he screamed, an animal rage now consuming his voice.

"Don't kill her, Jake," the driver warned. "She's not worth a murder rap."

"Don't worry, I wouldn't kill her," Jake growled. "Killing's too good for her. But when I'm done with her, she'll wish she was dead. Grab her arms."

The two men from the back seat pinned Leslie against the brick wall. Now all she had left were her legs. Kicking out, she tried to reach Jake first and then the others.

"Grab her legs," Jake yelled. "See that she stays still!"

After thirty seconds of fighting, they finally had Leslie completely secure, completely pinned to the damp wall. Now there was nothing she could do but wait. She had never felt so helpless. She knew that somewhere behind the light, Jake was readying his attack. But she had no clue as to what he had planned. Realizing she couldn't change whatever was about to happen, Leslie began to silently pray.

Dear Lord, I don't want to die. I can take anything, but don't let me die, not like this.

7

"Hold the light squarely on her face," Jake ordered. As the spotlight closed in, a strange, almost demented laugh accompanied his next words. "OK, if a rich broad like this says that she doesn't have anything worth giving us and she's too perfect to put out, then I guess that I'll just have to bring her down to our ugly level."

"What are you going to do, Jake?" the driver asked.

There was no answer as a jagged piece of glass came out from behind the light toward Leslie's face. It was the bottle that had been broken at her feet a few minutes before and now was hovering inches in front of her eyes. The harsh yellow spot-light caught every sharp ridge—every facet—of the shattered bottle. It was so close to her face she could even smell the lingering aroma of the scotch. Slowly, Jake passed the bottle back and forth in front of her eyes. As she followed it, he laughed. With each swing, the brittle points inched closer to Leslie's soft skin. Then, the motion stopped as Jake held the bottle directly in front of the model's throat. Out of the darkness, Jake's other hand produced the issue of *Fashion and Style*.

"Take a good look, Sweetheart. Take a last look at your pretty face and just remember if you'd just done what I'd asked you would've still looked like this tomorrow."

Leslie stared at the vision of female perfection that the man was holding. For what seemed like minutes, she focused on the face that was now featured on *Fashion and Style*, and also the ads from Buffalo Scotch and soon as the star of the Passion Nights spreads. What a perfect face it was! It had always defined her. It had opened doors for her since she was a little girl. Now it seemed perfection was condemning her as well.

"Well, Sweetheart," Jake's tone was now cold and harsh, "have you memorized the details? I hope so."

As the last of his words eased from his mouth, he dropped the magazine to the ground and yanked the bottle back behind the light. For a split-second Leslie relaxed thinking Jake was just playing a sick little game and he had no intention of following through with his plan. He just wanted to scare her into submitting. And if sex was what he wanted, then she might as well give it to him. But then, in a blinding flash, the bottle came back from behind the light and she saw the jagged edge coming at her face. Jerking her head to the side caused the bottle to miss her eye and, for an instant she thought it missed her, too, but as the weapon was withdrawn behind the light she felt a warm liquid rush down the side of her face. It was followed by a sharp pain quickly working its way down her cheek to the inside of her mouth. Unable to see or move, she didn't know just how badly she had been cut, but from the angle of the blow and the uneven edge of the bottle, she guessed that it was probably a pretty mean gash.

Shaking her head, she whispered, "Well, you extracted your price. I hope you're satisfied."

A wicked laugh greeted her remark. "Satisfied? I've only just begun."

Looking back to the left, she saw the bottle coming at her again and this time blood was dripping from the bottom. Before it struck, she fainted.

8

What is that moaning? Where is it coming from?

While shaking the cobwebs from her mind, the moans stopped. Still, unaware of where she was, Leslie once more let her mind ooze back to the darkness of sleep. Then she heard the moans again and this time they sounded closer.

Wake up, kid. The day's a wasting. Time to get up and see the world. But still the moaning and drowsiness kept her just beyond the realm of understanding, her mind protecting her for a few more minutes as she sank back into a deep, if troubled, slumber.

A few moments later, when a flash of light reflected above her closed lids, Leslie once again came close to trekking back into reality, but in her mind she was so far from the alley where she lay. She still believed she was in her New York bed. It was just another morning as she struggled to find the cover and pull it over her head. A strong force inside her tried to pull her back, not allowing her to enter the reality that was too horrible to consider. That force was trying so hard to protect her, but pull as it did it was doomed to fail. The real world wanted Leslie and it was bound to have her. It was time to get up.

As she attempted to rise sudden and severe bursts of pain shot through Leslie's face, jerking her back to the ground. Crying out, she suddenly and surely realized that she was not in New York nor was she in a bed. While she still didn't yet understand what had happened, she now began to sense that the moans she had heard were her own. Letting this fact sink in, she slowly tried to assimilate the events that had placed her where she was and how she got there.

Rolling over, she opened her eyes and tried to focus, but no matter how many times she blinked and strained, she saw nothing.

What kind of strange dream was this? Why couldn't she see? So many questions and no answers!

Shooting her arms in all directions, she tired to find a light to turn on or something to grab, but all her hands touched was the cool, humid air. A sudden wave of panic—a panic not unlike the kind a drowning victim feels when reaching for the surface while sinking deeper and deeper— caused her to violently jerk her head to the right sending a numbing pain straight to the depths of her brain. And now, facing to her left, she made out a blurry light. She couldn't tell where the light was coming from, or even what it was, but at least she knew she could see something. She wasn't blind! For a moment this stopped the

48

rush of her heart and the fear in her mind. As she calmed her nerves, she tried to think logically again.

What happened? Where am I? How did I get here?

For several minutes she tried to remember—to come up with an explanation, but no matter how hard she thought, no matter how many scenarios she imagined, she couldn't put together the answers to her questions. What's wrong with me? Why do I hurt so much? This has got to be a dream, but why does it feel so real?

Raising her left arm, she attempted to read the lighted dial of the watch that she never took off, but it wasn't there. Using her right hand, she searched her wrist for it, but found nothing. Puzzled, she let her arms drop back to the pavement. Resting for a moment, she once again attempted to clear her mind and not only remember what had happened, but to try to figure out what to do.

The sound of a car interrupted her thoughts. Turning her face to the point where she had seen the blurry light, she watched a vehicle pass by the end of what appeared to be an alley. The steady purr of the engine made her begin to question if this was a dream. Now it seemed too real! But, then again, a lot of her dreams seemed real.

"OK, Les," she whispered as if she were a bystander, "let's get up and walk over to the street. Another car is bound to pass by again and then we can find out what is going on."

Using her left hand to push against the damp pavement, she tried to move to a sitting position, but before she had even gotten her head six inches off the ground, dizziness overcame her and she fell back against the street. Not able to stop the queasiness and motion, she refrained from moving for several minutes until she regained a sense of balance. Then she repeated her efforts, this time managing to sit upright before the lightheadedness caused her to sink against the wall of the building. Her breathing had now accelerated and the world was spinning even more rapidly than it had before. She brought her knees up and in front of her body and propped them against her chest, using the heels of her shoes to keep herself from falling. Turning her eyes to the left, she tried to find and focus on the light she had seen just minutes before, but even it wouldn't stop moving. So, rather than attempting to catch and subdue it, she let her face fall against her hands and once again closed her eyes.

9

For the next few moments, she drifted into a light sleep, exhaustion and shock causing her to relax and forget about the pain. It was the noise of another passing car that stirred her back to consciousness. It was also when she felt streams of a warm liquid steadily rolling down her bare arms for the first time.

Was it raining? Raising her head and opening her eyes changed the course of the flow, causing it run down her face and enter her open mouth.

That wasn't water—water didn't taste like that. As she began to choke and cough, she suddenly realized her mouth was filling with blood.

Ignoring the dizziness, she spit and quickly pulled her right hand and arm from around her knee and touched her cheek. Her fingers practically stuck in the blood that was oozing rapidly down her face. She deliberately moved her hand along her jaw until two of her fingers slid under the skin and touched first her gums, and then her teeth. Extracting her hand from the wound, she eased it farther and discovered there was another huge gash just below her eye.

My God, what happened?

Afraid to touch or discover anything else, Leslie lowered her hand back to the ground and let her head fall against the wall. When she did, a new burst of pain sent another round of shock waves up and down her face. Moaning, she closed her eyes and dropped her other hand to her side. She felt a sharp prick when it hit the ground. Forcing her eyes open, she looked down, and after almost a minute of straining, managed to make out the jagged image of a broken bottle. Retrieving it, she brought it to eye level, but the darkness kept her from distinguishing anything more than what it was. Still, sensing it was something important, she held onto it, letting both it and her hand rest atop her knees.

Hearing the sounds of another car, Leslie once again glanced to her left. She watched as the car's lights shined down the street. In an almost absentminded way she observed the vehicle stop with its nose sticking just beyond a building's wall and out into the alley. For a moment, all she heard was the soft, steady gurgle of the motor, then came the slamming of a car door. Judging the distance from where she sat to the car to be a hundred and fifty feet, she realized that if she could just pull herself up and walk those few steps, she might get some help.

Setting her heels firmly against the ground, she used all of her strength to push her back up against the wall. Ever so slowly she lifted her body from the street, her shoulder blades rising brick by brick until she had fully straightened her knees. Almost erect, she took a deep breath and once again looked toward the car's lights. Hearing a man's distant voice, she strained to try to pick up the words he was saying. Remaining deathly silent, she listened, but he was too far away for her to understand. Figuring she couldn't be seen or heard, she knew she had to get closer. Using her left shoulder as a pivot point, she painfully pushed her back away from the wall and leaned on her left arm as she faced the end of the alley. Steadying herself, she set her sights on the car as if it were a target and began her walk.

Moving her right foot forward, she managed a small, unsteady step. The jarring this simple motion created caused a fresh round of pain to shoot through her jaw. Waiting for the searing sensations to fade to a milder throbbing, she forced her left foot to move six inches forward. Again she rested. Never before had Leslie exerted such effort. Never before had she pushed so hard. And never before had she accomplished so little. Twenty minutes after pulling herself off the pavement she was only twenty-five feet closer to the car.

Propped against the wall, she once more heard a man's voice, this time followed by the sounds of footsteps on a sidewalk. A moment later, a car door closed, and then the car jerked forward and began to move.

"Wait!" Leslie tried to yell, but the word remained caught in her throat. Trying again, she managed a small noise, but it was nothing like the word her mind had ordered her mouth to say. No matter what she did, her lips wouldn't or couldn't form the needed shape. As she watched the car drive off into the night she realized she was hurt much worse than she imagined.

Exhausted and weak, she rested against the wall for over five minutes, and then, knowing that making it to the end of the alley was her only hope, once more began to edge her way along the wall. With each step she grew weaker and the pain grew stronger. Tears, caused by both her mental frustration and the excruciating agony created by her wounds, mixed with blood dropped off her face and onto the ground, and still, she pushed on.

It took her an hour to make it to a spot just thirty feet from the alley's exit. From there she could see a little bit of the street, but there was absolutely no activity. No one had come by since the man in the car. Her mind and body were screaming at her to stop, sit down, rest, but like a marathon runner who could no longer feel her body, Leslie's heart was driving her to reach the street. As the moments passed, it was her heart that was losing the argument. If she rested, she would not get back up. But did just letting life fade away really matter?

Yes! Yes it did matter!

Pushing and pivoting off the wall, she lifted her right foot forward four inches, but instead of landing on solid pavement, it found a hole. Suddenly off balance, she fell forward, her reactions too slowed by both fatigue and the loss of blood to get her hands up in time to cushion her fall. Her face struck the ground first. Ironically, she no longer felt any pain, only a numbing sense of defeat.

Looking to her left, she methodically noted the fall placed her two yards from the wall she had been using as a crutch.

"Six feet," she whispered somehow believing that talking to herself might keep her from giving up. "Let me see, that is seventy-two inches. That's like a jump—a long stride. Too long a stride. It's over, Leslie. Either someone finds you here or you die. The wall is just too far away. Anyway, you don't have the strength to stand up again."

For a few moments, she allowed herself to give up, and then, after looking back down the alley and realizing how far she had come and how hard she had struggled she began to question her own logic. Shaking the negative vibes, she lifted her eyes and stared at the street.

Her father had always told her she could climb

any mountain by just taking one step at a time. He had used that as a motivating factor after she had broken her leg when she was six. It had sustained her during the days when she thought she would never get a good enough gig to pay the rent in New York. One day at a time, one step at a time, and one inch at time. That was the secret to success. And now, that mindset would define her.

"I can make it," she vowed. "Even if I have to crawl, I can make it."

Pushing off the street with her right hand and foot, she managed to shove her body a half-foot closer to her goal. Repeating the motion, this time using her left side she picked up another six inches. For the next five minutes, she crawled along the surface covering a little more than the length of her body and in the process losing both her shoes. Exhausted to the point of once again drifting into unconsciousness, her fingers and toes now cut and bleeding from digging into the asphalt, she stopped and began to let the sweet relief of sleep flow through her system, but just as she was about to nod off, another vehicle pulled up to the curb beside the alley.

Looking up, Leslie fixed her eyes on the car's lighted taillights. Hearing a door open and then close, she listened to high heels striding steadily along the street and then the sidewalk. Sparked by these sounds and a newfound hope they created, she pushed forward with her right foot and then her left, once, twice, and then a third time. This burst of power propelled her fifteen feet down the alley and to within ten feet of the back of the car. Somehow, she'd covered more ground in forty-five seconds than she had the last thirty minutes.

Resting for a moment, trying to find a second wind, she heard a woman's voice.

"Take my money will you, I'll call that stupid paper just as soon as I get to work. They're not going to rob me like this." Then Leslie heard what sounded like a fist hitting metal. "That'll show you," the woman angrily shouted. "No machine gets the best of me."

Suddenly the sound of rapidly moving heels echoed off the concrete. Panicked, Leslie crawled another step closer to the car. Swallowing a large mixture of blood and saliva, she lifted her head and tried to yell. All that came out was a gurgle. Attempting to clear her throat, she repeated the futile action. Meanwhile, a car door opened, brake lights flashed, and the woman and the car roared off into the night.

God, I was so close . . .

And with those thoughts, the model eased her head back down to the dirty surface and slowly drifted off. Too tired to cry, she simply gave in to her fate.

10

It was another slow night and early morning for the two nurses as they pulled duty in Springfield Community Hospital's Emergency Room. In their first five hours, they'd treated a woman who'd gotten her thumb caught in a bottle and a man who developed a rash after drinking a quart of grape juice. Otherwise nothing!

"How's the kid?" Marsha inquired.

"Dawn's fine now," Meg replied. "Evidently, it was just a virus. By evening, she was a live wire again. There's nothing like a kid to lift you up and pull you down all at the same time."

"Wait until she's a teen," the other woman warned. "There won't be many ups at all. If you don't believe me, ask my mother."

Checking an inventory chart, Nurse Meg Richards took a sip of a soft drink and sat down at the records desk. Her friend, five-foot three-inch, blue-eyed beauty who ran marathons as a hobby was Marsha Kolinek. Exhausted from boredom, she was leaning on the admitting counter, content to pass the predawn hours reading a newspaper the grape juice victim's wife had left behind when that couple had gone home.

"Did you read Dear Abby?" Marsha laughed. "I mean you won't believe this one."

Shaking her head, Meg looked up from her work, eased back in her chair and waited for Marsha to give the blow by blow.

"It seems there was this wife whose husband was a great guy through the week, but he wouldn't take a bath or brush his teeth from the time he got home from work on Friday until he got up Monday morning. Anyway this woman was tired of putting up with the flake, so she wanted to know how she could get him to clean up his act. Abby said . . ."

The ringing of a phone interrupted Marsha in mid-sentence.

"Hold it there," Meg grinned, reaching for the receiver. "I really do want to hear how this comes out. Springfield Community, ER, Nurse Richards."

Meg listened for a moment, smiled and said, "Nope. Nothing much going on here. If something doesn't happen pretty soon, I might just find a bed and take a nap."

The nurse turned back to her coworker. "Seems it's just as quiet up on the maternity wing. Just another night when nothing is happening or, in other words, it's fall in Springfield. Now, what was Abby's answer?"

11

Leslie Rhoads was pulled partially back to consciousness by a rush of cool air. Accompanying the breeze was a steady pitty-pat rhythm. Somewhere in the back of her mind, she noted both sensations, but, for a few moments, neither could yank her out of her mental hideaway. She was simply too far gone. Yet her eyes shot open and her mind jump-started when a blinding flash of lightning followed by a deafening blast of thunder rolled across the night sky and echoed up and down the alley were she lay.

Steadying her nerves, Leslie pulled her throbbing head off its resting place, rolled it to one side, and looked up the street. Noting how close the end of the alley was she resolved to try one more time to crawl forward. Rejuvenated by the rain, she pushed off with the right side of her body. The now wet surface acted as a lubricant allowing her to slide more easily. The harder the rain came down, the easier it was to crawl. Within five minutes Leslie had pushed herself to the gutter that separated the alley from the sidewalk. Her body split the gutter's rushing water into two distinctive streams, but as the rain fell harder and the water grew deeper, it soon was splashing off the sidewalk and into her nose and mouth. She almost laughed; she'd gotten this far just to drown.

Grabbing the bottom of a stop sign pole, she rolled herself onto her back. Closing her eyes, she let the cool rain pour down over her face, content that she had done all she could do.

"Well, Lord," she prayed as another round of lightning and thunder filled the heavens, "this is as far as I can go. It's up to you now." Within seconds, she fell back into a deep sleep.

12

Fifteen minutes later another car rolled up to curb. The driver left the vehicle running, quickly jumped out of the driver's side, dashed in front of the hood, hurtled a mud puddle, and raced under a storefront canopy. Shaking the rain from his arm, he dug under his coat and into his pants pocket. Retrieving three coins, he dropped them into the slot of a newspaper machine. When nothing happened, he fiercely jerked the machine's handle and let out an oath. Finding another trio of quarters, he repeated his actions with the same result.

After severely scolding the machine, he pulled his coat collar back around his neck and started to make a dash back to his car, but a flash of lightning illuminated something just to his left. His curiosity aroused, he edged toward the corner near the alley, staying under the canopy. Straining in the darkness to see through the heavy rain, the man waited for another lightning flash to verify what he thought he'd spied just seconds before. He didn't have to wait long. Soon another round of light filled the skies.

"My God!" he exclaimed, recognizing the form as a body. Too shocked to move, he just stared as another, this time more constant, blur of electricity lit up the darkness. Taking in the ghastly sight a final time, and then glancing around to see if anyone else was in the area, he rushed back to the front of his car, hopped in the driver's side, slammed the door, threw the vehicle in drive, and rushed away into the night.

Alone and unaware, Leslie lay in an ever-deepening stream of water, the rain pelting her face, mixing with blood and rolling down into the street. For now, the pain and the confusion were gone and her soul reached out to welcome a blissful release from her struggle—even if it was death.

13

The ringing of the ER desk phone caused Meg to glance up from the newspaper want ads. As she answered she was greeted by a loud humming, followed by some type of electrical interference. Hence, she could barely hear a gruff male voice.

"This is Joe Messa of the Springfield Police. I just found a woman in an alley, the victim of some type of assault. She's barely alive. My partner and I felt she was too far gone to wait for an ambulance. So we loaded her in the patrol car. We're about three minutes from you at this moment."

Noting the concern in her coworker's face, Marsha got up from her chair and inquired, "What's going down?"

Covering the receiver with her hand, Meg answered, "The cops just picked up a woman. They must be talking on a radio/phone patch— it's really hard to understand him."

Picking up a pen and paper, Meg turned back to the phone. Stretching, Marsha walked over to a point beside the records desk.

"Officer," Meg's voice was now coolly professional, "what kind of injuries have you observed?"

For a moment static again filled the receiver, then the man's voice, now a little clearer came back, "A . . . there's a whole lot of blood. She's been cut and probably beaten, but I don't know how. To put it mildly, she's a mess!"

"Where are the cuts?" Meg asked as she began to make some notes on the pad.

"Well, there was blood everywhere, down her clothes, just everywhere. Her face is bad. Hands and feet, too! Can't tell about much of anything else. She's barely breathing."

"Is she conscious?" Meg calmly asked.

"Naw," came the muffled reply. "She's not. At first I thought she was dead. But she's breathing and there's a weak pulse."

"OK, sir," Meg acknowledged, "get her in here as fast as you can. We'll be ready."

Even before the officer cut her off, Meg hit the page line of the phone and issued a calm but urgent request. "Dr. Robert Craig, please come to ER. This is an emergency. Dr. Craig to ER! This is an emergency!"

Dropping the phone into the cradle, she took a single deep breath and jumped up from her chair. Glancing over to the other nurse she cautioned, "Let's get ready for a bleeder. We'll probably need a blood type, transfusion, x-rays—a complete work-up. If the cop knows what he's talking about, it looks like we've got a touch-and-go here. We may need to call in some backup."

Pausing for a moment as she heard the thunder from the now passing storm she added, "Let's hope the cop's wrong."

Marsha hurried across the hall in to ER 1 and started getting the equipment ready for any and every situation. Meanwhile Meg rolled a stretcher to the ER's swinging outside doors.

"Meg," Marsha's voice rang out. "What have the EMTs done?"

"Not a thing," Meg hollered back, "the cops thought she was too close to dying to wait on a unit to get there. They're bringing her in their squad car. So we are going in blind!"

Talking as fast as he was walking, a young man rushed around the corner and charged into the room. "What have we got?"

Still looking out the door, Meg replied, "A woman—evidently beaten or cut up pretty badly—barely breathing. She was found in an alley . . . at least that's what the cops who are bringing her told me. They seem to think her face has been severely lacerated. That's all we know."

Grabbing the phone, the doctor alerted the lab to be ready to quickly analyze any and all tests that might have to be done and then ordered in two more nurses. Within seconds, Beth Rogers and Jan Greer arrived and were helping Marsha ready ER 1.

"They're here," Meg alerted the team as the fully lighted patrol car rounded a corner and pulled into the parking lot. "Let's get her in."

Charging out into the rain, Meg, Marsha, and Dr. Craig, guided the stretcher to the patrol car's back door. Pushing a cop out of the way, the physician jerked the back door open and leaned over the back seat. Pulling a flashlight from his pocket, Craig quickly surveyed the woman's obvious injuries then checked her pulse. Looking over his shoulder he barked at the nurses, "We're gonna lose her if we don't move quickly. She's lost an incredible amount of blood. Let's go."

Pulling her from the car, the three loaded the woman onto the gurney, pushed her past the two cops, up the ramp, and through the swinging doors. Letting go of the rolling stretcher as soon as it was inside, the doctor wiped the raindrops from his forehead and took another quick look at his patient, this time in room light.

"Get her into Number 1," Craig's head unconsciously leaning in the direction of the room. "Beth, get me a blood type and lots of plasma. We're going to need it in a hurry. Jan, find out what you can from the cops. They may have seen something that can help us. Meg, try to clean her up and see if we can find out how badly she's still bleeding. Marsha, get me her vitals."

Pushing her through a curtain and into the readied room, Meg grabbed the necessary cloths and gently began to wash the blood that had caked over the woman's entire face. Tossing cloth after cloth in a can, Meg finally exposed the first gash. "You poor baby." Just as she did, she heard Craig walk into the room.

"Doctor, if they are all like this, they're deep and uneven. This one goes clear through the cheek. The gum even had a deep gash. Look at this hole."

Glancing over Meg's hand, Craig stared for a moment, analyzing what he saw, and shook his head. "What kind of monster would do this?"

Meg shrugged her shoulders as she began to clean up an area around the woman's eyes.

"O positive," Beth announced walking into the room. "And I've got some with me."

Nodding, the doctor replied, "Let's get her started. Set it up on the right side. How's her breathing?"

"It's shallow, but it's regular."

"How much blood do you think she lost?" Meg asked.

Taking another look at her injuries, Craig replied, "Maybe four units . . . maybe more. She probably bled a great deal at first, but it seems to have slowed down some now."

Moving to clean up the patient's chin and throat, Meg noted her torn blouse. "Robert, do you suppose she was raped?"

As he felt her limbs for signs of injuries, he

shook his head. It evidently wasn't a concern in his mind at this time, but every nurse in the room shuddered at the thought.

"We'll get to that as soon as we save her," Craig then yelled through the closed curtain, "Greer, what have you found out?"

Sticking her head into ER1, Jan rattled off her report. "An investigative team is there at this moment looking over the scene. A man who was getting a newspaper discovered her and called the police . . . didn't give his name and he said that no one else was there when he was. The police don't think he knew anymore. At this point, that's about all they have."

Never once looking up while applying pressure and trying to stem the flow of blood from a large cut just above the eye, Craig replied, "Tell them to call us when they know anything else that might give us some idea of how this was done."

Finishing the injury cleanup, Meg took a moment to stare at what she'd uncovered. She noted that five different cuts were so deep that they had penetrated through the skin and muscle and into the inner mouth area. Her upper lip had almost been severed. Two huge gashes made a roadmap-like pattern beginning just to the right of her nose, and continuing into her left scalp. Another ragged one revealed the white glow of the skull. None of the cuts were clean. All were jagged and uneven. Besides the major damage, there were at least three-dozen smaller wounds.

"Robert," Meg almost whispered. "I've never seen anything like this. I mean going through a windshield doesn't do this much damage. What could have done this? This woman doesn't really have much of a face left."

The doctor nodded his head, and then looked behind him and hollered, "Jan."

"Yes, Dr. Craig."

"What's the name of that cosmetic surgeon down at the clinic?"

"A . . ." Jan went through her mental note cards finally finding the one she needed, "Dr. John Parks."

Applying pressure to another cut, Craig replied, "You'd better find him and get him up here." Then, almost as an afterthought he added, "Quickly!"

14

"Beth," Craig said as he once more looked at the injured woman's face, "start an IV. By the way, how are our vitals?"

Marsha took a quick check, reacting to what she saw, nodded her head, and then stated, "Rising. She's coming back a little."

"Good, let's get another unit in her." Looking up at Meg, the doctor, his voice now calmed by the good news his patient was rallying, said, "See if the cops have found out anything else. I want to know how this happened and if I should be looking for anything internal."

Exiting ER1 Meg discovered one of the policemen sitting in a waiting room chair drinking a cup of coffee. The man's expression was grim.

"Officer," Meg inquired, "have you got anything further for us?"

"Yeah," the policeman stood as the nurse approached. "I'm Jenkins. We got an initial report from the state's CSIs at the scene that they found a broken whiskey bottle, pretty much covered with blood. That must have been the weapon. They also found some personal belongings—some clothes, a bag, a magazine, and a purse. They haven't got an ID yet, but the bag had an airline tag giving a New York origination point and yesterday's date. So, she must have flown in last night. How she got to that alley from the airport is unknown—at least at this point."

Digesting the information, Meg began to thank the officer and then asked, "Couldn't you find out from the baggage tag who she is? That might help us locate someone who knows something about her."

"Probably," the man replied. "I'm sure that the

guys are running that down now. But just in case they're not, I'll call it in."

"Any idea how long she'd been there before you found her?" Meg's question was one that should've been asked first, but the shock of seeing the gruesome injuries had disrupted even her usually efficient manner.

"No," Jenkins replied. Then, after taking another sip of coffee he added, "She evidently crawled from the back of the alley because there was a lot of blood on the wall and the pavement there. It had dried and had not been washed off, so it had to have happened before it started raining. We brought her in at five-fifteen. It started raining at three-thirty. If she was on that last commuter flight, it got in around midnight. So, she could've been there as long as four hours."

"Remarkable girl," Meg sighed.

"Excuse me," the policeman replied, seemingly unable to understand the nurse's almost whispered comment.

Shaking her head and looking up, Meg said, "It was remarkable that she was able to make it that long having been so badly injured. It shows a great will to live."

Leaving the officer, Meg returned to the ER. "How is she?" she asked as she entered the room.

Reaching for another sponge, Craig replied, "She's getting stronger. She seems to be regaining consciousness."

71

Meg moved to a point beside the woman's right shoulder and looked down at her face. After once again studying the massive damage, she quietly said, "I wonder what she looked like."

"There's no telling," the doctor said. "Did you find out anything more?"

"Yes—a little." While still studying the injuries, Meg brought the team up to date.

"A broken bottle," the doctor's voice now showed a touch of controlled rage. "No wonder the cuts are so uneven and nasty. What kind of slime would do something like this?"

"Dr. Parks is here," Jan quietly noted.

Looking up, Craig nodded. A few moments later, a small, balding man in his forties entered the room. Noting his unshaven face and the shirttail hanging halfway in and out of his pants, Meg judged that Jan had gotten him out of bed. Nevertheless, as soon as he glanced at the woman, all signs of sleepiness shot from his face. Leaning over the woman, Parks stared at the injuries for only a few moments before signaling for Craig and Meg to follow him outside the room. Once in the hall, he offered his singular observation and then began his questions.

"That's the worst I've ever seen. It couldn't have been a car accident, at least not a normal one. How did it happen?"

"Somebody cut her up with a broken bottle."

The words projected from Meg's lips like they had been shot from a gun. Her voice was harsh, an anger threatening to expose itself on each separate word. And the more she thought about how this had been done, the angrier she became.

"How much blood did she take?" Parks inquired, while trying to shove the rest of his shirt under his belt line.

"Four units—so far."

Shaking his head, Parks scratched his head for a moment, then, after checking his watch, "She seems strong enough now, so let's get her into surgery just as soon as possible. I'll get my people here and do my best, but it's not going to help much. Not at first anyway." Then, once again picturing what he had just seen, he looked Meg in the eyes and added, "Wish I had a photo to know what she looked like before. There is damage on that woman's face that only God could fix."

"Yeah," Meg nodded, "but you can make her better. Whoever she is, whatever happened, she didn't deserve this. So, she needs the best now."

"Bring her up as soon as you can, Doctor," Parks said. "I'll get ready for you."

15

The patient was beginning to stir. By the time Dr. Craig and the nurse had reentered ER1 her eyes were open and trying to focus. Leaning over, Meg began to speak softly to her patient.

"Don't get excited," the nurse said slowly, hoping to calm any fears the woman might have. "You're in a hospital. Some policemen found you, got you here, and you are going . . ." Meg paused as she again surveyed the woman's destroyed face, after taking a deep breath to steady her nerves, she spat out what she felt was a lie, "You're going to be fine."

As Meg finished, the woman raised her hand, and upon finding Meg's, squeezed it hard. Nodding, the nurse reassured her patient, "You'll be fine. Just take it easy and we'll make all that pain go away very soon."

Her deep blue eyes never leaving Meg's face, the patient continued holding onto the nurse's hand. Even when Dr. Craig began to speak to her, the woman's focus never wavered.

"Young lady," Craig began. "Can you tell us your name? There wasn't any ID when they found you."

The patient tried to move her lips, her throat quivering, but all that came out was meaningless noise. Leaning back over her, he gently said, "Don't worry about it. We'll find that out later. Right now we're going to take you up to surgery and fix some of those injuries. You just stay calm."

Looking away from the patient, the doctor signaled for Jan and Marsha to wheel her up to the operating room. Still, the woman held firmly onto Meg's hand. For a moment, Meg thought she recognized something about the patient. As she watched her roll out of the room, she felt a tie to the victim—stronger than her normal nurse/patient bond. There was something about her. When the nurse finally pulled loose, a frightened look filled the patient's eyes.

"Strange," Craig's voice broke into Meg's troubled thoughts.

"What is?" Meg asked, still looking to the door leading to the surgical wing.

"How she took to you. Almost like she knew who you were."

"No," Meg shook her head while removing a glove, "I didn't recognize her. Who could, the way she is right now?"

"Are you sure you don't know her?" the doctor questioned. "The way she looked at you made me believe she knew you."

An exhausted Meg leaned against the admitting counter. "No, I don't know her, but my heart goes out to her. It's going to be tough to face life as she will have to. Reminds me of the young girl that was brought in two days ago."

"Dr. Craig," Beth announced as she returned to the room.

"Yeah," the doctor sighed, fatigue, both mental and physical showing in his voice.

Beth glanced at Meg before continuing. "The police are pretty sure they know who the woman is. Officer Jenkins is in the waiting room. You'll want to speak to him."

Nodding his head, Craig, joined by both nurses crossed the ER, rounded a corner and entered the small waiting area. The policeman was sitting in the corner looking at a magazine.

"Jenkins," Robert said as he crossed the room. "I'm Dr. Craig."

"Hi, Doc," Jenkins replied while getting up from his seat. "The woman we brought in—how is she?"

"She'll live."

"That's good," the big cop sighed, "I figured her for a goner. What about her face?"

"There'll be lots of scars. It'll never be like it was. Nevertheless, the important part is that she's alive. Your getting her here is a big part of that, too."

Shaking his head, the policeman rolled up the magazine and gently tapped it against his arm.

Finally, after seemingly searching for words, he began, "We traced her through the baggage claim," pointing at Meg with the rolled-up magazine, he continued, "just like the nurse here suggested. The victim's a New York model. In fact, she's a cover girl. She's even on this magazine." The officer tossed the periodical onto the chair beside him. Meg watched as it slowly unrolled to reveal the cover. She visibly shook when she saw the woman's face in the smiling photo.

It couldn't be!

Reaching slowly down, Meg picked up the issue. Hoping she'd been wrong, she took another long look. Her eyes filling with tears, she glanced back at the policeman. Her voice shaking, she asked, "Are you sure that this is the woman you brought in?"

"Yeah—real sure!"

"Meg," Craig asked. "So do you know her after all?"

Handing the magazine to the doctor, Meg took a deep breath. "That girl in the picture—that beautiful girl. That's the woman who we cleaned up. The reason she looked at me and grabbed my hand is that she knew me. She's my cousin, Leslie Rhoads. That face in the picture used to be hers."

Finding a chair, Meg once again studied the magazine cover. "I used to babysit her, even though I was only a few years older. There was a time when she and I were closer than sisters. I helped her with her makeup when she did local modeling—before she went to New York. I know her face as well as I know my own. And for the last hour I've been staring at her and I didn't even know who she was."

Looking back at the photo again, Meg whispered, "She was so beautiful. Heaven only knows what she'll look like now."

Meg dropped the magazine on the table and hurried back to her station. Sitting down at the records desk she picked up the phone, dialed a familiar number and waited for someone to answer. A few rings later someone did.

"Aunt Flo," the nurse began. "This is Meg. I don't know how to tell you this but . . ."

16

"How's your cousin?" Jan asked Meg as the nurse returned from making her afternoon rounds.

"Up until now," Meg began as she pulled a Kardex, initialed it, then returned it to its slot, "she has been so heavily sedated she's been unaware of the pain, the injuries, or what she can expect. Today, they're pulling her back into the real world and I wonder how she's going to handle it. With her injuries, it'll be a mind game more than anything else. I just don't know."

Opening a newspaper, Jan found a short article dealing with the investigation of Leslie's attack. After scanning it, she shook her head and tossed the paper in the trashcan. "Can you believe that it has been three days and the police haven't gotten anything of any substance? I mean, what are we paying these guys for?"

Looking up, Meg nodded and then added, "I think they're hoping that Leslie will be able to tell them something when she comes around. She may be able to give them a lead the crime scene couldn't. She's bound to know something, but when she'll remember it will be the million-dollar question. You know as well as I do that sometimes the shock keeps people from ever recalling a tragedy like that. If she can't, the cops tell me that the odds are the monsters who did this will never be caught."

Jan's eyes followed a rough-looking man as he walked past the nurses' station, down the hall, finally entering room 212. "That's another thing that bothers me," she complained.

"What's that?" Meg questioned, looking up and observing nothing out of the ordinary.

"Why don't the cops have somebody here protecting Leslie?" A mixture of anger and fear met in Jan's voice as she continued. "I mean when she does come to, she'll probably say something that will identify someone. So it makes sense to me that the person would try to kill her first. I jump every time anybody I don't know walks past her room."

Shaking her head, Meg tried to ease her friend's fears. "The cops aren't too worried about that. They seem to think that if whoever attacked her had wanted to kill her, he'd have done the job differently. The way she was cut up they seem to think that hurting her was what the person wanted. To them it looked like a revenge job. That's why they believe it must have been someone she knew. So, they aren't concerned with anyone coming to get her. And if you think about it, that makes sense."

Still not convinced, Jan shifted the subject. "How are her folks? I mean they've barely left her side since you called them."

"Pretty destroyed," Meg replied. "Aunt Flo in particular. You know how she was always so proud of Leslie and all her beauty titles and stuff. She put her in pageants when she was a baby. I think to Flo it's almost like a part of her died in the attack, too."

"Well," Jan understandingly answered, "the model did die. No matter what kind of magic Dr. Parks has up his sleeve, that face isn't going to work again. It'll be a whole lot different for her from now on."

"That's what worries me," Meg sighed. "Her beauty was what Leslie lived on for years. Even when she was little, she didn't play outside or roughhouse with the other kids because she and her mother were afraid that she might get bruised. Except for one freak broken leg when she tripped in the yard, she never got a scar, a blemish, or even a cavity, that's how much she was protected. She was always the perfect little lady. Kids used to make fun of her by saying that the wind blew around her, and that's the way it seemed. There was never a hair out of place. In some ways that made her pretty unpopular, in other ways, she was the Belle of the Ball.

"Her dance card . . . well, let's put it this way, with her looks, she never had to worry about having dates. Funny, deep down I always thought she seemed a bit lonely, even if she was always surrounded by large groups of people. But no one else thought that. After we got married, Steve called her an airhead because she didn't appear to be concerned about anything but the way she looked. Of course by that time she was into modeling a great deal and the mirror had to be her best friend."

Pausing for a moment, caught up in a memory from another place and time, Meg smiled a little, and after shrugging her shoulders continued. "I guess what I'm trying to say is, Leslie never had to work at being beautiful or liked. It was given to her. In some ways she never did develop very much in the way of a personality. So, now I'm worried that she never developed what it takes to go on with life after something like this."

"Maybe you're selling her short," Jan cut in.

"Maybe," Meg continued, "but I remember my little sister coming in mad one night because she had lost her boyfriend to Leslie. Gosh, Terri must have ranted and raved for over an hour before she finally said, 'If she didn't have her looks, she wouldn't have anything.' That statement has come back to haunt me a hundred times in the past three days. I keep praying that Terri was wrong, but deep down I'm afraid she's not."

17

When, a few hours later, Meg finished her shift, she convinced her aunt and uncle to go home and get some rest. With her mother babysitting Dawn, Meg took over the watch beside her cousin's bed. Looking down at the bandaged figure, she felt both pity and anger.

Why did this happen? Who could hate anyone this much? And why did Leslie come home without telling anyone?

There was no answer. At least not yet. So she let her head fall against the back of the chair. Closing her eyes, she tried to forget the present trauma and remember happier times. Soon she had fallen asleep.

About an hour later, she was awakened by a familiar voice calling her name. At first, she didn't respond, but when she heard her name a second time, she roused herself, gathered her senses and turned quickly toward the bed.

"Les," Meg whispered as the nurse rose bent over the patient, "how are you doing?"

"Meg," the faint voice came from behind a face covered with bandages. "I'm kind of sore."

Nodding, Meg smiled. "You have every right to be. You've been through a pretty rough time, but you're doing fine now."

Meg stared at the blue eyes that looked back through two holes in the white wrappings. There was such trust in those eyes. There always had been. Leslie had seemed to look to Meg for guidance and strength, and Meg had been her favorite babysitter even as a toddler. Now, even though the two of them hadn't been close in years, those eyes were once again looking to her and Meg wasn't too sure how to respond. But something needed to be said, so she charged forward.

"Your folks were here all day, but I finally convinced them to go home and get some rest. They looked like they were getting tired to me. Still, they'll be sorry they weren't here when you woke up. I hope they don't get too mad at me."

Forcing another smile, Meg asked, "Can I get you anything?"

"Could I have some water?" Leslie whispered.

"Sure," Meg responded, jumping up, finding a glass, and then filling it from a pitcher sitting on the nightstand. Inserting a straw, she placed the straw through a hole in the bandages left for just such a purpose. After a few sips, the nurse withdrew the straw and set the glass back on the bedside table.

After resting for a moment, Leslie slowly raised her arm, allowing her hand to lightly touch the side of her face. Feeling first along her cheek, she stopped for a moment, as if some kind of image had flashed into her mind, then she continued to examine the remainder of the bandaged area. Lifting her right hand to her eyes, she pulled it back far enough to note the wrappings on the end of her fingers. Dropping her hand back to her side, she looked back to Meg with a puzzled expression.

"What happened?"

"You don't remember?" Meg inquired.

Leslie just shook her head.

As a nurse, Meg had been asked that question at least a hundred times and each time the nurse had found a way to answer it while calming patients' fears and nerves. She had always been honest, but she had also known how to wrap that honesty in a package that would bring comfort and not more pain. But now, for the first time, she didn't know what to do. She had no answers and this fact must have been painfully evident to the woman in the bed.

Turning away from Leslie, she got up and walked across the room, pretending to check several flower arrangements to see if they needed water. Glancing back at the bed, she smiled and said, "Boy, we couldn't believe the amount of flowers you rated. This place looks like a garden, doesn't it?"

When she received no response, Meg realized that she wasn't going to be able to change the subject. She was going to have to meet this challenge head-on. Crossing the room, she returned to her chair. Leaning forward, she found Leslie's right hand and held onto it, saying a short prayer before she began.

"Kid," her voice was soft and serious. "You've been out of it for three days. They brought you in here very early Saturday morning and it's Tuesday morning now. You had evidently just come in by plane from New York when you got hurt. Do you remember any of this?"

Clearing her throat, she whispered, "I remember I was coming home—that is to Springfield. I came back to talk about an offer I'd received on a big modeling job. On the plane a couple of guys tried to pick me up . . ."

Before she could say any more, a suddenly

hopeful Meg questioned, "On the commuter flight to Springfield?"

Shaking her head, Leslie replied, "No, on the first part of the flight. I didn't even talk to anyone on the small plane. No one bothered me there at all." Pausing, Leslie once again placed her hand near her mouth, and then asked, "Why does it hurt so much just to talk?"

Gently pulling her cousin's hand back down to her side, Meg patted it, and whispered, "It will for a while. Don't worry about it. We'll get something for it in a second. Now, what do you remember about the airport?"

"It is kind of hazy," Leslie answered, after stopping for a moment to again study the bandages on her fingertips, she continued, "it's like a dream. I remember being alone. I was going to call Mom and Dad, but my cell was dead and it was so late I decided to get a cab. I called one and then waited for it to come get me."

Leslie pointed toward the glass. Meg retrieved it, positioned the straw, and studied her patient. Leslie was amazingly calm for a person who'd been assaulted so violently. That had to mean she'd didn't remember the attack. Maybe that was best. As she pulled the glass back and placed it on the table, her cousin continued her story in the same calm tone she had exhibited since she came out of her coma.

"While I waited, I noticed a huge poster of me

in the lounge." Suddenly she stopped, her eyes turned back to Meg, obvious embarrassment showing in them. "Meg, I didn't mean to hurt you when I took that job with Buffalo Scotch. I mean that is what the other driver was drinking when he lost control of his car and killed Steve. I shouldn't have done it. It was selfish. I didn't think about your husband or your loss. I let my own desire to further my career overrule my feelings for you. I know that must have hurt you. I'm sorry."

"Oh, Leslie," Meg answered in a comforting tone, "don't worry about that now."

"But," Leslie continued, not wanting to let the subject die, "I was too ashamed to even call you. No job is worth that. I should have turned it down."

Nodding her head as if to indicate she understood, Meg directed Leslie's thoughts back to the night of her arrival. "What happened after you saw the poster?"

"I walked over to it and then in this other store I saw a stack of *Fashion and Style* magazines." Leslie's eyes showed excitement as she asked her cousin, "Have you seen it?"

Meg didn't answer, she couldn't. A huge lump had caught in the middle of her throat. Nodding her head, she forced a smile at the very instant a tear involuntarily forced its way from the corner of her eye. Quickly glancing away, she reached for a tissue, and after wiping her eye, took a deep breath and asked, "Would you like another drink of water?"

"Yes," Leslie responded, "that'd be nice." After taking a long sip, she continued on the same line of conversation.

"You know, that cover has really put my career on the map. Carlee—she's my agent—thinks I'll get five or six more covers in the next year and I've been offered a big ad campaign. Of course, that's why I came home. I don't know if I should take it. It is not like that one for the whiskey company. This is more complicated and means a lot more work and exposure. All I had to do in that Buffalo ad was hold a bottle close to my throat and . . ."

18

Suddenly, with the thought of the photo shoot, a vague vision became a crystal clear image and present and past collided in a rush setting up a roadblock that stopped all of Leslie's other thoughts. Now there was only one scene and one reality and everything that was around her simply faded away. Like a shell-shocked war veteran, she was now back at the battle front and she was aware of nothing other than the horror that confronted her.

She felt sweat draining down her body and she smelled the damp, musty smell of old trash around. Yet, she could see nothing, only a bright light. Out of nowhere, a shooting pain seared her right cheek, and, directly in front of her eyes, a jagged piece of glass came into focus, blood slowly dripping from its broken edges and then it disappeared. Off to one side she saw an image of herself on the cover of a magazine. Then from out of the darkness, the broken bottle reappeared again, and Leslie jerked her head violently to the right, trying to avoid having it cut her face. Yet, as she jerked, she was held tightly in check and she couldn't move fast enough or far enough to keep from feeling the pain another time. When she did, she screamed.

"What is it Leslie?" Meg was now hovering directly over her, hands holding her shoulders, and pushing her back down onto the bed. But Leslie couldn't respond, she didn't even see her cousin, all she saw was a broken bottle that was coming again and again at her face, and no matter how hard she tried, she couldn't get away.

"No, God, no," she screamed as the nightmare went on. "Please don't," she yelled as she once more threw her head to the side.

While trying to hold Leslie down with her left

hand, Meg reached up and hit the call button with her right.

"No! Please stop. Don't cut me again!"

Leslie's screams carried down the hall as she tried to cover her face with her hands. Then, staring up, she watched as the bottle and the spotlight disappeared—she suddenly stood in front of her mirror applying her makeup. She was calmed and relaxed as she gently applied her blush with a small makeup pad. As the pad traced up her cheek it disappeared. Pausing for a moment, she looked back into the mirror and watched as she pulled her hand back. The pad now came out from under her skin. Dropping it on the table in front of her, Leslie glanced down and noticed that it was covered with blood. Looking back at her face in the mirror, she was confronted with a reflected image of a distorted mass of twisted and torn flesh. Throwing her hands up to cover her eyes, she saw them disappear under her skin. Screaming again, she tried to turn around and run from what her own face had become.

Seconds later, Marsha came running into the room. She stopped for a brief moment, and watched as Meg, now almost completely in the bed, appeared to be wrestling with the patient.

"Marsha," Meg shouted over Leslie's pleas and screams, "she's freaked! Help me hold her down so she doesn't hurt herself worse. If we can't get her calmed down, she's going to rip these stitches."

As Marsha grabbed her right shoulder and Meg put her full force on the left, Leslie began to fight even harder. Leaning over in front of her face, Meg began to softly repeat, "Les, it's me, Meg. Everything's all right. No one is going to hurt you. Look at me. I'm Meg."

Finally hearing the words, Leslie quit fighting and sank back against her pillow. As she did, the two exhausted nurses relaxed, too. For a few seconds, the three women caught their breath, then, Marsha, when she was relatively sure that the fireworks were over, refilled the water glass and gave the patient a drink.

"Meg," Leslie asked, obvious terror still filling her voice. "It wasn't a dream was it? Somebody really did cut my face with a bottle, didn't they?"

"Yes," Meg acknowledged, "they did."

"Is it bad?" Leslie asked, her eyes now riveted to her cousin's.

"I'm afraid so," came the quiet response. "You were cut up pretty severely when the policemen brought you in. You'd lost so much blood we thought you weren't going to make it for a while. But you're fine now."

"And my face?"

"It's got some healing to do," Meg replied, "but we are working on that."

"Why?" the model questioned. "Why would somebody want to hurt me?"

Marsha stared at Meg as the nurse patted her cousin's arm and answered, "We were hoping that you would know. None of us has any idea."

Thinking again, Leslie mumbled, "I can't really remember. I got in this cab and then—I just don't know. I remember being attacked but I can't remember why or by whom." Bringing her hands back up to her face, Leslie felt the bandages, and then began to cry. With each deep sob, her face hurt more. Marsha excused herself and returned a few minutes later with a syringe.

"Leslie," the nurse whispered, "I want you to roll over on your side. I'm going to give you something that will ease the pain and help you sleep. You need some rest now. When you wake up, your folks will be here and we'll have a doctor come by to tell you about your injuries."

After receiving the shot, Leslie turned back to Meg, and asked, "Is my career over?"

Swallowing hard, Meg smiled and evaded the question. "One of the top cosmetic surgeons in the state was the man we called to sew you up. He did his best work on you. So, don't you worry about it. It'll take a while, but you're going to heal up just fine. Now, just get some rest." Seemingly comforted by her cousin's words, Leslie soon drifted off into a deep sleep.

19

"That was crazy," Marsha announced as the two nurses stepped outside into the hall.

Meg nodded. "I was afraid she'd freak. I'm sure remembering what she remembered would cause any of us to react the same way."

"I hope this doesn't come out the wrong way," Marsha whispered, "but are you sure you should have told her that she was going to be OK? You know as well as I do that those scars aren't ever going to be completely fixed. Her career is over."

"Yeah," Meg acknowledged, "but after seeing the terror she felt when she relived the attack, and after hearing her pride when she spoke of the cover shot, I couldn't tell her the whole truth. Not now anyway. The fact she believes she'll once again be beautiful may be all she's got to live for. Until I find out differently, I can't take that away from her."

"Meg," Marsha softly explained, "you didn't take it away, but someone did, and nothing any of us says or does is going to bring it back. When those bandages come off Leslie will probably not even recognize herself. She's going to have to be prepared for that. I've met her folks, they're not going to be able to help her. They're just too close to the situation. But I can tell from the way she looks at you, she has faith in you, so you're going to have to be the one."

Marsha shook her head and strolled back toward the nurses' station. As she did, Meg sighed and turned toward her cousin's room. Before she pushed the door she said, "Leslie's not going to make it by simply having faith in me. She's got to have more than that or she'll fall and fall to a point where no one can pick her up."

"Did you say something, Nurse Richards?" a young man mopping the hall asked.

Looking up, Meg shook her head. She studied the unexpected interloper into her private thoughts before replying. In the past couple of months he'd become a familiar face. Yet in all that time she hadn't exchanged one word with him until now.

"No," Meg said with a smile, "I was just thinking out loud." After looking up the hall at the area that the man had already mopped, she continued, "The floor looks great. Thanks for doing such a good job, Jacob."

"Yes ma'am."

As the man went back to work, Meg reentered the room. Leslie was likely going to sleep through the rest of the night. Sitting down in the chair, the off-duty nurse figured she'd better grab some shuteye as well. But just about the moment she drifted off, the image of the alley where Leslie had been attacked leaped into her mind. If she couldn't shake that image, how was her cousin going to?

20

"Everything's under control," the man assured his friends. "The cops have no idea who messed up the woman's face. There's nothing to connect her to us."

The apartment was small, dingy, and dirty. Located on what locals called the other side of the tracks, this complex was home to those who were either down and out or keeping a low profile. Winos were far more common than Sunday school teachers and drugs were as easy to get as candy. To these residents breaking the law was a way of life and respecting the law little more than a front for their actions.

"How do you know we're safe?" A tall thin young man with a shaved head and arms covered with tattoos demanded. "I know the cops are digging. They've questioned everyone in the complex. Gives me the creeps!"

"I have my sources," the leader assured them.

"I can guarantee they're lost. They don't have a thing on us. Not for this or the other jobs we've pulled."

A heavyset twenty-year-old with a shaggy beard and long hair stood up. Sticking his hands into his pockets he yanked them inside out. "Nothing! I'm broke! We all are and because the cops have out extra patrols we're going to be that way for a while. If we'd let her go things wouldn't have tightened down as much. We could still be out working."

"We should have killed her," a fourth man offered. "Dead women don't talk. Jake, you're an idiot!"

The leader, fire in his eyes, rose from his seat and crossed the room with the grace and speed of a mountain lion. Before the other man could even raise his arm Jake landed a blow to the side of his head knocking him to the floor. Standing over him, Jake screamed, "Listen, she didn't see us. She doesn't even remember what happened. I wore gloves so there were no prints on the bottle. Even if she does remember, she had the light in her face. She couldn't see us. So, we are in the clear. And, if she does start to remember some-thing that might connect us, she can be killed. For the moment, we'll just move our operations to a different part of town and stay away from the airport."

"But I need cash now," the heavyset member of

the gang argued. "And that was an easy target."

Jake reached into his pocket and yanked out a wad of bills. He tossed them on top of the man he'd just knocked out and smiled. "Split this up. It'll last for a while. I've been putting stuff back for a rainy day." Turning, he glared at the others. "You need to learn that practice as well."

Jake moved toward the door of the small apartment. As he twisted the knob, he looked back over his shoulder and issued a warning, "Don't panic. This is under control. Just do your day jobs and let me decide when it's the time and place to pull our next gig. And please put yourself on a budget! Quit blowing the spoils the day after you get them."

The confident man walked out of the apartment into a yard filled with broken bottles, empty cans, and fast-food sacks. He studied the scene for a moment and shrugged. He was sure glad he didn't live here, but it was a great place to have his office.

21

Meg watched from across the hospital hall as Dr. Parks listened to the policeman's request for the third time in as many days. It had been an animated conversation, almost a chess match between two seasoned players who were not ready to give an inch. Finally, the cop took over. With flailing arms and rapid-fire dialogue he laid out what he needed. Nodding his head at one point then shaking his head at another, Parks waited until the officer was completely finished with his high-powered speech before checking the chart one additional time. Smiling, he closed the report and leaned against the hallway wall.

"OK," the surgeon agreed, "I'll let you see her."

"Well it is about time," the plain-clothes policeman replied. "I've got to know what she knows so that I can get this slimeball off the streets. We've already wasted days just waiting for her to snap out of the coma. We've got nothing and we need something. Darn rain pretty much washed away all our clues."

"I said I'd let you see her, not grill her," Parks fired back. The smile was gone as he pointed a finger at the man's chest. "You play this by my rules or you don't play it at all. If you get in there and try to pitch hardball, you could set this woman's progress back months—maybe even forever. I want you to put on your kid gloves and be real careful. Understand?"

Nodding the cop started across the hall.

"Not so fast," Parks caught the investigator with both his words and his hand. Glancing over his shoulder, the surgeon then summoned the nurse, "Richards, will you come over here? I want you to take note of everything I tell this man and then I want you to go in with him and make sure that he follows my advice."

Placing a clipboard on the station desk, Meg crossed the hall and followed the two men into a supply room. After the door had been securely closed the doctor began to speak to the policeman.

"I know that you have a job to do and I know that Ms. Rhoads is the one person who might be able to help you. So, I'll let you see her, if you don't go over certain boundaries. If you do, I'll see to it that you never visit anyone in this hospital again."

After looking the taller man in the eye, the doctor seemed satisfied he had made his point. Smoothing what little hair he had with his right hand, he continued, "We have Ms. Rhoads wrapped up like a mummy. I assume that in your line of work and with all the time you've spent questioning victims you have seen people that have had facial injuries before, and I also assume that you know this isn't the normal procedure. If you didn't know this, you do now, but I don't want my patient to know this. We have her wrapped to keep her from seeing herself until we think that she's ready to accept what has happened. Remember, this girl was a model—someone whose whole life was based on appearance—so don't dare do anything that will create more fear about her looks than she already feels. Remember, it has only been five days since the attack."

"Fine," the cop replied. "I'm not an insensitive jerk."

Parks nodded and then went back to his lecture, "Next, please remember that as fragile as our faces are our minds are much more fragile. While she wasn't raped, she was physically attacked and violated like no one else I have ever examined. This does things to the brain that we may or may not be able to change. One wrong word could be the key that warps this woman's mind forever, so watch it.

"Finally, at this point Ms. Rhoads is probably more frightened of what her injuries are like than she is the fact that her attacker is still running loose. I don't think that reality has really hit her yet, and when it does, it may shake her up a great deal. So please be as gentle as you can.

"If you understand all of this, and will live by it, you can go in now."

Captain Brian Rosatelli nodded his head before shooting back, "I have been on the force for more than two decades. I am fully aware of the fragile nature of the human spirit. I have been forced to interview men and women at moments when I would have rather left them alone with their pain or grief. Still, getting the truth is my job. So, rather than hold back, I had to push forward. And let me assure you this, I have usually gotten the information I needed without coming across as coarse or uncaring."

Parks nodded.

"And," Rosatelli continued, "I have a teenage daughter who is a cheerleader and honor student. Ever since this attack, I've had nightmares the woman attacked was my Jenny. I can't change what has happened to Leslie Rhoads, but I might be able to save someone else, maybe even my own daughter, from going through what she has been put through. Finding the man who did this is the most important thing on my mind and right now I don't have a clue. While I will try to be tactful and comforting, I will also do everything in my power to get a new angle that might solve this bizarre crime."

"Captain," Meg interjected as she stepped between the two men. "I think the ground rules have been established. Would you like to come with me?"

Nodding his head, he followed Meg and walked with her halfway up the hall to room 213. Pausing a moment at the door, Meg looked up at the officer and spoke, "I'll introduce you to Leslie. She's my cousin, and she and I are close. If I show some faith in you, I think it'll make what you have to do a little easier. She doesn't remember much—not yet anyway—but I sense by her reactions that more is coming back all the time. So, be patient. If you don't get what you need today, maybe you will tomorrow or the next day."

After taking a deep breath and smoothing her uniform, Meg pushed the room door open and sang out, "You've got a visitor!"

Looking up, Leslie first noted her cousin and then the man in the blue suit. Grabbing the remote and switching off the television, she waited for the introduction.

"Les," Meg said from across the room, "this is Mr. Rosatelli and he is a police officer who has been put in charge of finding out just what happened to you. You know he's got to be a great guy or I wouldn't let him come in here and bother you. So try to make his job as easy as you can. What I mean by that is don't flirt like you do with all the cute doctors. This guy's married."

Evaluating Leslie's response as positive and calm, Meg turned back to the officer and announced, "She's all yours."

"Hi," Rosatelli began crossing the room to sit in a chair beside the bed. "I'm sorry to have to bother you, but that seems to be a part of my job. First of all, I'm glad that you're feeling better."

"Thanks, and it's not that much of a bother," Leslie answered, "but I don't think I can help you much. I can't remember anything. I sure wish I could."

Taking out a pad and pen, the captain started

his questioning. He began at the beginning with her leaving New York. Then he patiently built her story in a slow step-by-step process. Everything went well until they got to the part where she arrived in Springfield. Then it stalled at about the same place as when Meg had first listened to the story. Trying several different ploys, the officer simply couldn't prod his subject into remembering any more than arriving at the airport. Sensing she might be getting edgy, he cut off his visit rather than frustrate his witness. Meg could tell Rosatelli wasn't satisfied, but she was glad he had the sense to know when to call it quits. The man did have tact.

"Ms. Rhoads," the policeman said while placing his notepad and pen back in his coat pocket. "I really appreciate your time. I'm going to leave my card here on this table and if you should think of anything else, please call me. I hope you won't mind if I look in on you again."

"No, come back anytime," Leslie apologetically responded. "I'm just sorry that I don't know any more."

"Don't worry," Rosatelli shrugged, "it'll come with time."

"I'll be back in a second," Meg told Leslie. She then followed Rosatelli out of the room.

Once in the hall, Meg said, "I appreciate you not upsetting her."

"No reason to," the man answered, "and thanks

for your help." Grinning he added, "Give Dr. Parks a good report on me." Then he walked off.

Looking up, Rosatelli recognized an old friend coming up the hall. "Mary Ann," he hollered, catching the woman's attention.

The attractive brunette smiled and then answered, "Well, Brian, did someone shoot you again?"

"No," he laughed as he extended his hand, "not recently anyway."

Setting her briefcase on the floor, the psychologist, a women Meg knew well, firmly grabbed the man's hand, shook it once, and laughed, "Then why are you here? I thought you didn't like any-thing or any place concerned with doctors or medicine."

"You're right," he grinned, "I don't. But this trip was business. As a matter of fact, I was seeing one of your patients."

The smile evaporating, the woman protectively responded, "If it is who I know it has to be, you didn't upset her did you? I don't really think that she's ready to be given much to carry at this time. She is much more fragile than she seems."

Cutting her off, the officer answered, "No, I didn't. I was the model of restraint. If you don't believe me you can ask the nurse," he looked toward Meg before finishing, "she was with me every step of the way."

Meg smiled. "He was a good boy."

Relaxing her jaw, Mary Ann, her tone still serious, asked, "Have you got anything new?"

"Not enough." Then, shaking his head the officer continued, "Who am I trying to kid? We don't have anything. No motive, nothing. We've just got some sicko who gets his kicks cutting people up."

"So," the psychologist probed, "you don't think that this was tied to those three or four muggings you had over the last month at the airport?"

"No, the M.O. just doesn't fit," he answered. "In those cases, all the thieves wanted was money. No one got hurt. I don't see why they'd screw up and do something like this. This is not just a simple robbery, this is real sick. It is just not like 'em. This is more like a Manson thing or maybe demon worship or something. You know the kind of thing that you shrinks deal with and cop shows like *CSI* wrap plots around."

"Well, you're the cop," Mary Ann answered. "I'm sure you know what you're talking about. And about the kind of people we deal with, a lot of them are overworked stressed-out cops. You sure you're not one of them?"

"Mary Ann," Brian bristled, not laughing at her joke. "If you get anything that could help us . . ."

"I'll call you," she assured him. "But from now on in, if you want to talk to Leslie Rhoads, you have to get my permission first. OK?"

Nodding his head the officer smiled and said, "Yeah, that works for me."

"Have a good day and give my best to your family."

Mary Ann waited until Rosatelli had disappeared before turning to Meg. "Did he upset her in any way?"

"No," Meg assured her. "He toed the line. But she still remembers nothing of the attack. And she has no idea how badly she's hurt."

22

A few minutes later, Mary Ann Cunningham was sitting beside Leslie Rhoads's bed. After the normal five-minute patter of polite conversation, the psychologist got down to work.

"OK, why didn't you call your parents to come pick you up?"

"It was too late," Leslie explained, "so I called a cab."

"You didn't mention that yesterday," Mary Ann said. "Why not?"

"Didn't think it was important," Leslie answered.

"Did you tell Rosatelli about it?" the doctor quizzed.

"No," the patient replied.

"What cab company?"

"I don't remember," Leslie shrugged.

"Leslie," she said while pulling a phone book from the nightstand. Turning to the yellow pages, she leafed through the book then stopped when she found what she wanted. "Look at the five companies listed on this page and see if you can remember which one it was you might have called."

Taking the book from Mary Ann's hand, Leslie held it up and studied the section where the cab companies were listed. She slowly examined each name. Shaking her head, she handed it back.

"OK," Mary Ann continued. "We might be able to jog your memory in another way. Your cell was dead so you actually used a pay phone to make the call." Grabbing the phone from the nightstand, she gently placed it in the patient's lap. "OK, Leslie. We'll see if this little exercise will help. Pick up the receiver while I hold down the button so that we don't really call anyone. Look over the list another time and dial each number on it. Maybe by repeating your actions, you can remember who it was you called."

Glancing at the first number, Leslie dialed the first six digits and stopped. Putting the receiver down, she stared into space for a moment, and then, as if assuring both herself and the psychologist, said, "This is it. The Blue Cab Company. I remember thinking it was strange when they picked me up in a white car without a light or any markings."

"A white car?"

"Yes," Leslie answered. "It was old and dirty white. I remembered thinking it was just like Springfield to have white cars working for the Blue Cab Company."

"What did the driver look like?"

"Gosh," came the puzzled response, "I don't remember. Then again, I never remember what cab drivers look like. I'm in cabs all the time in New York, but who looks at the drivers?"

"Well," Mary Ann assured her patient, "that's OK. This is a beginning. It is a really good beginning. Can you remember anything else?"

Leslie looked toward the ceiling as if in deep thought before shaking her head. "I don't even remember getting into the cab. It pulled up and then my mind goes blank."

"Nothing to worry about," Mary Ann assured her, sensing her patient's frustration. "We have made progress. You stay right here, I need to step out into the hall and do something."

She eased out of her chair and left the room. After the door had closed behind her she walked about twenty more feet, pulled her cell out and dialed a number she knew far too well. "Brian, I don't have much but I do have somewhere to start. The cab company she called was Blue Cab. They picked her up in a dirty white sedan. That's all she remembers."

Mary Ann waited a moment before ending the call with, "You're welcome." She then hurried back down the hall.

23

"I'm back," Mary Ann announced.

Hearing the almost silent whoosh of the door, Leslie saw not only the psychologist but also Dr. Parks. Mary Ann turned to face Leslie.

"I've asked Dr. Parks to come in," Mary Ann explained, "so that we might be able to go through questions you might have about your injuries, as well as any questions you have about what he did during the surgery. So, the ball is in your court. Speak freely! Ask anything you want."

Leslie's eyes darted between the two guests. For almost three days, she'd been aware of the wrappings and the pain, but she hadn't been allowed to view the damage, not even when it had been unwrapped each morning for the doctor's examination. She was curious and impatient. But now, when she was finally being given the opportunity to get answers, did she really want to know where she stood? Were the answers to her questions ones she really wanted to hear? As she reconsidered where this road might take her, Parks pulled a chair from the corner of the room and dragged it to a point where it touched the other doctor's. Leslie could now look at both of them without having to turn her head.

As the two medical professionals got comfortable, she took a deep breath and began, "When do I get to see my face?"

"Well," the surgeon took the lead, "before I let you see your face, I want the swelling to go down just a bit more. Just like with a busted lip or a black eye, the first few days after something happens, the discoloring, the swelling, the trauma, combine to cause a distortion of the natural features. I don't want you to have to endure seeing those things because they are too misleading. You will get the wrong impression. So, let's give it as least a couple of days. Then, I'll let you take a look and at that time I will explain more fully what we have left to do."

"There's more?" Leslie's voice showed a bit of surprise. She'd figured that all the surgery was completed. What more was there left to do?

"Yes," Parks responded. "You see, in cases like yours, the first thing we do is try to sew you back together in such a way that we match each torn or cut segment of skin with its mate on the other side. Then, after a time when the scar tissue has fully healed, we go back using more refined procedures and minimize the scars."

Scars! She really hadn't thought about dealing with scars. She didn't have a single scar anywhere on her body. What did he mean by scars? Couldn't he fix them where there weren't any? Isn't that what surgeons did?

"You said there would be more surgery?" Now more concerned, Leslie inquired, "How much and when?"

"It depends on the patient," the doctor replied. "Some people heal much faster than others. But a general time frame is between six months and a year. When all the procedures are completed most of the scarring that is left can be hidden through good makeup techniques, and this includes even those people who have suffered the most traumatic of injuries." The doctor's final inflection seemed to indicate to Leslie that she was one of those people. The psychologist must have noticed Leslie's reaction because she quickly jumped into the conversation.

"What Dr. Parks is saying," she explained, "is that it will take a while for you to fully recover. There are no quick fixes. You will feel fine in a matter of weeks, but it'll take longer to repair the damage that has been done; the results are worth waiting for."

Leslie let both doctors' words roll through her head and rebound within the depths of her reasoning, but the pictures those words conjured up were grotesque and frightening. A childhood visit to a military hospital burn ward jumped from the confines of her memory. It was there that she had been confronted with the specter of Iraq War burn victims, men whose faces had been melted or blasted away. Hopelessly ugly was the word she'd used to describe these men to her friends. She thought about a neighbor's son who had been one of them. Fortunately, he'd later died rather than having to walk in a world where people would have pointed and laughed. She now remembered the sickening feeling that had settled in her stomach when her father had forced her to kiss Jimmy goodbye. Now, as she thought back to that moment, she wondered if she hadn't become someone who was as ugly and unlovable as her neighbor.

Looking back to the surgeon, she urgently demanded, "Am I ugly?"

"You won't be," Parks assured. "I promise you that."

The words hit Leslie hard. He didn't say she wasn't, he only said she wouldn't be. So what did she look like now? Had she become one of the monsters Hollywood creates to scare people in the theater?

"Leslie," the psychologist's soothing voice

brought the patient out of her nightmarish thoughts, "you will never be ugly. Ugly is something that comes from deep within and spews out like a lava flow erupting from a volcano. It is not a part of the young lady I have gotten to know over the past few days. You aren't ugly, just injured, and we will fix that."

Picking up her issue of *Fashion and Style* magazine from the table beside her bed, Leslie took a long look at the cover and then dropping it in her lap, asked, "Did this die? Is it just a memory? Am I ever going to look like that again?"

An awkward silence filled the room. Then, in an almost apologetic tone, Dr. Parks answered, "Over time, we can get close, but the truth is, while we can do some remarkable things, you will never look exactly like that again. There will be scars, there will certainly be issues. But there is makeup to cover these issues up. And, you were lucky in that few of the muscles and tendons that control facial expression were damaged beyond repair. Hence you should have a full range of emotions that can be revealed when you interact with others."

She hadn't even considered that. Not only might she be ugly, maybe repulsive, but her face might not work right. Would spit leak out of the side of her mouth as she rested? Would she be able to eat or drink without having people turn away? Was she a freak?

Her fingers traced her bandaged face. Maybe because she had blocked out her memories of the attack, because she had forced herself to not think about what had occurred, she hadn't allowed herself to believe anything terrible had really happened. She had spent the past three days convincing herself that her injuries were just like a chipped tooth, easily covered or fixed. Now, even while hearing the real story from the doctors, she was fighting not to accept it. Just like a child who closes his eyes and hides under the cover to hide from the boogeyman, she wanted to cover the facts with a blanket of forced forget-fulness. Surely, if she did, she would wake up and begin her career again. It would be like nothing happened.

But now these two terrible people were so nicely and politely telling her she couldn't do it. They were stabbing her with images that were less than beautiful and preparing her for some-thing she didn't want and wouldn't accept. She was ugly! She was a monster! Leslie was dead. Without beauty, what was there?

"Leslie," Mary Ann's voice was calm and understanding, "are you all right?"

Nodding, the model indicated that she was. But she wasn't. She knew she would never be all right. Without her perfect face, she had no place in this world.

"If you understand what's going on," Mary

Ann continued, "and you don't have any other questions, then Dr. Parks and I will go on to our other patients. Don't forget, you can call me anytime you need me, and I'll drop everything for you."

"I'm fine," Leslie answered with absolutely no emotion.

With no other words, the two doctors got up and left Leslie alone with her thoughts and her fears. Picking the magazine up one more time, she stared again at the cover, and then like a high school quarterback trying to complete a Hail Mary, tossed it across the room. It knocked over an arrangement of flowers as it flew into a corner; water and a single red rose fell onto the floor. Overcome with emotion and filled with terror, she collapsed against her pillow and tried to pretend like this was all a dream. But no matter how hard she tried, the vision of the burn ward kept flashing through her mind. And what about her mother? Had she been pretending during her visits? During their talks had she been lying to her about being just as good as new? Or had they not told her parents the real outcome? Were they in the dark just like she was? Sobbing, she summoned a nurse and demanded something to put her to sleep.

24

As soon as his call from the psychologist ended, Rosatelli grabbed a phone book, looked up a number and dialed. He spoke quickly upon getting a response.

"Blue Cab, this is Captain Brian Rosatelli with the Springfield police. I need to know if you received a request for a pick-up at the airport last Friday. It was probably around or just after midnight?"

While waiting for the woman to check her log the officer hunched over his ancient metal desk, letting the breeze from a fifty-year-old Hunter ceiling fan cool his neck. Picking up a number three lead pencil, he pushed it across a yellow legal pad. Within a minute, an image of an old cat perched on a wooden fence emerged on the paper. The sketch showed a good deal of artistic ability. He was adding a second cat to the drawing when the woman came back on the line.

"Yes, a woman called us."

"Great! Where did you take her?"

"We didn't take her anywhere," the representative of the cab company explained. "She wasn't there when our driver arrived."

Drumming his pen against the desktop Rosatelli considered the information. If they didn't pick up Leslie Rhoads, then who did? Or what if one of their drivers is the sicko who committed this crime? Leaning back with the phone, he fired off another question.

"Do you have any white cars?"

"No," the lady responded with a hint of frustration. "They're blue. That's why we call ourselves the Blue Cab Company. If we had white cars we would have come up with a different name. Can you guess what that would be?"

"That's what I figured," Rosatelli replied, ignoring the sarcasm on the other end of the call. "Well, thanks anyway."

Looking out the window, he wondered where this little tidbit had taken him. It was almost as if the police gods were lining up against him. A violent crime with no motive and no clues! These types of attacks were usually associated with rage, not premeditated actions. Who did Leslie Rhoads know that hated her enough to scar her rather than kill her?

Glancing back to his desk, the captain turned his attention to finishing his drawing. Where did he go next?

25

With Jan on break, Beth Rogers was fighting to keep up with the demands of the hospital wing she was running single-handedly.

"Nurse," an elderly man's voice called out over the intercom.

Punching 218, Beth spoke into the small box, "Yes, what can I do for you?"

"I need something for my pain," came the reply.

"Just one moment." Checking the Kardex, Beth noted what it said and then once again spoke into the small white microphone, "Mr. McGregor, I'll be there in just a few moments."

Grabbing the meds from the drug inventory then marking the patient's card and the inventory sheet, she began to leave her station when another call came. Leaning over the counter she punched button 223 and asked, "What do you need?"

"Nurse," this time the voice belonged to a woman, "I was wondering if you have any of that ointment that the blonde nurse gave me last night. My wrist is itching like crazy."

"Just a moment." Finding the patient's card, Beth pulled it, checked it, and then pulled a tube of the ointment. Making a note, she returned the card to the Kardex. Picking up both the pill and the tube, she once again started down the hall. She hadn't gotten five steps when the intercom called her back to the station. Retracing her steps, she leaned back over the counter, noted the room number, and punched the button. This time she knew the patient without checking the card.

"What can I get you, Leslie?" the nurse asked.

"I'm out of ice," Leslie answered. "If it isn't too much trouble."

"I'll have it there in a second," Beth replied. Muttering to herself about when Jan would be getting off break, the nurse picked up an ice bucket and headed down the hall toward the ice machine. She hadn't gotten two steps when another voice stopped her.

"Why don't you let me do that? You look like you're real busy, and I'm all caught up."

Smiling at the janitor, Beth stuck out the ice bucket saying, "Thanks, Jacob, this goes to the woman in 213."

"No problem. I'll take care of her," he said as he turned to get the ice. Moments later, he slipped quietly into the room.

26

"Here's your ice," a male voice announced as the door to Leslie's room swung open.

Leslie had the lights turned down with only the television illuminating the room. She had lost herself in an old detective show rerun, and barely looked up as the man walked in. She was so engrossed in the storyline she almost didn't even hear him speak and didn't bother to look toward the door.

"The nurse had to run down the hall to give someone some medicine," he continued as he pushed through the entry, "so I brought it up for her. I didn't figure you would want to wait on it. Besides, the way the nurses talk about you, you must be pretty special. I think they said you were a cover girl or something, isn't it?"

Looking up for a moment, Leslie nodded, and then she returned her thought and vision to the television's twenty-seven inch screen. The janitor carefully placed several cubes of ice in a glass and then filled the glass with water from the pitcher sitting on a table next to the wall. Smiling, he crossed the room, and as he handed the glass of cool liquid to the patient said in a cheery voice, "Here you go."

The model took the glass in her bandaged hand, nodded her head as if to thank the man and then turned her attention back to the climatic scenes of the show.

"Do you think they will catch him?" the man asked as a criminal ran across an alley and tried to climb over a low brick wall.

"They always do," Leslie answered at the moment the hero's gun rang out from the back of the alley and dropped the hoodlum to the ground. "On TV, no one ever gets away."

"Yeah," the janitor acknowledged. "Of course, in real life, it's not that way. The crooks are usually smarter than the cops. At least, that's what I think."

For the first time, Leslie latched onto what the man had said and looked at him. In the television's flickering light, he seemed almost surreal. She figured him to be in his early twenties, his dark hair a bit too long in keeping with the present styles. His face was pockmarked, probably from years of fighting acne, and his eyes almost black as they shined like glowing embers in the dimly lit room. Glancing down, she noted not only his maintenance uniform, but also a small bandage on his right hand.

"Yeah," the man repeated after a commercial ended and the show's credits began to roll, "on TV, they always get their man." Looking back at Leslie, he smiled and said, "What happened to you?"

His question caught the model a bit off guard. Until now, no one had asked her that. Everyone who had seen her had known. After seconds spent toying with exactly how she should or could explain it, she finally said, "I was attacked and cut up by some men."

"Oh," the man answered as if he immediately understood the entirety of what she had said. Then, after brushing back his hair from his eyes, he asked, "Did they get them?"

She shook her head.

"You think they will?" he politely followed up.

Pausing for a moment, Leslie considered the question, and then answered in the most programmed of ways. "I'm sure they will."

"Have they got a suspect?" the man quickly asked, still sounding friendly, but maybe just a bit too interested.

"No," Leslie admitted, "they don't. I didn't see any of the men who got me."

Shaking his head, the man smiled and then sighed, "Oh well, maybe in time they will find them. I know a lot of guys at the station. Some of them are really good. Which cop did they put in charge of your case?"

Back on more familiar ground, Leslie quickly answered, "Captain Rosatelli. He seems like a smart guy."

"Old Rosey," the janitor laughed. "Yeah, he's OK. I've met him a few times. Of course, if you didn't see the guys then he probably doesn't have much to go on. So being good may not be enough. But let's hope for the best."

For a few moments, the room was silent except for the sounds of the television. It was an uncomfortable silence, one that hung heavy and foreboding like a London fog. What made her feel even more awkward was the way the man stared at her in the dim light. She'd been stared at many times, it had gone with being beautiful, but this seemed very different. It bothered her more with each passing second. It was as if he was counting the number of times the wrappings crossed her face, memorizing every detail.

"Hey, this is one of my favorite episodes," the man said as he glanced toward the TV. "Grissom gets to go to a bar and interact with bikers. It's great!"

Leslie nodded. This man's critical opinion didn't carry a great deal of weight in her eyes. No matter that he seemed to be making an attempt at being nice, she was tired of his company. She wished he had just dropped off the ice and left. No, she wished he hadn't come at all.

"Well, you don't seem too talkative," he said, breaking the long silence. "I hope I haven't caused you any pain or anything."

Once more, she didn't answer. As she kept her eyes glued to the set, she felt his on her. They were literally burning holes in her bandages.

"I'm sure you want to be alone," he announced, "and besides, I need to finish my work and check out. See ya!"

Smiling, the man crossed the room and left, but the strange atmosphere he had brought with him remained. Trying to shake her mood, Leslie returned her focus to the television. A few moments later, the door opened again. This time it was a familiar person who entered the room.

"I see you got your ice," a big smile accompanied Beth's greeting. Checking her patient's pulse, she added, "I've been busy tonight."

"That man," Leslie began, her hand pointing toward the ice bucket, "the one who brought me the ice, does he work here?"

"Yeah, has for about four or five months," Beth explained while noting the accelerated heart rate on the patient's chart. "He cleans up the place. Now, how are you feeling?"

"His voice sounded familiar," Leslie noted, completely ignoring the nurse's question about her health. "I wonder if I went to school with him."

"Naw," Beth laughed. "He had just moved here when he got the job. Came here from Chicago I think. I remember when he first got here he came on to us nurses a whole lot, but after the administrator spoke with him, he cut that out. Now, he kind of ignores us. Usually, he avoids even talking to us now. He's strange, but good help is hard to find when you pay as little as we do. He shocked me when he offered to get ice for you. Volunteering for anything is not like him. Anyway, if you think you have seen him before, I'm sure that it wasn't in Springfield."

"No, you're probably right," Leslie replied. Thinking about it for a moment she added, "You know it's not his face, but his voice that rings a bell. I know I've heard him speak, I just don't know where. I probably dreamed it or something."

"Maybe not," the nurse smiled. "If you do know him, given time it'll come to you. It always does. He didn't act like he knew you, did he?"

"No," Leslie shook her head as she spoke, "but even if he did, he wouldn't have recognized me with these bandages. Besides, he knew I was a model. He said something about it."

"Well," Beth offered, "even if you have run into him before, and even if you never can remember where, what difference does it make? As my grandma used to say, what you don't know can't hurt you. Now, I've got to get back to my Grand Central Nurses' Station, so you try to get some rest."

Nodding, Leslie took another sip of water and tossed the call box and the television zapper on the middle of the nightstand. Pulling her covers up to her chin, she soon relaxed and fell into a deep sleep.

27

A few hours later, Leslie awoke and sensed a presence in her room. As she opened her eyes she expected to see a nurse checking on her. But there was no one there. A shiver came from nowhere and caused goose bumps to cover her arms and back. Trying to ignore both them and the feeling of danger that created them, Leslie forced her eyes shut, only to have them spring back open when a sharp cracking sound broke the nighttime silence.

Ears straining, she attempted to ascertain from where the noise had come, but when no sounds followed, she gave up.

Must be the air conditioning or the pipes. That has to be it. There's no one in here, there couldn't be. Yet for some reason she couldn't relax.

Her senses now on guard, Leslie tried to quiet the noise made by her own breathing in order to inventory the sixteen by twenty foot room's other sounds. The first thing she noticed was a faint, slow, steady drip that seemed to be coming from the area of a sink. Tuning it out, she strained to hear something else. What she noted next was the almost silent rush of air coming from a blower by the window.

But there was something else as well . . . something more. What has been added?

Tuning the drip and rush of air out, she strained to hear something new. At first, there was nothing, just the normal quietness associated with a hospital at that time. Ten seconds became twenty and twenty became thirty and then she heard it. At first, it seemed faint and far away, but as she fine-tuned her ears, the noise became clear and close. Suddenly she knew what it was, and that knowledge created a rush of panic that raced through her body, freezing her thoughts and actions.

Where was it coming from? She had to ascertain that before she could figure out her next move. As she focused on the added sound, sweat beaded up under her bandages. She could feel it trying to find a path to roll down her cheeks. She wanted to reach out and press that point, but dared not move.

Holding her body rigid, she focused all her attention to her ears. They were now working too well. They confirmed to her mind what her heart already knew. Scarcely two feet from the foot of her bed she heard the sounds of steady breathing.

The minutes slowly ticked by, but she didn't dare move. As she feigned sleep, her bandages and gown slowly became soaked with her sweat.

And the sound of the breathing was still there. What could she do? If she reached for the intercom would he make a move to stop her? Was he here to finish the job he started in the alley? If so, why didn't he just do it?

Reopening her eyes, she tried to shift her body in hopes that she could make out the identity of the unknown intruder. But the low light and the way her head was positioned on the pillow kept her from seeing anything but darkness and shadows.

She had to find the call box. Slowly moving her hand, she searched the middle portion of the bed. It wasn't there. She then turned over in order to move her right hand over the pillow. If only she could find it, she could push one button and a nurse would come running. But where had she left it?

Of course, she had put it on the table when she'd turned off the TV. To reach it she was going to have to sit up. If she sat up, the intruder would know that she was awake. If he saw that, he'd probably make his move. So, she couldn't move. But what could she do?

After exhaustive minutes of thinking the only other plan that made any sense was doing nothing and hoping that a nurse would come by on her regular rounds. Up until that time, she was trapped.

Without moving her head, she glanced at the

lighted clock on a table at the far side of the room. 2:15! As the minutes slowly passed, she continued to stare at the numbers, trying to keep her breathing steady and her body still.

At 2:24, a sudden itch hit her right foot, but she fought the urge to scratch. 2:26, and the sensation was building to a point that demanded action, still, she fought it off. 2:28 and Leslie knew she had to get to her foot, but she also knew that she had to appear to be asleep. Taking a deep breath, she shifted her entire body to the right, rolling onto her side and bringing herself into a fetal position. Scratching her right foot with her left, she then steadied her breathing and pretended to remain in a deep sleep.

The minutes continued to crawl by and still the breathing got no closer to her bed. She knew she couldn't take it much longer. If something didn't happen soon, she'd have to make it happen.

2:41! Tiring of playing possum, she decided to employ a new plan. Her right hand was now resting on her pillow just inches from the nightstand. She slowly inched it forward. It took her over five minutes to find the bed's edge: When she did, she stopped and listened. The breathing had not moved, it was no closer. Maybe he hadn't noticed her actions.

Pushing her fingers along the nightstand's edge, she lightly brushed an empty glass. Easing her hand beside it, she paused again, resting for a full minute, and then reaching farther. A quarter inch at a time she moved her fingers along the table's edge. When she felt nothing, she repeated the motion, this time two inches toward the middle. Still, she found nothing.

Her nerves were now frayed, and a single sound, even something as harmless as a cricket chirping would have sent her into a complete panic. Tears of frustration now clouded her eyes; her mind was filled with anger caused by the nurses' lack of attention.

What kind of hospital are they running here? They need to keep a closer eye on their patients. Nurses were supposed to wake you up every ten minutes to make sure you were sleeping all right, so why wasn't one of them here?

Unable to find the call box, Leslie remained frozen on her side. The sweat that was pouring from her body had now drenched her bed and was beginning to burn her cuts. Throbbing pain compounded her misery. Tired, alone, and frightened, she began to almost wish for death.

Finish it. Finish what you didn't finish in that alley. Make your move and let me fight you one more time. As she waited for that battle another chain of events leapt into her brain. Leslie saw herself in a car, then in an alley. She saw a bright light and then she remembered seeing a bottle. Out of the darkness of the not so distant past she heard voices—voices that sounded as if they were a long way away. Then, there was one voice, this one much closer, so close she could hear his breathing, and there was laughter, a sick, coarse kind of laughter.

The scene that had so quickly jumped into her head instantly faded as she became aware of an even more threatening reality. The breathing was now closer. Afraid to look up she could feel a person hovering just above her shoulder. And even though she knew there were no shadows without light, she nevertheless felt the weight of a shadow covering her body.

Swallowing hard, she forced herself to remain silent, her breathing deep and her body rigid. For long moments, she waited for whatever was going to happen, but while the deep, steady breathing continued, nothing else transpired.

How Leslie wanted to cry out for help, to scream as loudly as she could, yet, she knew that even if she had tried, her voice would have been silenced by her own terror. In an attempt to gain some self-control, she forced herself to record every minute detail of each passing moment. As she did, her nerves began to calm, and her mind began to function logically.

The breathing sounded like that of a man not only because of the deepness, but the sound was from a large chest moving against a stiff shirt. He must have a cold, or maybe hay fever because of the rustle in the individual breaths. Based on where she sensed he was standing, she figured the man to be of average height.

OK, Nancy Drew, she told herself, you're doing good. What else can you figure out?

She noted a faint scent of cigarette smoke, as well as another odor that was familiar, but unidentifiable. While trying to place it, she became aware of movement—two quick steps, almost silent on the tile floor. Suddenly, she no longer felt the weight of the intruder's shadow. Letting her eyes slightly open, she watched as her room door eased open, and a dark figure exited to the hall. The room was now completely quiet.

Taking a deep breath, she waited for a full minute in silence, still scared to move. Finally, satisfied the man was not coming back, she sat up, reached over to the middle of the table and hit the call box. Within moments, an elderly nurse made her way to the room. By the time she'd arrived, Leslie had already flipped the night-stand's light switch and was sitting up in bed.

"What seems to be the trouble?" The nurse asked in a sweet, almost motherly voice.

"Someone was just in my room," Leslie hurriedly answered.

"No, that couldn't be," the nurse responded. "They would have had to walk by the station to get here or get out and no one has."

"Listen," Leslie urgently insisted, "there was a

man in here. I don't know where he came from or where he went, but he was in here."

"Calm yourself, young lady," the nurse said. "You've just had a bad dream. That happens a lot with folks who are on medication and sleeping in a strange place. You're perfectly safe here. You just sit still and I'll get you something to help you rest. I'll be right back."

Alone again, Leslie replayed what had just happened. She was convinced the nurse was wrong. It couldn't have been a dream. Besides she could still smell the lingering odor of cigarette smoke.

Getting out of bed, she dragged her IV slowly to the window and yanked back the curtain to check the lock. It was secure. Just as she was about to let the curtain fall back in place, she heard a car motor in the distance. Looking down, she watched as a dirty, white sedan eased out of a faraway parking place and edged into the street. Within seconds, it had turned a corner and driven out of sight.

Climbing back into bed, Leslie repositioned her IV unit, and pulled the covers up around her neck. It wasn't a dream. But why didn't he do something? Why didn't he hurt her? Why didn't he kill her? Why didn't he finish the job he started in that alley?

28

"Sorry it took so long for me to get away from New York and come see you," Carlee Middleton apologized. "But I guarantee I've been checking on you everyday."

"Yes, thanks," Leslie answered. "The nurses gave me the messages and the flowers are beautiful! I appreciate everything that you have done."

She knew from firsthand experience it was a pain to get to Springfield from New York City. And Carlee was busy, but Leslie was really disappointed it had taken this long for her agent to check on her in person. She'd thought she was Carlee's special model, the one she loved like a daughter. But maybe that commodity speech she presented at their last meeting was closer to home than Leslie wanted to admit.

"Well," the agent shrugged, "we've all been worried about you—been worried a lot. The other girls have been asking how you are every time they see me. It's nice to see with my own eyes that you are getting along pretty well."

An awkward silence followed as the agent seemed to struggle to find anything else to say. It was then Leslie realized that never before had they spoken about things other than work. Over four years of knowing one another and they'd never really gotten acquainted, at least not in a way that real friends do. It had never been more obvious than right now.

"Well," Leslie interjected, "have you seen any of our town yet?"

"No," Carlee replied. "I came straight to the hospital as soon as I flew in. Though, what I did see looks," she paused as if searching for a word, "quaint in an *It's a Wonderful Life* sort of way."

Nodding, Leslie completed the description, "And small. It must look like a real milk stop to you."

"No," Carlee reassured her. "As a matter of fact, the town I was from was even smaller than yours. Of course, that was a long time ago."

Another round of silence followed. Without work, there was just nothing to say.

Carlee got up and looked at the flowers. She made a big deal of smelling the plants and reading the cards before she awkwardly crossed the room and returned to her seat. Crossing her legs, she adjusted her skirt and then began to pick the lint from the material. She didn't quit fidgeting until Leslie broke the long silence.

"You know," Leslie began, trying to sound casual but not quite pulling it off, "I think that you should tell Passion Nights that I'm just not interested. Since I've come home, I've decided that I just couldn't do that to my folks. They wouldn't understand. I hope you don't think I'm stupid for turning the chance down, but for me it is the right thing to do."

Staring at a face that was wrapped like a mummy, Carlee nodded. Then, after a few more seconds of silence, added, "I think you're right. I agree wholeheartedly with your decision. I flew up here to encourage you to drop it. You're better than what they are asking for." Then, turning her head so her face couldn't be seen, she continued, "You don't need that kind of thing to make your career."

"Thanks for understanding," Leslie responded, her voice struggling to maintain the composure she didn't really feel. "I hope that turning this down will not cause you to drop me. I want you to still represent me when I get back."

"Sure, kid," Carlee whispered. "You know that you're number one with me."

"Thanks."

Carlee turned back as if to study the model's still beautiful eyes. Forcing a smile she said, "Your cover is the best-selling issue of *Fashion and Style* ever. They have had to do two more printings. Once people heard about what . . ." She didn't finish the sentence. Or maybe she just couldn't finish it.

"That's great," Leslie whispered. She knew

why it had sold out. It wasn't her face, it was what had happened to her. She was hot for all the wrong reasons.

"Hate to interrupt you ladies," Meg announced entering the room, "but Leslie has another visitor, and he's on a very tight schedule. If possible, he needs to see her right now."

"Well, we can't keep him waiting now, can we?" Carlee said, her tone indicating her great relief at ending the uncomfortable visit. "Leslie, you take care of yourself, and I'll see you soon."

"You are going to stick around for a few days aren't you?" Leslie inquired as Carlee got up.

"No, dear," Carlee quickly explained, "I have a flight out this afternoon. Got things to do. You know how those girls think I'm their mother. Can't do a thing without me. Now that you've turned down the Passion Nights gig, got to find someone in my stable who is right for it. Bye, now. Take care of yourself, kid."

29

Walking back toward the lobby, the agent passed a nurses' station, stopped and asked, "How bad are the cuts on Leslie's face? I mean, what's she going to look like when she is healed?"

Looking up from her work, Marsha Kolinek shook her head and inquired, "Are you a family member?"

"No, I'm her agent," Carlee explained. "That makes me almost like family."

"I would be violating the law to share any confidential information with you," the nurse replied.

"I understand," Carlee replied. "But can I possibly ask the question in such a way you could at least give me an idea?"

"I don't know what you mean," Marsha replied.

"Have you seen the report on the TMZ website on Leslie?"

The nurse nodded.

Carlee took a deep breath. "That report said that the doctors had never seen anything like this except in battle injuries."

"That is what the media has written," Marsha acknowledged. "And while I can't comment on this case, I can say a broken whiskey bottle with its jagged edges can do a lot of damage."

The visitor nodded before adding, "I've read a lot on this kind of injury in the past few days. From the nature of the attack I am guessing the loss of skin was extensive."

"Once again," Marsha replied, "I can't comment on individual cases."

The nurse's tone told Carlee everything she needed to know. This was not a simple car wreck or a freak kitchen accident.

"You say a broken bottle?" the agent asked. "That wasn't in the news stories I read."

"And I shouldn't have told you," Marsha whispered. "The police don't want anyone to know. They're holding it back, hoping to use it to catch the man who did it. So don't tell anyone."

Carlee shook her head. "I won't. The scars, you think she will have some scars when this is all over?"

The cat was out of the bag, so Marsha felt she had little choice but to continue. Still she chose her words carefully. "In cases like this there will always be scarring. When skin is badly damaged there is no way for a perfect restoration."

Shaking her head for a moment, Carlee nodded and whispered, "Thank you." Minutes later, she had found a cab and was headed to the airport. As she rode along the highway, glancing at the town Leslie called home, she didn't notice much of anything. She was far too lost in her own thoughts.

This accident had really messed up her plans. Suddenly, her best product had been taken off the market. Who did she have in her stable that had the right look for Passion Nights? There had to be someone to take Leslie's place. Maybe Rachel Collier or Taylor Stone? She'd push those two to anyone.

Then a second thought hit her. She had a drawer filled with unpublished shots of Leslie. A few calls and she would likely be able to sell those to magazines and online sites. But she'd have to move fast. The public's fascination with the girl would only last so long. Probably the best way to do it was to leak the news of the unpublished stuff to *Entertainment Tonight* and let them stir the pot. Meanwhile, she'd have to get the photos organized and figure out what they were worth. She wouldn't be making the millions she'd planned on making off Leslie, but she could still cash in during the short-term.

She made two quick calls to contacts to get the ball rolling before the cab even arrived at the airport. After getting out and taking a final look around, she grimly smiled. She knew she would never come back to Springfield nor would she ever see Leslie again. She didn't want to. Her once pet model was not perfect. It was time to move on and find another woman she could market. In the meantime, she could still make some money and buy some time by giving the world the before photos of the model whose face was no longer perfect. It wasn't a pretty picture, but as she had told Leslie, she was a commodity and you had to sell when the market was right. Still, she sadly realized, this was not going to make nearly as much money as the Passion Nights gig would have. Unless . . .

Pulling out her phone, she scanned her

directory. A few seconds later, she was talking to a friend in Los Angeles.

"Jim, Carlee here. You know the model I had that got attacked?"

She waited a moment and then cut in, "Yeah, that's the one. Well, she was literally carved up with a broken bottle. Cut her face to shreds. She has gone from beauty to the beast. My contract with this woman is still good, so I own a hunk of everything she does for another eight months. What do you think about a movie about her life and the attack? You know, small town girl goes home to safe little town and gets carved up."

Carlee stood by the curb and tapped the toe of her three-inch pumps as she waited for the movie producer's answer. As she listened, she smiled.

"That's even better," she said. "A true-story slasher flick! The teen audience would eat it up. It would be perfect in 3-D. Could be worth millions to us. Why don't you get to work on that angle and see if you can find the money to produce it quickly! We need to move on this while the iron is hot."

Carlee nodded a final time before concluding, "Call me when you have wheels on this thing."

Dropping the phone into her pocket, she smiled. This might just work out OK after all. It was all about marketing, and maybe marketing Leslie would be easier now than when she was perfect.

30

"Good morning." Brian Rosatelli's greeting was friendly, but very businesslike. Before either Meg or Leslie had an opportunity to reply, he had found a seat, pulled out a notebook, and began talking. "I was surprised when I found a message from you on my desk this morning. You've got something else for me?"

Catching her breath, then trying to shift mental gears from making small talk with Carlee to giving straightforward information to the policeman, Leslie nodded and launched into the story of what had happened during the night. Both the cop and Meg listened intently as she explained. When she finished, she shrugged and looking to the two, asked, "It wasn't a dream was it? I'm not crazy, am I?"

Shaking his head, the captain turned to Meg. "Is there any way that someone could have gotten in and out of here without going by the nurses' station?"

"No," Meg answered. "Not unless . . ."

"Unless what," Leslie demanded from her bed.

"Unless they had a key to a back door," Meg noted, "and we always keep it locked."

"How many people have access to those keys?" Rosatelli asked.

"No one really," Meg shrugged. "And in another way, everyone. Besides the administrator, who has one of his own, we keep the only other two keys in a desk drawer in the station desk."

"Would you see if they are there?" Rosatelli asked.

Nodding her head, Meg exited the room. Turning back to Leslie, Rosatelli asked, "Have you got anything else?"

"Yes," she quietly announced. "Last night I remembered a little more about the attack. I don't know if it will help or not."

"Go ahead."

"Well," Leslie struggled to explain: "There were voices. I didn't know them, but in the alley where they got me, there were voices. Someone was also holding me. It was more than one person."

Scratching his head, Rosatelli thought for a moment. "Leslie," his words were now carefully thought out and deliberate, "when the Blue Cab Company got to the airport that night, you weren't there. They don't have white cars, so it wasn't them that picked you up. It had to be whoever hurt you that drove that car. Can you remember anything about the car or the people in it?"

Shaking her head, Leslie shrugged. "Only that

it was a dirty, white sedan. Like the one that pulled out of the parking lot last night."

"What do you mean?" Rosatelli asked.

"After the man left, and after the nurse went to get me some medication," Leslie explained. "I walked over to the window—it took me a little while because I had to push my IV—and in a far parking lot a white car started and drove down Jane Street. It turned at the light. It was like the one at the airport. I don't know if it was the same one, but I think that it was like it."

Considering the woman's story, the cop got up from his seat, walked to the window, pulled back the curtain and looked out. "Was it the parking lot right below us or the far one down that hill?"

Grabbing her robe, Leslie threw it around her and got out of bed. Pulling the IV to the window, she looked and pointed. "It was the far one and there was enough light for me to know that it was white. My vision's good," she added in an attempt to convince not only the captain but also herself.

They were still staring out the window, studying the cars, when Meg returned. Both of them turned to face her as she entered. The nurse began by nodding and then offered, "One of the keys is gone. No one knows who has it or how long it has been missing, but it's not there."

"Ms. Rhoads," a note of satisfaction showed in

Rosatelli's tone, "I don't think you had a dream. To show you how strongly I believe this, there'll be someone here tonight to make sure no one comes into your room." Turning back to the window, he asked Meg, "Who parks in the far parking lot, the one down the hill?"

"It's supposed to be for employees, why?"

"Maybe nothing," the captain shrugged, "but maybe a big break. Is there a record of the types of cars that the staff drive?"

Shaking her head, Meg answered, "No. We just get a permit sticker and put it on. We don't have to fill out a form that lists the kind of car we drive or anything."

"Oh, well," Rosatelli smiled, "that'd have made it easy, but there are other ways to find out who drives a white sedan, if they work here." Directing his eyes back to Leslie he asked, "Do you have anything else? It doesn't make any difference how minor it might seem."

"Not now," she apologized. "I wish I did."

"Don't worry," he smiled, "you've given us a lot today. I'm sure that more will come back to you later. I'll talk to you again soon."

After leaving the patient's room, Rosatelli stopped by the admitting desk and inquired, "Do any of your employees drive an older white sedan?"

The old woman behind the desk looked up from her work and asked, "Why?"

"It's a police matter," Rosatelli replied flashing his badge.

"I really wouldn't know," the woman replied. "I don't pay much attention to what folks drive. Cars aren't important to me. I'm still driving the same '62 Rambler that my dad bought me back when I was in high school."

Rosatelli smiled and handed her his card. "If you see a white sedan, call me and tell me who's driving it. Now, where can I find the hospital administrator?"

"Mr. Willis's office is down the hall and to the left."

"Thanks."

After Rosatelli rounded a far corner, a man asked, "What did the guy want, Betty?"

Looking up, the receptionist noted another employee. Smiling she answered, "Oh, probably some kind of parking violation or something, you know how cops are. He was asking if I knew of any employees who drove a white sedan. Like I'm going to keep track of what everybody drives!"

"Oh, well, you know cops," the man responded. Checking his watch, he pushed his mop and bucket back to a storage room and then returned to the front desk.

"Betty, if anyone asks, I've got to run out and pick up a few supplies from downtown. I'll be back in about an hour. OK?"

Looking up again, Betty nodded and then asked the man, "Jacob, when you get back could you see if you can get the cord on my printer fixed? It has been shorting out again."

"No problem," the man yelled as the door shut behind him.

31

Later that afternoon, while attempting to lose herself in a soap opera, Leslie heard a soft knock on her door. Grateful for the diversion, she clicked the television off, sat up and sang out, "Come in."

"Leslie?" a tall, dark-haired man asked as he pushed open the door. "I hope that you don't mind seeing an old friend. I mean it has been a long time."

He stopped just a couple feet inside the room, waiting for some type of signal from the patient, something to assure him it was all right to approach her, but Leslie didn't move. She was too caught up in a mix of old memories and confused emotions to breathe, much less talk.

As he waited, the man's steel blue eyes stared intently at the woman. If he was bothered or shocked by the bandages on her face and hands, he didn't show it. His strong jaw even dropped a little, revealing a quick, deep smile.

Leslie took a deep breath, but still said nothing. Her mind was much too busy trying to tie this image to a memory and the bridge she was mentally constructing wasn't getting completed. There were still gaps, big ones!

The visitor's deep blue suit, his pressed white shirt, and his silk tie fit perfectly. Taken together, they revealed a man who seemed completely confident in himself. His posture, the erect, strong stance, echoed the same image. In his right hand, he held a flower box and in his left a paper cup. What did that say? For the moment, she didn't care. She thought she'd solved the riddle.

"Hunter?" Leslie questioned. It looked like him, but Hunter Jefferson had been thinner the last time she had seen him, and he had certainly not been the fashion plate that this man was. Of course, high school had been a long time ago and she knew that people grew up, changed, matured, but somehow she had never pictured Hunter as much more than a jock. Could this seemingly sophisticated man be him?

"Yeah," he smiled coming closer to her bed, "you remembered. I thought I might have changed too much. After all, it's been six, almost seven years."

"That long?" Leslie replied unbelievingly.

Of course it had been. Hunter and she hadn't

seen each other since the night of graduation. He'd taken a job in another state then headed off to play football somewhere in the South. She had gone to a summer modeling school and briefly to college before dropping out and heading to New York. In that time, he hadn't even crossed her mind. Now, here he was, and the feelings that he brought with him were so good—so very good!

"There are times," Hunter began, finding a seat and handing her the flowers and glass, "that it seems more like a thousand years. As a matter of fact, it is sometimes hard to believe that we were ever that young or that free."

Placing the glass on the nightstand, Leslie opened the flower box. Inside she discovered four pink roses. Shaking her head, she looked up and exclaimed, "I can't believe that you remembered!"

"Yeah," he laughed, "you were the only girl I ever knew who picked pink over red. The cup has a chocolate shake from Big Al's. I remembered that, too."

Laying the roses on the bed, she picked up the glass, took a long sip and then shook her head again. "Hunter Jefferson."

They both grinned at each other for a moment, and then, after taking another sip, Leslie broke the ice. "Do you know how long it has been since I had a shake this good?"

"No," the man replied. "You've got me there. I

bet it has been a long time. I'm sure that they don't make shakes like this in New York."

"It was my senior year," Leslie said, a hint of nostalgia in her tone. "We were selling candy to raise money for the class trip and I ended up having to come up with enough cash to pay for the four boxes I ate at school. I was really upset because the money was due and I didn't have enough. And then you took me to Big Al's and bought me a shake. I remember that I cried at first, and then I laughed and laughed. The one thing I don't remember is how I made up the money?"

"You didn't," Hunter laughed.

"I didn't?"

"No," he explained. "I'm surprised that you don't remember. You conned me into paying for the boxes. I believe you said that you would pay me back later. With interest, you now owe me . . . Don't really guess it matters now."

After they both laughed, Leslie queried, "I really made you buy them? That sounds like me doesn't it?"

Agreeing, Hunter added, "I also had to buy all your leftover spirit ribbons, four magazine subscriptions, two sweatshirts, and one of those stupid spirit hats."

"I made you do that?"

"Well," he grinned, "you made me feel sorry for you, and then I bought them. I was a pretty easy mark for you."

"Oh well," Leslie grinned. "I was immature then. Let's drop the old days. I'd like to know what has happened to you since then."

Leaning back in his chair, Hunter's eyes lit up as he recalled past times and glories. Smiling, he crossed his ankles and relaxed. "The story is both complex and simple. I can sum it up with it seems like a lot has happened, but in truth it might not be much at all. I certainly haven't had the kind of success or fame you've had. It has all been kind of boring stuff."

"Tell me," Leslie begged. "I bet you've done a lot of things that I never dreamed of."

"Well," Hunter shrugged, "maybe a few things you didn't dream of. Let me see now, where should I begin?"

He closed his eyes for a moment and folded his fingers together over his knee. He left her hanging for at least a minute, and then began his story.

"You probably knew that I went to Alabama on a football scholarship, but what you likely didn't know was that I tore up my knee my freshman year and never played another down. My career was over before it really began. I was pretty disillusioned. I kind of gave up for a while. You probably remember I never paid much attention to the books in high school, I didn't think I needed them. So, when the knee went, I dropped out and came home."

Almost forgetting about her bandaged face, Leslie reached out and patted his knee. "I'm sorry. That sounds tough."

"Kind of minor compared to what some folks have been through," he humbly added. His eyes stared deeply into hers for a moment and then he picked up his tale, "I worked here in town for a while, lived at home, and tried to pretend I was still something special. I wasn't, and when Dad had a stroke and died, that fact became pretty clear. Mom couldn't feed both of us on her paycheck, so I had to look for something that paid real money."

Leslie shook her head. "So sorry about your dad. He was such a nice man. He built my folks' home."

"Yeah, he did, and the homes of a lot of other folks here in Springfield as well. But I had trouble even hitting a nail with a hammer, so that was out. For somebody with my experience, there wasn't anything I could do other that stock shelves. So I had two choices—work at a menial job and talk about my old glory days or I could go back to school, work my way through, and try to learn how to be something other than a worn-out Friday night hero.

"Being a bum may have been boring, but going to school scared me to death. So it took six months of boredom to send me back to school. It wasn't Alabama this time, but it was a college—

152

Hardin over in Elmwood—and I did learn how to study. I finished in three years and then I got a law degree. Came back here a year ago and I now work at the offices of Brown and Brown. Alan Brown, I think he and your cousin Meg dated in high school, has taken me under his wing and taught me a great deal. I've taught him a few moves on the YMCA basketball court, too. Anyway, that's it. That's the whole dull story."

"You did it on your own, too," Leslie chimed in, "not many people can say that."

"I think," Hunter grinned, "doing it on your own is a nice way of saying I blew it when I had someone else paying for it. But don't worry about it. I'll take what you said as a compliment. And speaking of doing it, you've set the world on fire. That touchdown I made to win the game against Broadway has been long forgotten, but everybody talks about you. You're famous. You've made a lot of us proud just to have known you."

"Yeah, maybe." Leslie could sense she was blushing, though the bandages hid that fact. "But in the real world, I wasn't that much."

"Don't put yourself down," Hunter shot back. "You've always known what you wanted to be and you became that. The rest of us struggled and searched and floundered around a lot. You never had to do that. You wanted to be a model for as long as I have known you. Leslie, you've always been solid."

Though she wasn't going to admit it, it felt good to hear someone talk about her that way. She'd wondered if anyone back home had cared about her after she'd left, much less noticed that her face had found its way into a few magazines. Yeah, at a time like this, laid up in the hospital, it felt really good.

Changing the subject, Leslie inquired, "Well, what about the women in your life? You didn't mention them."

"Nothing to mention," the man lamented. "I've had as much success in that field as I did on the college gridiron. I think I've just been too busy to look. At least I hope that is it. I'd hate to think that I'm too ugly."

"You're far from ugly," Leslie laughed. "I know what you mean when you talk about being too busy. I barely have time to talk to a man, much less go out with one. Do you remember that time at the drive-in when we piled into Jinx's pickup?"

Over the course of the next hour the two high school friends relived old times and shared the experiences of the recent past. Their conversation was broken up only when Meg came in announcing that visiting hours had ended. When the nurse wouldn't give in to their demands for more time, the two said goodbye and promised to talk again.

32

"Hunter's a great guy," Meg noted after the door closed behind him.

"Yeah," Leslie sighed. "There is a lot more to him than I figured there would be."

"It's kind of a shame what happened to him in football," Meg added. "He probably would have played in the NFL."

"Well," Leslie stated, "bum knee or not, he seems to be doing all right."

"Yeah," Meg agreed. "He was able to adapt and grow. A lot of people can't change when something unplanned or disastrous happens. Hunter may have struggled for a while, but he bounced back. Did he tell you about what he does at church?"

"Hunter?" Leslie's incredulous look matched her voice. "Hunter's going to church?"

"Yes he is," the nurse smiled. "He started going after his dad died. Now he works through the outreach program with kids from the poorer families. He takes a lot of juvenile cases—kids who have gotten into crime and drugs—and tries to give them some direction. His name still means something here. Everybody has heard of his football exploits and that helps him win some points with the kids. He has done a great deal."

"Well," Leslie sighed, "before this afternoon I figured he would end up a drunken, egotistical washed-up jock. I guess he had a lot more potential than any of us ever gave him credit for."

"He did and we all do," Meg answered. Checking her watch, she straightened the towels by the sink, and then, crossing the room sat down beside her cousin's bed. Taking a deep breath, she suddenly changed her tone and manner.

"Leslie, you've got to face something, too."

"What do you mean?"

"When those bandages come off," Meg began, "you aren't going to look like you did on the cover of *Fashion and Style*."

"Oh, Meg, I know that. I realize it will take a little more surgery and I'll have to learn a few tricks with makeup. Don't worry about me. I can do that. And I'm sure Carlee can get me some new gigs when that is over. I just consider this a vacation from my career."

Shaking her head, Meg solemnly noted, "Leslie, when Hunter blew out his knee, he worked hard at bringing himself back. As good as the surgeons were, and as much therapy as he did, he never could run and move like he once had. He had to change the way he thought and looked at life."

"I get that," Leslie said, "but running

4.4-second forties is not something I have to worry about. All I have to do is pout, smile, or act bored."

Meg reached out and grabbed her cousin's bandaged hand. "There is no easy way for me to say this to you. I mean even your mother won't listen to me. If I can't get through to her, I don't know if I can get through to you. Still, I've got to make you understand. A little makeup and more surgery are not going to do it. Time is not going to do it. Leslie, you are probably never going to model again. The damage that has been done is too great.

"If you go into tomorrow believing that there is a magic potion; if you go in there thinking that you are going to see something that is beginning to heal and look like the way you have always looked; you're going to be crushed. Not only that, but your reaction will crush your mother and father. You must get ready to accept that life is going to change and that you are going to have to change, too."

"Meg," Leslie insisted, "I know that you don't want me to be shocked by the stitches and stuff, but it can't be that bad. I mean I saw this model who had been cut and . . ."

"Leslie," Meg cut in, "the night they brought you in, you were cut up so badly that I didn't even know who you were. And if I didn't recognize you—your cousin who practically was a sister to you—then maybe you will realize just how bad your cuts were. We can't take a face like that and remake it into the one you had before this happened. I wish we could, but we just can't."

Silence filled the room for a few seconds, and then Meg, her voice now shaky and her eyes filling with tears added, "And your folks haven't seen the stitches, so they don't know how bad it is either. Leslie, you've got to be strong to handle this and then you have got to accept it and go on. It's not the end of the world unless you choose to make it that way. I once thought—you know when Steve was killed—that my world had ended, but it went on, and now it is very good again. It is not the same, and I still hurt, but I've proven to myself that life can still be sweet and wonderful and fulfilling."

The nurse stopped, patted her cousin's hand, and looked deep in her eyes. "Leslie, do you understand?"

"Meg, you told me Dr. Parks was the best."

"He is. You were in the best hands you could have been in. But the damage was too great. You'll probably have surgeries for years and by then it will be too late to model even if you do end up looking like the old Leslie."

"Meg," her voice drifted off and Leslie's eyes fell to the bed. A day that had been so good now seemed so dark.

"Listen, kid," Meg continued, "I probably

broke every rule in the book by telling you what I just did, but it is the truth. Tomorrow will be a day when you get to see yourself again. Please remember to look deeper than you ever have before. If you judge yourself with the standards by which you've always judged yourself, you will fail. Tomorrow you will discover what you are made of, so tonight you need to take a long inventory of what is important."

"And what is important?" Leslie asked.

"What's on the inside. That's how folks really judge anyone. At least folks who matter."

Getting up from her chair, Meg smiled and said, "I've been off duty for a while and I need to go get my daughter. Your folks are coming up in a few minutes. Please give them my best. I love you, kid."

Stepping out into the hall Meg wondered if Leslie could take it. Could she see what she was going to see tomorrow and move forward? Meg hoped so, but deep down she thought Leslie coming through tomorrow without having thoughts of suicide would be a long shot.

As she walked past the waiting room, she noted the cover of the current edition of *Fashion and Style* on a table. Picking it up, she took a long look at the photo. What was under that beautiful face would be revealed tomorrow. Shaking her head, Meg dropped the magazine in the trash and walked out into the afternoon sunshine.

33

Leslie slept fitfully and when morning finally did roll around she felt the kind of nervous anticipation usually reserved for the moments before the beginning of a big event like a modeling session, exam, or wedding. While she wasn't getting her photo taken, dealing with a major test, or being married, she was about to experience an instant that might just as radically change her life. This was the moment when the bandages came off and reality was revealed. And after Meg's warnings, Leslie was facing that prospect with great anxiety.

As the moments ticked by, Leslie attempted to lose herself in the idle chat of morning talk shows, but the drama of picking out just the right kind of paper towel or why the third world politicians always painted the United States as the bad guys failed to capture and hold her attention. She saw the screen but didn't absorb the images it was displaying. In reality, the noise and the pictures played to an audience of hospital furniture and bare walls.

She was now getting real food after spending a week on liquids, a week that she whiled away hours dreaming about everything that could be chewed. And now that it was here, it meant nothing. As bland as the morning shows were, breakfast was worse. It was a tasteless mixture of powered eggs, burned bacon, and cold toast accompanied by colder butter. None of it stimulated Leslie's palate. She just played with the meal. The nurse had just taken her tray away when Leslie's folks arrived.

"How are you doing, my poor baby?" Florence Rhoads's voice rang out as she entered. In her early fifties, she swept across the room and hovered by her daughter's bed. Johnathon Rhoads smiled at his daughter and took a seat on the far side of the room. It was obvious that Florence was the head of the house and her husband was little more than an ornament, much like the flashy bracelets that adorned the woman's wrist.

Johnathon had never been outgoing, not even as a child, but when he had accepted Florence Hankins's proposal, he had been forced to draw even deeper into himself. His wife was the star and he had seemingly adapted to the backup role and worked to provide her with all her needs. Their daughter had been one of Flo's projects, along with the garden club, historical society, and countless other organizations. He had simply been there for the important events and paid for all the necessary gowns. He, too, was a fashion plate simply because his wife dressed him. And

161

even now, at a moment when he should have been involved in every segment of his daughter's treatment, he seemed to be nothing more than an obscure shadow; an aging, two-dimensional image with no life.

Leslie had often wondered what her father would have been like if he had asserted himself. He was handsome, tall, and erect, with blue eyes like hers and a quick smile, but his good looks only came alive in photos. In real life, he was perceived as a black and white vision in a full-color world. It was almost as if he wasn't really there.

Flo was a different case. With her carefully groomed blonde hair, her perfect makeup, her long nails and tailored suits and dresses, she appeared to be a practicing member of the upper crust. But the practice went for naught as she was caught in a middle-class world. She had wanted so badly to be someone special, and when life had dealt her a middle-of-the-road hand, she had pushed to maintain the appearances of something more. She had gotten so caught up in the quest for image that she had pushed her daughter into the arenas of interests that had eluded her.

In Flo's mind, Leslie had been born beautiful and this was the next best thing to being born rich. Flo had seized upon that gift and pushed her daughter into the little beauty contests, then plays, then modeling, and finally into leaving college and using what God had given her in New York. Over the years, she had constantly lectured her daughter on the fact that she herself had wasted her own beauty and the opportunities by marrying a small-town boy and settling for a life that any woman could have. Leslie couldn't do that and Flo would be there to make sure she didn't.

Due to the mother living through the daughter, the Rhoadses' home had become a testament to Leslie's career. In every corner of every room there were photographs of the beautiful girl— pictures of her as homecoming queen, a twirler, a cheerleader, and a model. It was a shrine to her success, a museum that captured her beauty, but very little else. And that was because Flo saw her daughter's whole value in the incredible face and body she'd been given by birth.

"Hi, Mother," Leslie's greeting held little of her mother's charm or enthusiasm.

"Well," Flo began as she took her gloves off and placed them in her lap, "today is the day. We finally get to see just what kind of doctors they have here in Springfield. I'm hoping that they did a better job on you than they did on me last year when I had the mole removed. I mean, you can still see where it was. I told Johnathon we should've gone to St. Louis, Cleveland, Nashville, Atlanta, or New York and seen a specialist, but he didn't want to drive me, so I settled for what we had here, and when I get under a makeup light, I can still see proof that your father was wrong again." Turning toward her husband she added, "Isn't that right, dear?"

The man nodded.

"Anyway," she continued, "I told your father the night that you were hurt, why couldn't this have happened in New York. I mean they have good doctors, not these small town quacks that are here because they couldn't cut it anywhere else. I just hope they were able to do a better job on you than they did on me." Reaching into her purse, Flo pulled out a compact, studied her face carefully, and then exclaimed, "See, here it is. Can you believe that mole would leave a scar like that?"

Leslie starred at the spot that her mother showed her, but saw nothing. Still, she nodded, figuring it was safer to agree than open up a new chapter in the story.

"Leslie, Aunt Flo, and Uncle John." Meg's voice carried a forced enthusiasm as she stepped into the room. "I just saw Dr. Parks coming up the hall. I think he was waiting on Dr. Cunningham. When she gets here, we'll begin." Moving closer to the patient, Meg leaned over the bed and whispered, "It's going to be OK, kid. Don't worry about anything."

The next few minutes passed slowly as Meg and Leslie were forced to once again listen to

Flo's mole story and then another one about the poor quality of people who were now attending their church. She was launching into a critique of local shopping when the doctors arrived.

"Mr. and Ms. Rhoads, Leslie, how are we today?" Dr. Parks asked as he entered the room. "I think you all know Dr. Cunningham?"

Mary Ann nodded and took a place by the window. Walking to the foot of Leslie's bed, Dr. Parks smiled at his patient and then addressed everyone.

"None of you have seen Leslie's face yet. We thought it best to keep it under these wrappings until some of the swelling and discoloration had gone away. Still, we are a long way from being finished with our work. When the scar tissue that you will see today heals then we will do more surgery, and then more work after that. So it will take time for us to completely deal with the nature of what has happened here. If anyone here is expecting a miracle cure, just change your thoughts right now. It will take time for us to fully rebuild her face.

"Now, I would like Mr. and Ms. Rhoads to wait in the waiting room until we are through with the process."

"But," Flo began.

"No buts, Aunt Flo," Meg cut in. "Leslie needs to be the first, not you." Opening the door, the nurse escorted the two parents to the lobby and then returned to the room. Closing the door, she stood beside the doctor, a place where her cousin could clearly see her.

Turning on the light above the bed, Dr. Parks looked over his shoulder and asked Mary Ann to open the shades. With a sudden rush, sunlight lit up the room. Picking up his scissors, he began to cut away the wrappings.

Looking into the doctor's eyes, Leslie watched as the man examined each new area as it was exposed. Her heart raced as more and more of her face was uncovered. Her hands, hands that were slowly closing and opening, were clammy and cold. Her stomach was doing flip-flops and every muscle in her body was taut.

After the final bandage was removed, Dr. Parks carefully surveyed his work. Nodding his head, he glanced over at Meg and announced, "It was really a stroke of luck that we have not had to battle any infection. And the stitches are healing nicely. The color looks good at this point, too. In a way, we are further along than I thought we'd be."

Looking back at Leslie, he smiled. "Leslie, from a medical standpoint, things are going very well. As a doctor, I feel very good about what I'm seeing. But, just because I feel good about it as a doctor is not the same as you feeling good about it as a person. What I'm seeing and what you are going to see are two completely different visions.

"I'm looking at the end of a long road. I'm looking at your face as if it were a canvas with just a sketch roughly drawn on it. From this sketch, I will in time be able to complete the painting. But you must remember it is not even a half-completed work. So don't let what you see influence every one of your hopes about the way you are going to look for the rest of your life. Things will only get better from here. If you had seen yourself the night they brought you in, you would understand just how far you've already come.

"Now, Meg, if you will get me a large hand mirror, I think that it's time we allow Leslie to see her face."

Meg crossed the room to a table where she had earlier placed a large mirror. Picking it up, she took a cloth, wiped it clean, and then returned to the patient. Placing the mirror face down at Leslie's side, she stuck her hands into her pockets and silently said a short prayer.

"Are you ready?" Dr. Parks asked his patient.

Leslie didn't answer. A wave of fear rushed through her body, a fear that almost brought her heart to a stop. A part of her wanted to rewrap her face, to put off looking at herself for a while, to pretend that she still owned the face that graced the cover of four million copies of *Fashion and Style*. It would all be so much easier to hide behind the mask, to leave the unknown the unknown, to not see and therefore not believe, to deny rather than accept. But she knew that she couldn't do that.

Glancing up at Meg, she stared deeply into her cousin's warm, brown eyes. There was a certain comfort in knowing that Meg was beside her. There was an even greater comfort in knowing the nurse was staring at her without grimacing. So maybe it wasn't so bad.

Looking back at the doctor, Leslie nodded her head, grasped the mirror's handle in her right hand, and then hesitated and asked, "Would it be all right if I did this with Meg and no one else?"

Dr. Parks glanced over to Dr. Cunningham, who nodded. As he got up, he said, "We'll be right outside. When you're ready, I want to explain more fully what we have done and what we will do in the future."

When the two doctors left the room, Leslie looked over at her cousin. Smiling, Meg whispered, "It's just you and me, kid."

"That is the way I wanted it," Leslie replied. "I've got to know before I have to face Mom. You're going to have to help me."

"I will be there for you."

34

Taking a deep breath, Leslie lifted her arm and drew the mirror directly in front of her face. It took her eyes a second to focus; when they did, they locked onto the image in the glass, not moving, not even blinking.

"My God," she breathed, "Meg, what kind of horrible joke is this? This isn't me! This isn't even a face." Jerking the mirror back to her side, she frantically looked at her cousin. "Is this it? Is this the best they could do?"

"It is only a start," Meg assured her.

"Start?" Leslie moaned, "If this is a start, the race is over. My God, why didn't they just kill me? It would have been a whole lot less painful."

Leslie's heart was racing. Tears were clouding her eyes. She wanted to scream, but couldn't. She wanted to run, but there was no place to go. And even though she was no longer looking at the reflection of her face, the image was still there, burning a hole in her brain.

"Look at me, Meg," Leslie sobbed, "I'm a freak. The only thing I've got left is a pair of blue eyes and a set of perfect white teeth. What kind of nightmare is this?"

"It's the kind of nightmare you make it," Meg calmly reassured her. "Look back in the mirror."

"No!" Leslie shot back.

"You have to," Meg retorted. "You are never going to be a cover girl again, but you can still be something special. When Dr. Parks is done, and with the right kind of makeup, you won't be a freak, not unless you decide to make yourself one."

"I didn't do this," Leslie snarled, pointing to her face and suddenly remembering something else from the night of the attack. "Some monster did this and he wouldn't have if I had let him rape me. It would have been a whole lot easier to have lived with that, don't you think?"

"Look back in the mirror," Meg ordered. "The window to your soul is in those eyes. Look at them." Grabbing the mirror, the nurse held it in front of Leslie's face.

The woman stared at the image for just a second and then spat, "There is no soul. Not anymore. It died with my face!"

35

Meg spent five minutes trying to settle Leslie down before she felt it was time to allow her parents to get their first look at their daughter's face. As she stepped into the hall she noted the confrontation she feared might erupt had.

"She's my daughter," Flo yelled at Dr. Parks. "I'll go in there now if I want to. You can't keep me out. She doesn't need to be with her cousin, she needs her mother!"

Jumping up from her chair, Flo pushed past Meg and raced across the hall. Before anyone could stop her, she had opened the door, entered the room, and walked to her daughter's side. What she saw stopped her in her tracks. Pulling her hand up over her mouth she locked on the deep, red scars that ran jaggedly all over her daughter's face. Through unblinking eyes she took it all in. Then in a voice that dripped with rage she screamed, "What have you done to my baby?"

Meg moved towards her aunt, but before she could speak, Dr. Parks had made his way into the room and shouted, "Ms. Rhoads, please control yourself."

Looking past the doctor who had just entered

the room, Flo yelled, "Johnathon get in here. These butchers have ruined your daughter."

Meg looked to Leslie. The injured woman's jaw was slack, her blue eyes reflecting a hurt so deep it would have been impossible to measure. This was last thing she needed, but there seemed to be no way to stop Flo's biting rage.

As Leslie's father entered, Flo whirled around and pointed toward the bed. "Look at her Johnathon, just look at her. Look what they've done to my beautiful baby."

"Ms. Rhoads," Mary Ann Cunningham cut in.

"Don't you try any of your soft soap on me," Flo barked. "You aren't going to cover for the inept surgery of your colleague." Flo looked beyond the woman and to the doctor. "I'm going to sue and I'll make all of you pay. No one can do this to my little girl and get away with it."

Turning back to her daughter, she stared again at the scars and then, her tone softer, added, "Don't worry, honey, I'll take care of this meat cutter. Then I'll find someone to fix the mess he's made."

For Meg, that insult was the final straw. Though it was anything but professional, she felt the need to fire off a verbal assault of her own. "Shut up!" Meg screamed stepping between her cousin and her aunt.

"How dare you talk to me in that manner," Flo spat back.

"How dare you say anything," Meg answered. "Now, get out of this room!"

"I beg your pardon," the woman exclaimed.

"You heard what I said," Meg's voice was full of resolve. "Move."

Looking past Meg to her daughter the woman snapped, "It's just like you, taking the side of this miserable place. Your job is more important than your cousin's care. You always were selfish."

"Get out this door this minute," Meg demanded, pointing toward the exit, "and don't come back until you can actually treat your daughter with the gentle kindness she needs and the staff with the respect they deserve!"

Flo's eyes locked onto Meg. The staredown lasted only a few moments before the weaker of the two women glanced back to her husband. "Come on, Johnathon, let's get out of here. We need to call a lawyer." Beginning to move toward the door, she then added, "But I'll be back, and each of you will pay. You can't keep me away from my daughter for long."

"Uncle John!" When the man heard Meg's voice he stopped in his tracks. "You stay here."

"Come on, Johnathon," Flo yelled as she opened the door, "don't listen to her."

Looking at Meg's locked jaw, the man didn't move. Pausing for a moment, he finally said, "You go ahead, dear, I'll be with you in a second."

"You old fool," Flo said bitterly as the door swung closed.

Slowly walking across the room, Johnathon paused at his daughter's side. Nodding his head and smiling, he softly whispered, "You're still my beautiful little girl. Nothing or no one will ever change that."

Forcing a smile, Leslie reached out and took his hand. Squeezing it tightly, she took a deep breath and sighed, "I know I'm ugly, Daddy. Let's not pretend. But it wasn't the doctor's fault. If I had just given in to some demands, I'd still look like I did. In truth, I wish they'd just killed me."

"Leslie," Johnathon whispered, "don't say that."

"No," she quietly answered, her tone echoing a deep, haunting sadness, "I wish I were dead. But mom needs to know Dr. Parks didn't do this. So don't let her do anything that you don't want her to do. For the first time, stand up to her. Do the right thing. I'm tired of you being kicked around."

"Uncle John," Meg's voice caught the man's attention but didn't stop him from continuing to look deeply into his daughter's eyes. "She won't always look this way. With time she will be close to what she was. No one could have done a better job than Dr. Parks. I think that Leslie knows that and I want to make sure you do, too."

Nodding his head, Johnathon squeezed his daughter's hand one more time and then slowly walked out the door leaving Leslie alone with the two doctors and Meg.

For several moments, no one said anything. The scene they'd all just experienced had taken a heavy toll on them. Finally, Leslie broke the ice.

"How much better can I get?"

Walking across the room, Dr. Parks pulled a chair up to her bed and began to explain. Leslie listened as he told her about how the scars would heal, then there would be more surgery that would make the scars smaller. Sanding would even make them less noticeable, and finally, new kinds of cosmetics would cover most of the scars that were left.

"So someday," Leslie inquired, "I'll be able to come close to being normal?"

"Yes," the doctor replied, "as the years go by, you'll come closer and closer to the way you looked last week. Now, because of certain bits of nerve and muscle damage, your smile, the way your mouth moves, and other facial expressions will be different. But it will be a thousand times better than it is now. As I said, this is just the beginning."

"Thank you," Leslie stated, her clear tone indicating a degree of courage. "I deeply appreciate all that you've done."

"Les," Meg cut in, "this will sound hollow now, but you've got to remember that you're lucky to be alive."

"I'm not feeling lucky," Leslie sighed, "but it is what it is."

"Do you need anything else?" Dr. Cunningham asked.

"No," Leslie shrugged, "just a few minutes alone with my cousin."

"OK," the psychologist replied, "but if you do need something, please give me a call." Taking a final look at her face, Dr. Parks added, "Leslie, we'll take the stitches out tomorrow and then we'll let you go home. You will probably rest better there than here. I'll check on you this afternoon."

36

After the doctors left, the two women sat silently for a few moments. Neither looked at the other. Finally, Leslie issued a simple request, "Meg, would you close the curtains please? And while you are at it, turn off the lights."

Within seconds of the request, the room was dark, bathed only in the dim light that showed through the bottom of the curtains.

"You were right," Leslie sighed.

"About what?" Meg asked.

"About my face. It's worse than I led myself to believe. I really wish I had died."

"You don't mean that," Meg softly replied.

"Oh, yes, I do," Leslie sharply responded. "They could have closed the casket, no one would have ever known." After letting the words roll off her tongue, the woman began to allow a few stray tears to cloud her eyes. Trying hard to choke back sobs, she finally raised her arms and drove her fist into her bed. "I thought I was going to get through this and maybe bounce back. Maybe even . . ." She failed to finish, letting the words linger in the air like a thick morning fog.

"Maybe what?" Meg finally asked.

"Oh, it is too weird now," Leslie sighed. "I mean it is too far out."

"What?" Meg demanded.

Forcing a laugh, one filled with pain, Leslie whispered, "I even dreamed a little dream about falling in love with Hunter." Forcing another laugh, she added, "It would be a one-sided love affair wouldn't it?"

"I don't know about that," Meg answered. "I think that he probably had some similar thoughts when he came by here to see you. You have a lot in common."

"Yeah," Leslie replied. "He has a railroad track going across his knee, and I've got Grand Central Station carved into my face."

"That's not what I meant and it is not funny."

"What's the matter, nurse?" Leslie's tone was

now sharp. "I thought humor was an important part of the healing process."

"Listen," Meg's voice was calm and low. "Acceptance of reality and then a desire to beat the worst and become the best is what is needed to bring healing. That and a lot of love and faith."

"Faith?" Leslie questioned. "Do you know that if I had never heard that word, if I had not been so steeped in what was right and wrong, I would have taken the Passion Nights contract and stayed in New York. I would have never come home to talk with my folks about the rights and wrongs of doing it. That is what faith and God got me. Faith made me ugly. And do you really think that my mother could love a face that looked like this?"

"I can," Meg replied.

"Yeah," Leslie shot back, "maybe you're just glad that I'm no longer so much prettier than you are. After all, I'm the one who kept you from being the most beautiful girl in our family. Now you've got the title, don't you? I guess this worked out just fine in your eyes."

"You know that's not true!" Meg shot back. "I think that you need some time alone. I think that maybe you need to take a deeper look into that mirror and see if your beauty is any more than skin deep. Maybe I was wrong, maybe it isn't. Maybe all you are is just etched on the surface."

Meg paused and reached for her cousin's hand. "I told you yesterday that I loved you. I meant it.

I don't care what you look like, and what's more I never did. I just know that you can put it back together and if you want some help, I'll be there."

"Fine," Leslie replied. "I'll give you a buzz. Now, you're right, I do want to be alone."

As Leslie's deep blue eyes shot hateful arrows at her cousin, Meg set her jaw, rose from her seat and moved toward the door. As she opened it she took a deep breath before looking back to the bed. "You are still beautiful. I see it, and you will in time."

37

For the next few hours, Leslie sat in the dark, alternately crying and cursing. She was filled with a rage—an anger not so much directed at a moment or a person, but at God. She couldn't believe that He could do something like this to her. After a while, anger gave way to pity. She was wallowing deeply in this pool when she heard a knock on her door. Ignoring it, she sank back into her thoughts.

"Les?"

She immediately recognized Hunter's voice.

Great! This is just what he needs to see.

"Les?" he whispered again.

A voice inside her told her to play dead, to act as if she was asleep. Still another voice, a much smaller one, one that was still a part of her dying faith, yelled louder. It demanded company; it demanded another soul to share her pain. It was the latter voice that won.

"Is that you, Hunter?" Leslie called out from the darkness.

"Yes," he answered. "May I come in?"

"I guess so."

Leslie watched a small beam of light created by the opening door shoot across the far side of the room. Within seconds, it had disappeared. Stumbling in the dark, the visitor finally grew accustomed enough to the dim light to feel his way to a chair parked beside her bed.

"Kind of dark in here," he noted as he sat down.

"Yes," Leslie agreed and then added a lie, "but the light has been hurting my eyes, so I've kind of kept everything closed off."

"That's fine," Hunter responded. "Don't need the light to talk. This kind of reminds me of the time you and I sat out under the stars on the elementary playground. Gosh, we must have been freshmen and it was so dark that we couldn't even see our hands in front of our faces. It was strange, even as dark as it was, with only the dim light of those stars, I thought that you looked more beautiful than any girl I had ever seen."

Leslie's lips didn't move, they couldn't. She didn't know what to say.

"Les," Hunter said, "might be dark, just like it was way back then, but I can still see the life in your eyes. Do you know that there were times when the only thing I ever looked at were your eyes?"

Leslie fought back tears as her visitor continued to speak, "Meg told me that they cut you out of your mummy suit today. I bet you were happy to get rid of those things. I always thought bandages itched."

He waited for a response, and when it didn't come he continued, "I hear you are going to get to go home soon. Are you going to your folks?"

Up until this moment, Leslie hadn't thought about where she would be going. Suddenly it dawned on her she would have to be going back to the home of her youth. New York was out for now and there wasn't anywhere else. Nodding her head, she finally responded, "Yes, I guess I'll be going to Mother's for a while."

"Well, home cooking will probably taste pretty good for a change," Hunter laughed. "I mean it has got to be better than constantly eating out in New York."

"Oh, I don't know," Leslie added, "Mother's never been a very good cook. She never seemed to have time."

"Les," the man's voice was now a bit nervous.

"After you get out and back on your feet, I was kind of hoping that you and I could go out. Maybe see a show or maybe even eat at Big Al's. You know, do the things we used to do. I think it'd be fun."

The room filled with an awkward silence as Leslie struggled to find a way to answer her old friend's proposal. When no easy answers popped into her head, she used a standard one. "Well, I don't know how long it will take me to get back on my feet, and besides, I've heard that you can't go home again. Didn't some famous author say that once? So maybe reliving the old times wouldn't be such a good idea."

The dark room was silent for a moment, then Hunter's voice filled the void, "You know, you're probably right. When we go out we don't need to try to find the past, but rather discover the future. We're both different now and the world's different, too. We'll have to look for new adventures—do things we've never done.

"A big circus is coming to town next week and that's one thing we never did. I've never even been to one. Maybe we could go?"

"Hunter," Leslie's voice rang out harshly. "I don't think that you'd want to take me out to Big Al's or even the circus. If you did they might confuse me with one of the freaks."

"Oh, I don't know," he laughed.

There was only one way to put this man out of

his misery and that was with the truth. Reaching up, she jerked the pull string that served as the switch for the light that hung over her bed. As the light flashed on, it temporarily blinded both her and her guest. As he blinked his eyes, trying to get accustomed to the sudden brightness, she shouted, "Do you see what I am? Do you see what I look like? Do you realize how stupid you must be to ask me out? I'm not the beautiful little girl from the starlit playground. I'm . . ." Her voice trailed off as she couldn't force herself to finish what was lying so heavy on her heart.

Her eyes could see Hunter as he casually studied her. His face hadn't changed its expression; his blue eyes showed no traces of disgust and his body hadn't gone rigid. Finally, he smiled and said, "I didn't know that you didn't like the circus. I think it'd be great fun and I still want to take you, but maybe you'd like to have our first date be dinner at my place. You said your mother wasn't a good cook, well I am!"

"Hunter," Leslie pleaded, "don't do this to me. Don't pretend that I'm something that I'm not. Walk out right now. I'm not going to blame you. You don't have to follow through just because you're a gentleman. I'm hideous, I know that, and you don't have to try to fake your way through something you didn't ask for."

"Les," Hunter smiled. "I didn't buy that line about your eyes hurting today and I certainly knew from the bandages that the attack did a number on your face. I just want to spend some time with you. Now, I can understand if you aren't comfortable out in the real world yet. It takes a while, but no matter where, I want to spend time with you. Please, don't deny me that."

"I think you're stupid," Leslie sighed. "Or blind."

"Neither," Hunter replied. "I just know the value of an old friend and that beauty that I still see in those eyes."

"Fine," Leslie nodded. "My first night out of the house, I eat dinner with you. It will probably beat Mother's cooking by a long ways. But if between then and now you change your mind, I'll understand."

"I won't change my mind," Hunter grinned. "Now, if you will excuse me, I've got to get back to my office. I'll come by tomorrow."

"Thanks for coming by," she said. "And you don't have to come back."

"I know I don't," he replied, "but I will."

As he left, Leslie hit the call button. Within moments, Meg entered her room.

"I owe you an apology," Leslie sobbed.

"No," Meg whispered, "you don't owe me anything. Now, would you like something from the real world for dinner? Our janitor is going to pick up some food from Big Al's. All of the nurses have decided to pig out."

"Yeah," Leslie sighed, "how about a shake?"

"Let me run and catch him."

Meg hurriedly rushed from the room yelling, "Jacob, could you pick up a chocolate shake for my cousin?"

"The girl who was cut up?" the man asked.

38

"Everywhere I look I hit a dead end," Brian Rosatelli's voice displayed all the frustration he was feeling. "None of the white cars match."

"What do you mean, Cap?" patrolman Bruner inquired.

"You know the slashing victim?" The captain explained. "Well, she saw a white car pull out of the employee's parking lot a few nights ago and it was like the car that picked her up at the airport. Well, I've checked on all the employees who have white sedans. Three of them are unmarried women, and the fourth, a janitor named McCleod, told me that his car has been broken down for at least a month. He's been using his aunt's blue truck. It's a dead end. Someone else must have used the lot that night and there is no way that we can find out who."

"What about security cameras?"

Rosatelli shook his head. "None out there. It's not like New York or L.A. where everyone has every angle covered. Those TV shows make it look like there are cameras showing every part of the world all the time. Fat chance! There aren't any in the hospital hallways either."

The lack of cameras was normally something Rosatelli pointed to with a sense of pride. There wasn't that much crime in Springfield. The old Midwestern values were still in place. Most folks left their doors unlocked right up until the moment they went to bed. Yet now that a violent crime had occurred, this lack of full coverage was frustrating. At no key point in this case was there a single scrap of video footage. Not at the airport, the alley, or the hospital! Like it or not, Springfield was going to have gear up its security in order to protect its citizens during this more violent age.

"Is the car all you have got to go on?" Bruner asked.

"Yeah, Charles," Rosatelli admitted. "The woman never saw her attackers and she doesn't really remember much anyway. So there's a madman on the streets and we are helpless when it comes to finding him. We don't have a clue, except for a white car, and there are just a few thousand of them around here."

Bruner shook his head. "Cap, that may not be the case. As she was picked up at the airport and we have had nothing since, it could have been someone passing through who just took advantage of the moment. Kind of an impulse thing! The guy might be a thousand miles away now."

"Yeah," Rosatelli answered, "I've considered that. Even spent a full day online looking at other crimes in other places. Figured I might see a pattern. But nothing! Then there is the nature of the attack. What was the motivation? Cutting someone up with a broken bottle signals this was a personal crime—one motivated by deep animosity toward the victim. Yet she wasn't hated. And there was no sexual assault. In the norm, there would have been. None of the clues fit. She had no enemies, no ex-boyfriends, no jealous friends, no one with an agenda against her."

Picking his cell phone up off the desk he moved quickly toward the door. Glancing back over his shoulder, he said, "Well, I think I'll call the hospital and see if Ms. Rhoads remembered anything else. Maybe she can give me something else to go on."

"Hey, Cap," the patrolman asked, "have you put it on Crime Stoppers? Maybe you could get someone to call in if there's a reward. Money often trumps fear!"

"It's going on the air next week," Rosatelli answered, just before he left.

As he stared out on Springfield's calm streets, he scratched his head. This one made no sense at all. With crimes, there are always whys that lead him to a who, but not in this case. There simply is no reason for anyone Leslie Rhoads knew to do this to her—no reason at all.

39

"Boy, this place sure is dark," Flo Rhoads complained as she walked into her daughter's hospital room. "Why don't you turn on the lights?"

"Great idea, Mom," Leslie answered. "Why don't we put out a sign and charge admission, too." She raised her voice to mimic a carnival barker, "Come one, come all, see the freak! Catch her now and we guarantee you won't sleep for a week."

"Yeah, you look horrible," Flo replied, "but we will make them pay."

"Who, Mom?" Leslie answered. "Who are you going to sue? The doctors did what they could and we don't know who cut me up. Why don't you just grow up and face the facts? This is what happened and this is the way I look."

"I don't have to do that," Flo shot back. "Somebody's going to pay and pay big for taking my daughter from . . ." The woman paused as her eyes locked onto Leslie's face.

"Come on, Mom," Leslie pushed her, "finish it." She waited for a second, and when her mother said nothing, Leslie added, ". . . taking my daughter away from me. Not my daughter's face, not her beauty, but her whole being. To you, it's like I died. In fact, you would rather I had died!"

"That's not what I meant and you know it." Flo's weak apology failed to ring true.

"Mom," Leslie's voice was filled with bitterness, "the first words out of your mouth when I was born were not, 'Is she healthy?' but 'is she beautiful?' You used to brag to everyone about how beautiful I was from day one. Was it that day I became your project? After all, ever since I can remember you have spent your life telling me, forcing me, to be all the things that you said you could have and should have been if you'd had better parents or a more suitable husband. Lucky for you I was beautiful because it gave you something to live for. Now, I'm not beautiful, but I'm reasonably healthy, and it's not enough. You see, I can't become the things you wanted to be anymore. You can no longer look on the cover of a magazine, see my face, and imagine that it is you. Now your daughter is just another person and I'm not the person that you want. I'm an ugly person, so for someone like you, I have no value. I'm not someone you can be proud of anymore!"

Flo turned her face toward the window, crossing her arms under her ample bosom. Leslie waited for a few moments to see if the woman would put up an argument, even a weak one, but it was quickly apparent there was none coming.

"Mother, I've spent my life being a computer that you programmed and operated. You molded me into a successful model, but what kind of person did you mold me to be? I don't know who I am beyond my face! I don't think there is anything in me except my beautiful face and this body. And, if that is the case, then my life is over. Admit it, you think it is. You think that without my face, I'm worthless. So, you want to sue somebody—anybody—to make sure I, and probably you, have the money my beauty would have earned."

"Honey," Flo pleaded, "you deserve some money. I mean you were almost at a point where you would've been worth millions. Your agent told me about the perfume promotion. It would've made your career."

"Wait a minute," Leslie interrupted her mother, "I came home so that you would talk me out of that ad. I thought you would freak over the nudity. I mean, what would those little old ladies in your garden club say when they saw me naked?"

"Oh, Les," Flo's tone was now sad and low, "the nudity would've been no big deal. You would've been famous. It was just an ad. And it would have showed your real beauty. It would have made your career. I wouldn't have stopped you from being the envy of every woman in the world. That is what I always wanted for you."

"That's great, Mother!" Leslie exclaimed. "I spent my life trying to live up to your godly principles in order to be the kind of good girl you wanted, and when it meant a career break, those things meant nothing. Now, I realize you only put up a token fight against the booze ad so that you could have something to hold over me. It had nothing to do with Steve's death. You didn't once think of the pain it might cause Meg!"

Leslie was on a roll and she wasn't going to let up until she had revealed all the deep-seated grudges she had been holding against the woman who'd given her life.

"Do you even know who I am? Am I your daughter or am I just a series of still photographs, a series of beautiful images caught momentarily by a digital camera, and then framed like a bunch of first place trophies? You better decide, because if all I am is Leslie the model, Leslie the beautiful face, then I died in that alley. So, why don't you dig me a grave?"

"Now honey . . ."

"Don't, Mother, don't even start. Why don't you just get out of here? I'll call you when it's time for me to come home. Oh, and please buy a bunch of veils for me to wrap my face in so you don't have to look at it ever again. Or better yet, have a mask made from the cover of *Fashion and Style*. Then you could pretend I am still that beautiful baby you dreamed of and held onto for so long."

Putting up no argument, Flo Rhoads smoothed her hair, grabbed her purse, and pushed out of the room. She didn't even bother to mouth a goodbye.

In the darkness of the room, Leslie continued to fume. She was angry, not so much at her mother—she had long accepted the fact that her mother did not look beyond the surface at any-one—what was upsetting her were the questions that she couldn't answer about herself. Without a beautiful face, she didn't know if she had any value. She had never been the center of attention at parties because of her humorous quips, spark-ling concepts, or deep insights. She had impressed people by flashing her teeth or batting her eyes. It'd never taken any more than that, and she wondered now if she had anything else to give. Was that all there was to her? She had never been so grateful when her thoughts were interrupted by a ringing phone. After pulling on the light cord she found the receiver and answered.

"Hello."

"Leslie, Captain Rosatelli here. Listen, I've drawn a blank on the white car. Have you come up with anything else?"

"No," Leslie answered, "I don't know anything else." Pausing a moment, she brought her left hand up to her face, letting her fingers linger on the rough stitches. As almost an afterthought, she inquired, "When are you going to get this guy? I want him put away."

"So do we, Ms. Rhoads," Rosatelli assured her. "And we are doing all we can, but . . ."

"No buts," Leslie's voice was suddenly rough and coarse, almost as if she was channeling her inner Flo. "If you were a real police force rather than some hick organization, you'd have him. Listen, he ruined me, I'll never work as a model again and I want to see him pay."

"Well, we're doing all we can, and I'm sure that we will get our man. You don't worry about it. Call me if you think of anything new."

Minutes after Leslie hung up, Meg strolled into her room. She was wearing a blue skirt and a white and red blouse. She looked a lot more like a model than a nurse.

"Well," Leslie inquired, more than a bit put off by her beautiful, stylish cousin, "where's the uniform?"

"Even I get days off," Meg responded. "I see you're using the lights today."

"I had to turn it on to find and answer the phone," Leslie explained as she reached up and pulled the off switch. "Why did you come by?" Her inquiry was anything but friendly.

"Well, to see you. Your mother called and said that you were not having a good day. And my mom wanted to see Dawn anyway, so I thought I'd check on you."

"Mother doesn't know what she's talking about," Leslie shot back. "She's the one not having a good day. I'm fine. Bored, but fine."

"Yep," Meg smiled, "judging by your tone, I'd say that you're handling everything just perfectly."

"Well," Leslie snidely answered, "how would you feel?"

"About the same as you," Meg admitted. "I might even be a little madder. You wouldn't believe the person I became when Steve was killed. I'm really glad you didn't see me then. I was almost demonic. And while I don't want you to sink to the level I did, I'm glad that you're fighting. That's good. And even though I wouldn't want to tell her this, I think that you said a few things that your mother needed to hear. If you hadn't told her, I might have. But, you need to put that behind you and start dealing with what's real. And you need to cry. I put that off when I lost Steve, and I wish I hadn't. You need to admit how deeply hurt you are and let it out."

"I've been trying," Leslie replied, a softness returning to her tone. "I just can't cry. I'm too angry to cry. And worse yet, I don't have any answers. I do know that I want the guy who did this caught and punished."

"Sure, we all do," Meg quietly agreed. She paused a moment before softly asking, "And what about the face? Have you looked at it today?"

"No." The reply was short and direct.

"Well, it still has a long way to go," Meg admitted, "but more of the redness is gone and it does look better. The stitches are ready to come out. As a matter of fact, Dr. Parks is going to remove them this afternoon. Then he'll let you go home. I told your mother that I thought it would be best if I picked you up and took you to her house. Do you mind?"

"No," Leslie replied, shaking her head, "that would be a whole lot better than having Mother get into it with Dr. Parks again. I don't need another scene like the one we had yesterday."

"Fine," Meg's voice was reassuring. "I'll be back in a few hours. Do you want me to get you something? Anything?"

"Meg, is there a specific time I'll get released?"

"No, not really," she answered.

"Good," Leslie stated. "I don't want to walk out of here until after dark. OK?"

"Sure kid."

"Thanks," Leslie smiled, "I knew that you'd understand."

40

"Hello, Les."

"Hi, Hunter!" Leslie answered. "How are you doing?"

"Fine." His voice was so clear he sounded as if he was in the same room not across town. "A more important question is, how are you doing?"

"Well, I must be pretty good," she explained. "They're letting me out of here and sending me home later this evening."

"Want me to drive you?" There was an eagerness in his voice she couldn't fathom.

"No, thanks a lot, but I promised Meg that she could. It'd mean a lot to her." Leslie had almost choked on her overstatement, but no matter what Hunter had said the day before, she still wasn't comfortable with him seeing her scars, particularly not in normal light.

"I can understand that," Hunter's tone was still enthusiastic, "I'm just glad you're going home. I probably didn't tell you this, but my apartment is just a few blocks from your folks' house. You probably know the spot, 115 Hubbard, Chapman Square Apartments."

"Yes, I think they were building those when I

left for college," Leslie answered. "Aren't they made out of brown brick?"

"You got it," Hunter laughed. "Ugly brown brick. But it's not bad for a carefree single guy. What time are you going to get home? I'll come over and see you."

"I don't know what time, but if you don't mind, why don't you give me a little time to settle in with my folks before you drop by." A part of her really wanted to see Hunter, but a bigger part of her wanted to retreat into a dark world, one without visitors. She was sincerely hoping that home would be a place where she could hide.

"No problem, maybe later in the week."

"Just call," Leslie suggested.

"OK, I need to get back to work. Bye."

"Bye."

She was still confused over whether and if she wanted to see him as she set the room phone back in its cradle. She wanted company and she dreaded being locked in the same house as her mother. But then there was her face. It might be easier just to maintain a friendship via the phone. That way she wouldn't have to wonder if he was focusing on her scars or on her heart.

As she stood beside her bed, she caught a glimpse of herself in the mirror. Though she knew the scars were there, it still shocked her. They were deep, red, and angry. It was like someone had torn a handkerchief in a hundred pieces and then tried to piece it back together but with the wrong color thread. Running her still bandaged fingers over her face, she sighed. They felt even worse than they looked. It was like touching a relief map.

"Anybody home?"

Leslie's eyes left the mirror to her cousin. "Yeah, I'm here."

"Feeling OK?"

"I'm fine, Meg. They took the stitches out, gave me some meds. It's good to have the IV out. But I don't know if I'm ready to leave. I think it might be easier to be a freak in a hospital than to be one out there." Leslie pointed to the window.

"Come on," Meg smiled as she patted her cousin on her back, "let me help you pack."

The room was silent for a few minutes as the two women pulled together the few things Leslie had at the hospital. It was Meg who broke the silence with a question that was far off the previous line of conversation.

"What do you want to do with all of these flowers?"

"I don't want to take them home," Leslie answered as she looked around the room. "But there sure are a lot of them."

"A lot were from other parts of the country," Meg explained. "It seems you have a lot of fans."

"Had a lot of fans," Leslie corrected her.

"How about if I ask one of the nurses," Meg

suggested, "to give them to some of the folks who haven't gotten anything during their stay?"

"That'd be fine," Leslie agreed. "Maybe something good could come out of this."

"Why don't you wait here," Meg said, "and I'll tell Molli we're leaving and that she will have some floral deliveries to make. Why don't you call your Mom and give her the word we'll be there in a few minutes."

Picking up the phone, Leslie dialed the familiar number and waited for a response. "Dad, this is Les."

She waited for a moment and then assured him, "I'm fine. Meg and I will be there a little later. Tell Mom I'll see you soon."

Walking over to the mirror, Leslie took another long look at the scars that lined her face. Grabbing a brush, she attempted to comb her shoulder length hair in a Veronica Lake style that at least hid a few of them.

As she slipped the brush into her purse, Meg came back in. "Do you think Hunter could fall for me now?"

"I don't know," Meg admitted. "But I feel that if he'd have fallen for you a month or a year ago, he could now. You're still the same person on the inside."

"The inside isn't what I'm talking about," Leslie sadly nodded. "A month ago I would have wowed him with a flash, a wink, a smile, and a face that could have moved most any man. I can't do that now and I don't want to be a charity case for anyone."

"You?" Meg said as she raised her left eyebrow, "A charity case?"

After sitting back on the corner of the bed, Leslie asked, "Do you remember Blanche Ward?"

"No," Meg shook her head, "the name doesn't ring a bell."

"Well, Blanche was in my class, and she was very nice, smart, even funny, but she was also very plain. And she was overweight. I was thinking about her last night. Tommy McCall took her out after he broke up with Connie Seymour."

"Wasn't Connie the girl with the long blonde hair and the body that wouldn't—well, you know?" Meg laughed as she motioned in a swirling manner.

"That was Connie all right," Leslie smiled, "except I think that your top motion should have been a bit more pronounced. Everything about Connie spelled sex appeal. I used to marvel at her walk. I swear she threw her hips so far from side to side that she could close the locker doors on both sides of the hall with her hips."

"There was a girl in my class like that," Meg said as she put a few more items in a bag.

"Anyway," Leslie continued, "Tommy took Blanche out a few times and she fell head over heels for him. She would wash his car, do his homework, followed him around like a little lap dog. There wasn't a moment when she wasn't thinking about her Tommy.

"It lasted for about a month. Then Tommy dumped her and went back to Connie. I don't think Tommy meant to hurt Blanche; he was only trying to prove to himself that there were things more important than looks. In a way it was a noble effort, but the effort caused Blanche a great deal of pain. When she fell back to reality, she fell hard. She withdrew for the remainder of her high school years. I mean she was there, but her personality was missing. And then, she went to college somewhere downstate. No one I know has heard from her since."

"Tough," Meg noted. "Not easy being a high school girl."

"It is more than just high school," Leslie said. "Tommy took Blanche out for the wrong reasons. He just wanted to prove that he was a good person with some wonderful qualities. That he was more than just a good-looking guy, but that he had a big heart and mind that saw deeper than a face or a body. So, it was really a missionary date. Something to make him feel good about himself."

"In relationships, there is pain," Meg suggested. "You get hurt several times before you really find love."

"But," Leslie cut in, "isn't that what Hunter's

doing? Am I just a feel-good date? Is he talking to me for missionary reasons? Kind of like the way he volunteers to work with problem teens?"

"I don't think so," Meg replied.

Looking back toward the mirror, Leslie again ran her fingers over the scars. Shaking her head, she pulled a scarf from her purse and tied it in such a way that it covered both her hair, and the bottom part of her face. Finally, she put on an oversized pair of sunglasses. Looking back at her reflection, she nodded her head. She hadn't completely covered the mess, but she had managed to hide the majority of it.

"You ready?" Meg asked.

"Yeah," Leslie responded while turning to face her cousin.

"Well," the nurse mused, "I see that you have dressed for the occasion."

A bit put off by her cousin's remark, Leslie shot back, "You didn't expect me to go out like I looked, did you? I mean people would stare."

"They will now too," Meg softly informed her, "but it's your decision. If that's how you want to look, that's fine with me. By the way, your sweater's beautiful. I wish that I could look that good in jeans, too."

"You do," Leslie shrugged, "but does the way I'm covering up my face look that weird? By the way, I don't want a wheelchair. No way!"

"I tell you what," Meg assured her. "I have to

roll you out the door, but as soon as it closes, you can get up and walk on your own. And by the way, you look all right, that is, if you are trying to hide something."

"I am," came the blunt reply. "Now will you check if anyone is in the hall before you wheel me out."

Glancing out the door, Meg called back, "It's all clear."

The short hundred-foot trip to the back door was the longest that Leslie ever remembered making—longer than any runway during a show or stage during a pageant. Rather than having each foot draw her closer, it seemed that each one put her farther and farther away. Finally, after what seemed like hours, she made it. She was just getting out of the chair when an older couple strolled up the walk.

"Good evening, ladies," the gentleman said.

Panicked, Leslie glanced at the sidewalk and hurried out the door into the night air. Once in the parking lot, she raised her head as her eyes searched for her cousin's familiar yellow Mustang. Spotting it, she surged ahead, almost like she was running a race.

"Wait up," Meg hollered as she doubled her steps to catch up. "You're supposed to take your time and at least act like you are feeling a little bit sick. I mean, after all, you just got out of the hospital."

Ignoring her cousin's pleas, Leslie maintained her pace, stopping only when she arrived at the passenger door of the car. After she loaded the bags in the trunk, Meg hopped in the driver's side and buckled up. Looking over at her cousin, she smiled and waited for her to do the same thing.

"Let's go," Leslie urged.

"As soon as you buckle your belt," Meg responded.

"Oh for God's sakes, Meg," Leslie snapped back. "We aren't going that far."

"Yeah," the driver admitted, "but most accidents happen close to home. Besides, if I had to make a quick stop, you'd go flying into the windshield."

"It couldn't hurt me any more than I am now, so what's the difference?"

"The big difference," Meg smiled, "is that you would bleed on my interior and this car is the only possession of real value I have in the world. I don't want you smashing the windshield or staining my interior."

Shaking her head, Leslie submitted and snapped her belt into place. Smiling, Meg flipped the key and once the engine caught, backed out of the parking lot and headed down the road. She had driven four blocks before either of them spoke.

41

"I don't think Hunter is pulling a missionary dating trick on you."

"What?" Leslie asked.

"Like what's-his-name did to Blanche," Meg answered. "I think that you're dreaming up a bunch of stuff when you're talking about romance. I mean Hunter is probably looking for a friend, someone to share some old times and make some new ones. The last thing you need to do is worry about whether he loves you. There's more to life than just love, or for that matter, more to love than just looks. You ought to think about that. Don't cut yourself off from a friend that you may need just because you think that you're different. It's OK to be scared, but don't let fear control you. After all, if you can walk through Central Park by yourself or grow up in the same house with your mom, then surely you can find enough courage to handle whatever happens in your relationship with him."

Leslie didn't respond to Meg's words, but they did make sense, and having Hunter consider her just a friend would make dealing with her own problems much easier. After all, a friend could readily overlook scars and flaws. So, she would just have to make sure that the relationship remained nonromantic. Of course, convincing her heart to do that would be far easier than convincing her mind.

"We're here," Meg announced as she pulled the car into the driveway. "I can see your mother waiting on the porch."

Glancing up, Leslie caught her mother's stocky form marching down the front steps and toward the car. Her father was waiting just outside the door.

"Leslie Marie," Flo's voice boomed across the yard and likely alerted everyone on the block to what was happening, "how I do wish you would have let me bring you home. My Cadillac would've been so much more comfortable than Meg's old sports car. I mean the ride must have been terrible, especially with your injuries. Come here, honey, and let me help you across the yard."

Shaking her head as she exited the car, Leslie looked across the street and saw Mr. and Ms. Boyd sitting out on their porch enjoying the night air. Now realizing her mother was putting on a show for the neighbors, she decided to change the rules of the game.

"Mom, I'm fine. It was my face, not my feet that suffered the most. I'll make it without your help." Then, as Meg popped the trunk on the car, a mischievous grin crossed Leslie's lips. "But

Mom, if you do want to help, why don't you grab my bags."

"A . . . a . . . a . . ." Flo stammered as she looked into the dusty trunk. "A . . . Johnathon, why don't you be a dear and come down here and get your daughter's things. I better walk alongside of her, just in case she stumbles or something."

"I'd better help her up the stairs," the man answered with a smile. "You get the bags."

Meg nodded, smiled, and slipped back into her car. After her eyes met Leslie's and Leslie nodded, she started the Mustang and backed out of the drive. Leslie's eyes followed the yellow car until it drove out of sight.

Leslie stayed up long enough to eat a bit of the food her mother had picked up at a deli and then begged off to go to her room. As she closed the door a strange kind of feeling settled over her. All around her were visible signs of the past, pictures of her with old friends, at high school dances and at slumber parties. From a large bulletin board hung dried out Homecoming mums, cheerleader letters, and funny notes. Pennants and posters covered the walls and old books and diaries lined two white shelves. In all the years she had been gone, her mother had changed nothing. This room was almost like a shrine.

Sitting at her desk, she opened a drawer and pulled out a desk tray filled with old letters. Under the tray were some snapshots and finally her senior annual. Putting the letters and photographs back, she closed the drawer, picked up her yearbook, and wandered slowly across the room to her bed. Lying down she began to leaf through the pages. She stopped when she got to the one that showed *Springfield High's Most Handsome and Most Beautiful.*

Looking back from the page was a much different Hunter. He didn't possess that self-confidence that he had on the two days she had recently seen him. He was good looking, but in a juvenile sort of way. On the other hand she appeared very much like she had on the cover of *Fashion and Style.* While Hunter's pose looked unnatural and therefore a little awkward, she looked so perfect that the image seemed a bit staged. Hunter looked eighteen, she looked twenty-five. Now, just at the moment he'd caught up with her, he had left her far behind. He appeared like he stepped off the cover of *GQ* while she belonged on *Monsters Illustrated.*

A slowly creeping depression seeped into the room as she continued to study the annual's pages. Feeling the emotions begin to play with her ability to think and keep things in perspective, Leslie closed the book and got ready for bed. Turning out the light, she glanced out her window and down on the street that had changed so little during the time she had been away.

As she stared out into the moonlit street, a tug-of-war was being waged in her mind. A part of her begged to escape to old memories while another facet asked her to accept what she had become. Somewhere she heard a laughing, the kind of laughing the wicked witch had employed in *The Wizard of Oz*. Trying to find its point of origin, she soon realized it was coming from deep within her own head.

42

In New York, Leslie had never watched television. With her busy life and work schedule, she simply hadn't had the time. Now, it seemed, it was all she did. From the time she got up on her first day staying in the house where she'd grown up to this moment, almost four days later, she'd done nothing but eat, sleep and bury herself in game shows, soap operas, and syndicated reruns. By doing so, she avoided having to listen to her mother run down the quality of local doctors and lawyers as well as the horrid leadership of the social clubs that seemed to take every spare moment of her life. During these rants, the more her mother talked, the louder Leslie turned up the volume on the TV.

Even though a host of family friends had come

by, except for Meg, Leslie had refused to see anyone. When company came she hid in her room, the TV blaring, and ignored her mother's knocks on the door. She couldn't bear the thought of revealing how she looked to those who'd once known her beautiful face. The strange thing was that her mother seemed to want to put her on display. Flo was taking some kind of perverse pleasure in using Leslie to attack the local medical community and police force.

Leslie did take Hunter's calls. They chatted about old times, his work and local happenings, but when he suggested coming by for a visit, she cut him off. She was not going to let him see her either. She didn't even look at herself. For the entire time she had been home, Leslie had refrained from using direct light and she had not allowed her folks to open the shades. By living in the dark, she kept everyone else there, too.

On a Friday afternoon, Leslie's fifth day at home, Flo strolled into Leslie's room, marched up to the TV, turned the set off, and looked toward the bed where Leslie had been curled up. "Honey, I really do want to stay here with you, but if I don't go to the Garden Club meeting heaven knows what Gladys Short will pick out to go in front of the new library. That woman thinks that she is such an expert on plants and landscaping just because she got a degree from Iowa State University. I mean, what can you learn in college about things like that! You're born with that skill, you can't teach it. I know so much more than she does about what looks good. If you don't believe me look at her front yard. I told the landscaping service where everything should be placed."

Leslie just nodded, grabbed the remote, and turned the TV back on. A nostalgia channel was showing an old black-and-white episode of *Gilligan's Island*.

"Fine, Mom," Leslie mumbled, keeping her eyes glued to the flickering images of the skipper and his first mate, "I'll be fine."

When, a few minutes later she heard her mother's car pull out of the driveway, Leslie said goodbye to the professor and the movie star, turned the television off and got out of bed. Wandering through the house she fully embraced the gifts of silence and solitude. Finding her father's old tomcat curled on a living room windowsill, she sat down beside him and began to stroke his head. Glancing up, the cat momentarily studied her, then once more shut his eyes.

"Spot, you've been in some fights since I left," Leslie told the uninterested cat. "Your ears are shredded and that scar across your nose proves you may have lost a few more battles than you've won. Age must be catching up with you.

"Kind of funny how the world goes on no matter what happens to us. I mean you could get run over tonight on your rounds and except for Dad missing you for a few weeks nothing would really change. That's the way it is for me, too. The modeling world is going on, someone else is doing the campaign that supposedly only I could do and Springfield just keeps being Springfield. Unfortunately, this all happens with me being very much alive. If I'd only died then things would really be back to normal.

"By the way, how do you take Mother's grating complaints all day long?"

Glancing up from the cat, Leslie noted an old blue truck parked across from her house. It appeared very out of place on a street that boasted only the finest in upper-class American cars. As she looked closer, she noted a man was sitting inside the old vehicle and appeared to be staring at her house. Passing it off as someone waiting for a neighbor to get home, Leslie turned her attention back to the old cat. A few minutes later, she got up from her seat and returned to her room to watch television.

Gilligan was now over, but *Mr. Ed* had taken over the screen and for the next half hour it was the horse, of course, who grabbed the young woman's attention. After the talking horse rode off *Tales of the Gold Monkey* came on. She gave it five minutes, grew bored, and walked to the kitchen to grab a snack. She was chowing down on potato chips when she heard the doorbell.

Ignoring it, she continued to eat. Finally, after seven rings, she gave in and ambled to the front entry.

"Hunter," she exclaimed as she cracked the door a few inches. Why was he here? Hadn't she made the point that she didn't want to see him face to face?

43

"Hi," the handsome man replied. "I got off early today and seeing as how it was such a beautiful afternoon, I thought that I'd come by and see you." As he finished, a rumble of thunder could be heard in the distance. Looking back over his shoulder at the approaching storm, he grinned and added, "Well maybe it will be a beautiful day for a few more minutes, and then a really great one if you're a duck." He grinned and asked, "You're not a duck, are you?"

Keeping the door cracked she replied, "No."

"Didn't think so."

Leslie stared at Hunter for several moments, not talking nor opening the door. She was unsure as to the next move. She wanted him to come in, but she didn't want him to see her. Finally, when the thunder rumbled again, he broke the silence.

"I'm going to get wet if I continue to stand out here much longer. If I do, I may melt. I'm just that sweet. So, could I come in?"

Nodding, Leslie pulled the door open enough to allow him to step in and then pointed toward the den. Excusing herself, she ran up to her room, and then, after applying a thick layer of makeup and putting on a large pair of sunglasses, came back to visit. Walking across the room from her visitor, she found a seat on a sofa in a dark corner. After she had sat down, he began the conversation.

"I've been getting the feeling that you're avoiding me. I mean, I've tried to wrangle an invite over here to see you and every time I mentioned it on the phone, you've put me off. Now, I want to know the truth, is it my deodorant or my mouthwash? And if it is one of those, don't worry, I've changed since the last time I saw you."

Laughing, he continued, "But seeing as how you are way over there and I'm way over here, you couldn't know that, could you? So, I'll just come over to where you are and prove it."

She didn't want him to move. She didn't want him to get closer. But he reacted before she could speak. Jumping up, Hunter literally bounced across the room in four quick strides and plopped down beside Leslie. Smiling, he inquired, "Well, how do I smell?"

Shaking her head, she raised her hand and moved her hair more over the right side of her face. After she had accomplished that, Leslie shrugged her shoulders and answered, "Fine."

"Good, now we can talk about real important stuff like am I getting my shirts bright enough or do you think I should switch to New Tide?"

Swallowing a laugh, Leslie looked over the top of the sunglasses and stated, "I'd definitely consider a switch, beginning with where you shop for shirts."

"That's cold," Hunter shot back.

"No," Leslie grinned, "that's honest."

Checking out the pattern on his shirt, Hunter's look turned much more serious as he asked, "What's wrong with it?"

"Nothing," Leslie laughed, "but I had you going, didn't I?"

A bemused look returning to his handsome face, the lawyer relaxed on the couch and placed his hands behind his head. "Boy, I've missed you."

"You just talked to me yesterday," Leslie answered.

"No, not that way," Hunter explained. "I've missed being around you. I don't know how to explain it, but the two times I've seen you, even when you were in your mummy costume, it has been like finding a part of myself that I thought was gone. Do you understand?"

Shaking her head, Leslie indicated she didn't.

Casting his eyes back toward hers, he stared into her sunglasses, obviously struggling to find the words to explain his feelings. "Les, the people that I know from my high school days, they're still here. Most of them have never gone away and because of that their perspective on life hasn't changed. It doesn't make any difference that I'm a lawyer, because to them I'm still and always be that old high-school jock. So visiting with them makes me feel old, like my life has all been lived and I'm just marking time until they cover me up with dirt.

"But from the moment you and I talked, I felt strangely alive. I mean you seemed to want to know that I have changed and you accepted that. It was like you wanted me to share my current life with you. When we talk on the phone, it's not about something that happened in high school, it's about a case I'm working on or a kid I'm helping. And you sound interested in that part of me. That's nice and it makes me feel so good."

Leslie hoped the words he'd spoken hadn't registered on her face. She didn't want him to see how conflicted she was. Maybe the sunglasses could hide that fact. Yet they wouldn't for long. As she tried to mask her emotions behind the shades, he slowly reached over and lightly grabbed the corners of the frames, gently pulling them from her face. Reacting too late to stop him, Leslie turned her head toward the far wall.

"Don't," Hunter softly requested. "Don't turn away from me. You don't have to. You're a living, breathing person to me, not an image on a magazine. I want to see your eyes, to read them, to know that you are understanding what I'm saying. In order for me to do that, you have to open up those blue windows to your soul."

Hunter gently took Leslie's deeply scarred chin in his big left hand, carefully missing the cuts, and turned it back toward him. Looking into her blue eyes, he smiled. Glancing down for a second, she took a deep breath and then allowed her eyes to return to his. Forcing a crooked smile, the only kind she could now make, she nodded her head.

"I figured that you understood," Hunter's voice was soft and reassuring, "but I had to know.

"Leslie," he continued, letting his hand drop from her chin, "you can't close the whole world out. Not now, not ever. It's kind of like playing solitaire. If you play that game the only person you ever beat is you. The only person who wins is you, too. There is more to life than that. The person who walks away from the world also walks away from himself. Once you do that, only fear, loneliness, and bitterness remain. I won't let you do that, at least not without a fight."

Leaning against the couch, he crossed his legs

and looked out across the room. On a far wall hung a huge photograph of Leslie. It had been taken her first year in college. As he studied it, he began to tell a story.

"For the past few weeks, I've been working with this sixteen-year-old kid named Kip. Kip's nice looking, bright, and from a good family, but he has spent the last few years constantly in trouble with the law. Last year he was sent to a juvenile home for three months, and they say when he got out he beat up the kid who ratted on him.

"He refuses to let me help him. He's mad and even he doesn't know why. He is doing drugs, probably involved in petty theft, and I don't know what else. But he stays alone and as long as he lets his pain eat on him from the inside, he strikes out. And he is not the only one, I've got a dozen or so guys like that I'm trying to help, and I'm not getting anywhere."

Stopping, Hunter looked back at Leslie, shook his head and said, "Don't let this stop you from growing, from reaching out, from being all the wonderful things you can be. I don't know how you must feel, nor have I ever had anything happen to me that would allow me to say that I can identify with you. But I do think you're very special, and besides I'm selfish enough not to want you to lose that specialness, for my sake, if not for yours.

"Now, let's go to my place and let me fix you dinner."

"No," Leslie's response was direct and fast. "I don't think I should go out yet."

"Don't try to sell me that," Hunter answered. "I checked with Meg, you can go out, and she thinks it would be good for you. Besides, I think that it would be better for me."

Shaking her head, Leslie struggled to find another excuse. "My mom and dad will be home soon, and I should help them put something together for supper. I mean, what kind of daughter would I be if I just took off at the last moment?"

"A normal one," Hunter answered. "How many times have you helped with supper this week?"

"None," came the meek answer.

"Fine, tonight you will," he assured her, "but at my apartment. You can peel the potatoes and wash the dishes."

"Hunter," Leslie pleaded, "I'm not ready to get out yet. I mean . . ."

"You mean that you don't want anyone to see you. I understand that and I've got an answer. Wait right here."

Running outside, ignoring the fact that it was now pouring, he yanked a plastic sack from his car and came charging back into the house. Reaching into the sack, he pulled out two large, plastic masks. Holding them both up in the air, he asked, "Do you want to be Donald or Daffy?"

Shaking her head, she pointed to Daffy. Tossing the mask to her, he slipped the other one over his face. Doing his best Donald impression, he continued, "Call your dad at work, tell him where you're going to be, and then get an umbrella, because it is raining cats and dogs. Of course, we are ducks, so what do we care?"

Leslie raised her right hand to stop him from grabbing it. "I don't want to be your charity case," she explained. "I don't want you to look at me like those kids you try to help. I don't need or want to be saved or pitied."

He smiled. "My friends aren't charity cases. My friends are people who give me something I need. In reality, I'm the charity case. I am a very lonely person who is tired of eating on my couch by myself. Please take pity on me."

After studying him a moment, she finally nodded. "Let me go call Dad and give me twenty minutes to put on something that will go with this mask."

44

Hours later, long after the rain had stopped and the supper dishes had been washed and put away, and just after Hunter had won his third straight game of Scrabble, Leslie stretched and looked at her watch. "Hunter, it's practically midnight. I've got to get home."

"You've got a curfew?" he asked. "Haven't you outgrown that a little? I mean did your mother call every night while you lived in New York to make sure were tucked in bed by ten?"

"No!" Leslie protested, "but you've got to understand that this is my first night out since . . ." Suddenly it dawned on her that she hadn't thought about the attack or her face in over seven hours. Bringing her hand up to her cheek to make sure that the scars were still there, she looked quickly at Hunter who was just waiting for her to finish her sentence. Letting her hand fall to her side, she finished, "Since I came back to town."

"Yeah," Hunter smiled, "and this has been the best evening I've had since I don't know when."

Getting up to put their two empty coffee cups

back in the sink, she caught a glimpse of a woman's photograph sitting on a desk in the bedroom. Noting that Hunter was caught up in putting up the board game, she set the cups down and wandered into the room in order to get a closer look. She had just picked up the framed picture when Hunter's voice came from somewhere behind. Embarrassed, she quickly returned it to its spot.

"An old flame," Hunter explained.

"I'm sorry," Leslie mumbled, "I had no business . . ."

"You know her, don't you?" Hunter asked.

As she more closely studied the photo, an involuntary wave of jealousy rocked her. The woman in the picture was beautiful; she was blessed with huge brown eyes, wavy, long dark hair, and had an assured and confident smile. She was someone that Hunter would have been attracted to and a woman he would have looked good with. She glanced over the top of the photo at the man's bed and wondered how many times this woman had slept there, how many times he had told her that he loved her. Setting the photo back on the desk, Leslie shrugged her shoulders and said, "No, I don't know her."

"Oh, Les," Hunter teased, "of course you do. That's Blanche, you know Blanche Ward? Of course, she was little bit bigger in high school. Anyway, she and I went out for a while. Ended last spring. She got married last week to Tommy McCall. You remember him, don't you?"

"That's Blanche?" Leslie couldn't believe it. "It can't be, she was such a plain girl."

"Yep," Hunter assured her, "and I was best man at her wedding. You know the saying, always a best man, never a groom."

Smiling, Leslie looked up at Hunter and said, "It is late and I do need to get home."

"Do you want me to wear my mask?" Hunter inquired, "or are you no longer ashamed to be seen with me?"

"I'll chance it," Leslie responded.

Neither of them spoke on the short trip home. Maybe it was because neither of them seemingly wanted to do anything to break the mood. So, when Hunter's car pulled up into the driveway, it came as no surprise the vehicle was filled with nothing but the sounds of two people breathing. Leslie finally broke the awkward silence.

"I had a great time."

"So did I," Hunter assured her. "How about tomorrow night? And before you answer, I just want you to know that I have a weak heart and unpleasant negative answers might bring on an attack."

"I wouldn't want to do that," she laughed.

"So, you'll go?"

"As long as it's someplace not in public," Leslie answered. "I'm just not ready for that yet."

"OK," he agreed, "how about my place and you cook?"

"If you'll wash dishes."

"It's a deal. Six o'clock. Let me walk you to the door."

"No, Hunter, I'm a city girl. I'll walk myself. Drive carefully going home."

As Hunter's Jeep roared off into the night, Leslie lingered on the front porch for a moment, drinking in the damp, warm August night air. Happy, maybe truly happy for the first time in years, she'd momentarily forgotten about the tragic moments of a few weeks before. Reaching into her purse, she found her key, and after taking one last look at the now clear sky, opened the door.

As she closed and locked it she noted an old, blue pickup turn a corner and roll down the street, slowing as it passed in front of the house. The two passengers exchanged some words before the driver stepped on the accelerator and the truck sped off into the night.

45

Carlee retrieved her cell from her purse and walked over to her office window. She smiled as she noted Mike Irvin's name pop up on the caller I.D.

"What have you got for me?" she asked.

"A great deal," came the reply. "I've come up with a proposal that would be worth about a million to you. But, I need to warn you, the production company has a few requirements."

"What do they want?" the agent asked.

"They want a script that includes a few elements that didn't actually happen."

"Not surprising," Carlee replied, "I'm guessing something to juice up ticket sales."

"We're on the same page," Irvin assured her. "Here's the deal. They know that the attack on the Rhoads girl occurred before she did the perfume ad. So she'd never done any nudity. They want to write into the script that she was a big perfume model. Thus, they can work nudity into the script and use that image as the driving force behind the attack."

"Yeah," Carlee said, sitting down at her desk, "the sex angle. All the nudity and violence will make this film a 'must see' by the demographic this type of story appeals to. And, as it is based on a true story, people will believe this is what really happened rather than what really did happen. It makes sense and that kind of sense makes money, too. And our truth will be the one that is believed by the masses."

She propped her feet up on her desk and leaned back in her chair. Leslie Rhoads's career might be over but she was turning into a gold mine for the agency.

"Anyway, Carlee," Irvin's voice brought the woman's focus from a headshot of Leslie on her desk back to the phone call. "The studio needs to know if Ms. Rhoads will have any problems with this kind of adaptation."

"It doesn't matter," Carlee assured him. "I own her image and her story as a model for a few more months. My contract is iron-clad solid, and it runs through a part of next year. Thus, I have control over what goes in the script, she doesn't. I've checked with my attorney; she can do nothing about the direction we go."

"That's what the backers need to know. Can you have your lawyer fax his statement on this issue to their offices?"

"No problem," Carlee answered as she leaned forward, picked up a pen and made a note on a legal pad.

"One more thing," Irvin said, "is there any

progress on the case? Have they arrested any-one?"

"No," Carlee replied.

"Good, we don't need them to ever capture the guy who did this. If he's still out there and this movie makes cash, we can do sequel after sequel with this guy. It could be the biggest cash cow you ever had."

Carlee smiled. "Keep me informed. When you get contracts, let me know. As soon as I sign this deal, I want to release the information to the media. We have to keep this publicity rolling."

The agent set her phone down on her desk. If they actually did catch the guy who cut up Leslie, it would cost her some big bucks. Yet, she wasn't worried. She'd been to Springfield. She'd seen the town enough to know the police force was not up to this challenge. The guy who attacked Leslie would likely remain scot-free forever.

Looking back at the headshot, Carlee frowned. If only the model had done some nude work before she'd been attacked. Those pictures would be worth a small fortune now and they would sure make marketing the movie even easier. Oh, well, too late to kick herself for that move. At least she'd figure out how to make big money out of damaged goods.

46

"Jake, it's been a month."

"Jim," the man snarled, "it's been a month. What's the deal?"

"We need to pull another job," the big man pleaded, "my funds are low."

"Too soon," Jake announced as he leaned over to the window and watched kids play football on the litter-filled lot just across the street from the apartment complex. "Police are still hauling everyone in and giving them the third degree on the model job. Just too many patrols out there right now. With all those eyes the odds of getting caught doing even a small heist are too big."

"But I need some cash," a teenager argued. "I need it bad. They just don't give drugs away, you know."

"Come back tomorrow," Jake assured the kid. "I'll have some for you. I got a safe source, and I know what will make you feel real good."

The bigger man got up from a well-worn chair and crossed to the leader's side. Staring the boss in the eye, he posed a question that was on all their minds, "What about the woman? Are you sure she's not going to remember something to put the cops on our trail?"

Jake grinned, "Louie, what are you concerned about? All you did was hold her; I was the one who cut her up. So if I'm not worried, why should you be? I can assure you she has no clue as to who attacked her. I doubt if she's even talked to the cops since she left the hospital. But I know where she is. And if things get a little hot, it won't be too hard to silence her before any of us fall into the cops' web."

"Why not just do it now?" Louie argued.

Jake shook his head, walked three feet toward a far wall and stepped on an inch-long roach. Smiling, he glanced back to the big guy. "If you have the stomach for it; go ahead. But make sure you aren't spotted, or leave DNA evidence behind, and you can't make any other mistake that could lead the cops back to you. And, if you think you have problems sleeping now, wait until you're worried about being nailed for Murder One. That'll keep you looking over your shoulder for the rest of your life."

"Yeah," the big man agreed, "I guess so. But as long as she's alive it gives me the creeps."

"Not me," Jake laughed, "I'm loving that she has to look at herself in the mirror each day. I promised to make her ugly and I did. I can't begin to explain the satisfaction I feel when I think of that. I put her in her place. I took that holier-than-thou attitude and brought her down to the gutter. She may not know who I am, but she'll never forget what I've done."

His lips formed into a smile that was both wicked and haunting. It was so unnerving that the other two men in the room looked away in a combination of disgust and fear.

"You are too stupid to understand," Jake snickered. "It's not about how much money we get from a stick-up or even how much pain we inflict. No, it's about power. Each time we pull a job, we make those we hit feel powerless. And that makes us superior. We essentially own them because we have shaken them to the core. They live their lives scared they might run into us again. Because of us they have nightmares that will never end."

He rubbed his hands together and turned back to face his confederates.

"Who could ask for anything more?"

47

The attack, as she now called it, had placed Leslie on a roller coaster of dynamic swings in emotions. She began each day by looking in the mirror. Just a mere glance at the image reflected in the glass caused her to sink into a deep depression, made even darker by her mother's constant talk of lawsuits. Nothing, not even the daily routine of watching television show after show brought her any relief. Then, at just the moment when she thought life was nothing more than a black hole, Hunter would come by.

Her nights with Hunter were filled with one-on-one conversation, old movies, board games, and listening to him talk about his work. On these evenings, she forgot about her problems, her pain and her own fears, and became a carefree participant in life. She lived only for these moments.

"Aren't you tired of my place?" Hunter asked as he put away the Trivial Pursuit board.

Her scarred face aglow, she laughed and responded, "I feel more at home at your place than I do at my own."

"Well," Hunter answered, "I'm at home, too, but I'm also getting tired of it. I need a break."

She knew what he meant by a break. He'd been hinting at it for weeks. He wanted to go on the town, grab a meal at Big Al's, take in a movie at the Multiplex, or go bowling. Just thinking about doing any of those things rocked her even more than the nightmares that often plagued her sleep.

Looking nervously across the living room, Leslie swallowed hard. Speaking in her sweetest voice she tried to charm the man who'd become her only contact with the real world. "Oh, Hunter, you know what just being with you means to me. I'm not ready to face the world. I need a little more time."

"I'm not going to make you, Les," he assured her, "but I do want you to do more than just hang out here. Tomorrow, let's go to the lake. My sister has a cabin there, and a boat, and we could ski for a while, and then watch the sun go down from the deck. I think that would be a blast. And the setting is certainly a lot better than my place."

"Are you sure that no one else is going to be there?" Leslie demanded.

"Not a soul."

"OK," Leslie gave in, "as long as it is just you and me."

"Now, about tonight," Hunter began.

"What?"

"I need to work with one of my kids," he explained. "He's going through a rough time and he needs some guidance. So, let me take you home now and I'll pick you up at say—two—tomorrow afternoon."

Trying not to sound too disappointed, Leslie replied, "Sure," and then after pausing a second she added, "might need some time at home anyway. Tonight's as good as any."

She'd only been home a few minutes when Meg called and offered her a chance to come over to her place. Forgetting about giving Hunter the line about needing to be home, Leslie jumped at the opportunity to get away from her mother. It had been two weeks since she had visited with her cousin, and she could hardly wait to update her on all that had happened. If she couldn't be with Hunter, Meg was a great second choice.

Two hours later, after a great homemade chicken dinner, and after Meg had put her daughter to bed, the conversation took on a much more serious tone.

"Your scars are healing nicely," Meg observed. "I think that Dr. Parks did a great job."

"Oh," Leslie's hands involuntarily drew to her face as she spoke, "they still make me look like a freak. When I stare at them, they remind me of my first few attempts at sewing on the machine."

"Well," Meg assured her, "Dawn didn't seem to notice. And if a two-year-old doesn't point, then you have a good start. Let's remember there will be a time, after several more surgeries and some sanding, when they'll fade to almost nothing. Your memories and fears will probably linger longer than the visible signs of what happened."

Meg took a sip from a glass filled with Coke. "Have the police uncovered anything else?"

"No," Leslie's answer sounded more indifferent than vindictive. "They're pretty much at a dead end. I guess whoever did it might never get caught. It would help so much if I could just remember his name."

"You heard a name that night?" Meg inquired.

"Yes, I know I did, but even in my dreams, whenever I get close to remembering it, I go all foggy."

"Well, the mind is a funny thing," Meg answered, sounding more like a nurse than a cousin. "Sometimes the images are brought into sharp focus by seeing or hearing something completely unrelated to the event. Maybe you will hear or read the name that you heard and then it will all pop back."

"I wish that it would happen soon. The farther I get from that night, the less I want to have to relive it in a trial."

Nodding her head, Meg got up from her chair and put a disc in the CD player. After punching the play button, she took a seat on the floor, crossed her legs Indian-fashion, and leaned against the couch. Closing her eyes, she let the music fill her head as if bringing back the memories of the moment she first heard these notes.

Watching her cousin, Leslie strained to recognize the voice of the singer, but while it sounded very familiar, she couldn't place it. Finally, after letting the first selection play out, she broke the silence.

"Who is this?"

Opening her eyes, Meg brought her knees up to her chest and wrapped her arms around them.

She listened to the opening words of the second song before replying. "It is obvious that you are younger than I am. If you were my age, you would know Louise Mandrell. She was one of Steve's favorite singers. This was his favorite album and I discovered it the other day when I was cleaning up some stuff. The song he loved so much was called 'Save Me.' "

"It's nice," Leslie nodded. "Maybe I need to start tuning into some country." Listening to a line in the song, she then added, "Speaking of taking someone away to the moonlight, I think I'm falling hard for Hunter."

Smiling, Meg got off the floor and returned to the couch. Staring at her cousin for a moment, she grinned, "And he for you?"

"I don't know," Leslie admitted. "I'd like to think so. I mean he sees me all the time and he says wonderful things, but I'm just not sure."

"You think he may just be thinking friend-ship?" Meg asked.

"Could be," Leslie sighed. "He hasn't made any kind of romantic moves on me. Just a nice good-night kiss on the forehead. In a way, it is unlike any kind of relationship I've ever had. Maybe it's my face. Maybe that's why he can't really kiss me or hold me like a lover."

Not letting a second pass, Meg jumped back with, "Maybe it's the environment."

"What are you talking about?" Leslie demanded.

"How can you know what you have unless you view it in the light of the real world? I mean you and Hunter have spent the last month hiding in the dark. You can't build a life with someone else that way, nor can you live your own life that way. You're hiding, and in a way I don't blame you and I understand, but you've got to get back in the real world someday."

"I will," Leslie promised. "I'm just not ready yet."

"Leslie, I don't mean to sound like a preacher, but I want you to think about your whole life, not just the last few weeks. Why did you come home to talk to your mother about the Buffalo Scotch ad? The reason was that you knew that she'd say take it, and then you could point to her and tell folks you wouldn't have done it if she hadn't thought it was a good idea. Why did you come home this time? To do the same thing! Your mother would have given her stamp of approval on the perfume ad campaign and then you could have taken off your clothes, and it wouldn't have been your decision. If you got any negative feedback, you could point to Flo."

"But . . ."

"No buts," Meg cut her off. "What I'm saying is it goes back through your whole life. It was the reason you dated some people and didn't date others in high school, and why you chose to quit school and go to New York. Flo kept you under

236

her thumb. Your whole value system is based on her judgments. And she has made it easy."

"No, wait just a minute," Leslie argued. "I was in New York, on my own, and did what I wanted."

"Maybe you did," Meg replied. "But Flo was controlling how you felt about yourself then, and she is even doing it now. Your mother thinks that you look terrible. She thinks she has been given a freak for a daughter. So, when you look in the mirror you see a freak, too. Think about it for a moment, when it came to crunch time, did you ever make up your own mind about anything in your life or even how you look? Your mother, the woman you say grates on your nerves like fingernails on a chalkboard, sets the standards as to how you feel about yourself."

The room took on a strange silence, broken only by the music. Minutes passed, and neither woman looked at the other. Finally, only after the CD had finished playing its final selection, Leslie piped up.

"I don't know what you just said has to do with me and Hunter. And I don't need my mother to point out to me I'm a freak. All I have to do in look in the mirror. Look at me, tell me I'm not one!"

A cold stare emanated from Meg's face, followed by an even frostier reply, "Yes, you are a freak!" She let the word sink in, watching as her cousin's eyes took on a look of disbelief. Then, right at the moment Leslie was hitting bottom, Meg added, "But you're a freak because you choose to make yourself one."

Meg let her words hang in the air for a few seconds and then launched into a story, "Do you remember Coach Collins's wife?"

Leslie nodded.

"What do you remember about her?"

"Well, she was outgoing, vivacious, and a lot of fun. Had a personality that wouldn't quit. Everyone wanted to be around her."

"What about her face?"

"What about it?"

"The whole left side had burn scars," Meg explained. "Don't you remember the stories? She and the coach almost lost their lives when their house burned right after they got married."

Thinking back, Leslie did remember the story, but while she knew that Carol Collins might have had a little scar on one side of her face, she couldn't remember just how. As Leslie became lost in her thoughts, Meg pulled an old high school annual out from a bookshelf. Leafing through the pages, she found the picture she was looking for and handed it to her cousin.

"I don't remember the scar being that big," Leslie said looking at the photo. "I could have sworn that it was just a mark."

Pointing to another picture, Meg asked, "What about Missy Schmidt? She was a dwarf and she didn't let it stop her. She was even chosen a Homecoming Princess. If you will turn back a few pages, you'll note that she was class favorite, too. She could have been a freak, but she chose not to be.

"Now, if you want to spend your life behind huge glasses and only going to places where other people aren't, you're going to not only cheat yourself, but cheat everyone else in the world, too."

Touching her face again, Leslie let her fingers trace the jagged tracks, lingering on the deep ones beside her mouth and across her nose. Shaking her head, she pulled her hands back to her side, and breathed, "I just don't know."

"Listen, Les," Meg explained, "I probably had no business being so hard on you. I'm probably expecting too much too soon. I know you need to grieve and to heal emotionally, but I don't want you to sell yourself short. Hunter has been so good for you, but he can only do so much. You have to walk on your own, without him always being there to protect you. I love you like a sister and I don't want to see you get hurt, but some-times it's the pain that heals us."

48

Meg's words played over and over again in Leslie's head right up until the time Hunter knocked on the door the following afternoon. Seeing his face, noting his quick smile, gave her the lift she needed to once again forget her problems, at least for a while.

"Les," Hunter laughed a few hours later as he pulled her from the water into the boat, "you're still not a good skier. We must have dragged you for thirty feet that time. When you fall, which you have done really well, you're supposed to let go of the rope."

"Well," she replied as she grabbed a towel and dried off, "it has been a few years since I've tried."

"Tried is the operative word here," Hunter shot back. "As I remember, you couldn't ski when we were in high school, either."

As he fired the boat up and headed for the lake cabin, Leslie sat in the back and watched the wind blow through his hair. She couldn't believe how good he looked in his swimsuit, just how well he had maintained his body. Smiling, she knew she was with the man of most women's dreams.

Stretching her long legs, she also was sure she still had a body that turned heads. She was confident that no one on the lake looked better in a swimsuit than she did. Yet, once, when a boat had passed close to theirs, she noted a man staring not at her figure, but at her face. His expression showed he was more than a little shocked. He quickly turned to his girlfriend and then pointed back to Leslie, but, by that time, she'd already grabbed her sunglasses and turned her face the other way. That one scene, completely unnoticed by Hunter, had brought back her fears. Over and over again in her mind, she had heard the word freak. It would be hours after that incident before she was again able to relax.

Hunter cooked a wonderful meal but Leslie had eaten little. Later, after they'd watched the sun set over the beautiful, placid blue water, he built a roaring fire. Now dressed in old jeans and a cotton blouse, Leslie relaxed in front of the flames, and in a matter of minutes, fell sound asleep. But the sleep was far from restful.

In her dreams, Leslie found herself mingling in a large crowd. The smell of popcorn and cotton candy hovered around her, and the sound of an old-fashioned calliope was playing in the background. She smiled at Hunter as he pointed to a large group of people gathered in front of a tent. Latching onto his arm, she followed him as they pushed their way to the front of the line.

Reaching into his pocket, he purchased two tickets, handed them to the man, and he and Leslie walked in.

The first thing they saw was a man with four arms who could play guitar and a banjo at the same time. In the next booth a fat lady, reputed to weigh over seven hundred pounds, sat in an oversized chair eating a huge sack full of donuts. Within the next few minutes, Leslie observed a snake man, a pair of Siamese twins, and a cone-headed boy. Still, the best or worst, depending upon the customer's perspective was evidently yet to come. A large crowd had gathered at the last booth. Many of the patrons were in an obvious state of shock, too caught up in the grotesque scene to move. Others, perhaps more hardened, were pointing and shouting barbs at the exhibit. Overcome with curiosity, Leslie released Hunter's arm and with childlike exuberance and curiosity ran to the booth. Shoving her way to the front, she looked up and was greeted by a woman whose face was covered with scars. As she studied the horribly disfigured woman, Leslie turned her head, completely repulsed. Then it hit her. She knew the freak. The woman in the exhibit was someone she'd seen somewhere before. Lifting her eyes, it was as if a mirror had been pushed in front of her face. The woman who made everyone sick was Leslie.

Suddenly she heard the crowd begin to shout,

"Freak, freak, freak!" Forcing her way back through the mass of angry people, she ran back to where she had left Hunter, but he wasn't there. Looking behind the screaming crowd, now pointing and screaming at her, morbidly following every move she made, and there, in the front of the mob, was Hunter. His face was distorted in a look of anguish and pain and he had joined the chorus. At the top of his lungs he was yelling, "Freak, freak, freak . . ."

"Wake up, Les," Hunter whispered gently shaking her shoulders. "You've been having some kind of dream."

Opening her eyes, Leslie reached out and grabbed Hunter, pulling herself into his arms, hugging him like she had never hugged anyone before. Crying, she let her tears run down her face and onto his shoulder, her sobs, shaking both their bodies.

"Hunter," she pleaded.

"Yes," he softly answered.

"Love me," she begged.

"I do," he assured her.

"No, not that," she answered, wiping her eyes, and then staring into his. "I want you to make love to me."

Looking at her for a moment, Hunter released her, and eased back against a chair. Staring into the flames, he took a deep breath and shook his head.

"Why not," Leslie demanded. "Am I that horrible to look at?"

"It's not that, Leslie," he quietly answered.

"Sure, it's not that," she fired back as she quickly unbuttoned her blouse. "If I had given you this chance in high school, you would have ripped my clothes off before I could have changed my mind. But now, now that my face has been ruined, you're not interested. I sicken you, don't I?"

Turning his eyes back to the fire, Hunter didn't answer.

"Boy, that's great," Leslie lashed out. "I put my faith in you. I think that you're interested in me as a person, but now I find that I'm just another charity case. You took me on to try to make me feel good about myself, to fix my life, and then you were going to walk away. You don't love me, if you did, you'd make love to me. Can't you even look past my face? My body is still to die for!"

Standing up and marching across the room, Leslie flipped each of the cabin's lights off. The room was now dark except for the uneven glow of the flickering flames.

"OK, Hunter," Leslie snarled, "the lights are off. You can't see my face. You can pretend that I looked the way I did a few months ago. So, with that thought in mind and no lights on to prove it a lie, I shouldn't turn your stomach. You should be able to kiss me and not get sick."

Though he looked toward her, he still didn't move.

Now angry and embarrassed, she flew across the room, stood over him and screamed, "Why don't you say it? Why don't you just say it? I'm a freak, an ugly, scarred freak. Why don't you just admit that you couldn't love me if I was the last woman on earth? You couldn't touch me if I stripped naked and wore a mask over my hideous face. I'm not a woman; I'm a monster! And that's what I'll always be. Nothing will change that, not now and not ten years from now."

Her anger expelled, Leslie turned and ran out the door, across the grass and to the dock. There, leaning against the railing, she cried out, "It just isn't fair. I hate you, God. You made me unlovable. You made me a freak! Why couldn't you have just let me die?"

Consumed by her own pain, thinking she was alone and forgotten, she fell to her knees wishing she had a gun she could put to her head and end her suffering. A few seconds later, two strong arms lifted her upright and a man's voice whispered into her right ear. "Les, you're not a freak. I'm proud to be with you, so proud that I want you to go to church with me tomorrow morning."

Turning to face him, the woman shook her head, and then, proving just how deeply she had been hurt, snapped, "Oh, that proves it. You'll take me to church then everyone can see what a wonderful person you are for helping the poor woman. You'll come off like a saint and I'll look just like what I am, a charity case . . . what did we call it in high school . . . missionary dating. Well, I may be the charity case, but I'm not going to let you use me to look like a saint. Not now and not ever."

"That's not it," Hunter quietly assured her. "I love you. I love you more than I have ever loved anyone in my whole life. The problem is, I'm not going to live a lie by letting you live one."

"And just what does that mean?" she demanded.

Looking out at the water, the man shook his head, obviously struggling to find a way to gently answer her. After seemingly examining every inch of the lake's surface he finally spoke. "I love a woman that you don't even know. You look in the mirror, and you see someone who is ruined. You see a woman whose public life is over. You see someone without value or worth. I look at you and see someone who has so much to give. I see hope, and you see hopelessness. I see light, and you see darkness."

As she leaned against the dock's railing, she continued to glare; listening but not accepting what he was saying. What she wanted him to admit was that he saw her the way she saw herself. She'd accept nothing else.

"Leslie," his voice remained soft and kind,

"I've spent the last few weeks trying to help you, that is true. But in the process, I have found that I've not helped you at all. You're still too caught up in what the world thinks about the way you look to realize that—as trite as this may sound—beauty is only skin deep. I thought I could get you to realize that, but I couldn't in high school and I can't now.

"The only person who can reveal to you who you really are is probably you. As long as you look in the mirror and see someone who is worthless then that is what you are going to be. And I don't go to bed with anyone who is worthless. I'm better than that and if you had any kind of feeling of self-worth, you wouldn't demand that I do that or anything else to prove my love for you."

"Are you finished?" Leslie bitterly bellowed as she buttoned her blouse.

"I guess so," Hunter answered.

"Then take me home!" she demanded.

Neither of them spoke on the forty-minute drive back to Springfield. During that seemingly endless trip, Leslie was fighting a mental war. One side of her brain demanded she consider what Hunter had said and the other demanded she accept herself at face value. As she grew closer to home, that uglier side was winning the battle.

As Hunter pulled into the driveway, he noted

that one of the family cars was gone. "Where are your folks?"

Showing no emotion, Leslie answered, "Out of town. They'll be back tomorrow night."

"Are you going to be all right by yourself?" Hunter asked.

"I'm a big girl," she shot back, "I lived alone in New York, remember?"

"At least let me walk you in and make sure everything is all right."

"Forget it, Hunter. I can manage."

Jumping out, she slammed the passenger door with all of her might, stormed across the front yard, unlocked the door, and tossed it open. Not bothering to even glance over her shoulder, she entered the house and threw the door shut behind her. Not stopping to turn on a light, she ran upstairs to her room, pitched her purse and bag into a corner and collapsed on her bed. As she lay there staring at the ceiling, she heard Hunter's Jeep back out of the driveway and fade away into the night.

Though she didn't want to, it was time to let go of the emotions she had been bottling up for months. Her heart, suddenly overcome with overwhelming pain, pushed her body to begin to shake with deep, mourning sobs. Forcing herself to her feet, she crossed the room to her dressing table, took a long look at her mirror, and then, grabbing an old jewelry box, heaved it into the middle of her reflection.

She moved to the window and looked down at the scene beneath her. A blue pickup pulled up to the curb just in front of the Rhoads's home and, after letting the motor idle for a moment, the driver turned off the ignition, and lit a cigarette.

Who was he? Why was he here now? Leslie continued to study the truck for another five minutes, then, after tossing the cigarette butt out the window, the driver restarted the vehicle and rumbled off into the night.

49

After the truck disappeared around the block, Leslie turned her attention back to her room. Flipping on a bedside table lamp, she examined the remnants of what had been her dresser mirror. The broken glass brought a deep sense of satisfaction. She'd killed the ugly image that was her face for the moment. But just killing it once didn't satisfy her. She needed more.

She marched from her room, down the steps, and to her parents' downstairs bathroom. Flipping the switch to bring some illumination, she stepped in front of the sink. There was that face again, staring back at her from another mirror. She frowned and breathed, "I hate you," before opening the medicine cabinet. Scanning the shelves, she finally discovered the object of her search in the middle of the third one. Grabbing a half-full bottle of pills, she hurriedly left the bathroom and headed for the kitchen. Beside the sink was a glass she'd used earlier in the day; she filled it with tap water and then walked to the den. Turning the television on, she switched channels until she discovered an old horror movie, and tumbled into a chair.

"Well, Mother," she said to no one as she spilled a handful of pills into her palm, "I finally owe you one."

In this case, she did. Flo had been employing prescription sleeping pills for decades. Leslie had always believed it was because on dark and sleepless nights, her mother couldn't confront just how sad and bitter a person she was. Now, the route of escape for Flo offered the promise of an even more fulfilling and lasting one for her daughter.

Dropping the empty bottle to the floor, Leslie looked at the red and blue pills filling her right hand. They had peace written all over them. This was what she needed. Sleep! The kind that never ended!

No reason to take them all at once; she had all night long to accomplish her mission. Picking one of the tablets out of her right hand with her left, she popped it into her mouth and chased it down with a sip of water.

One down! The second one followed! Then the third! Five minutes later, she polished off the fifteenth pill. Now it was time to lean back in the chair and wait.

How long would it take? Ten minutes? Maybe longer? Sitting there staring at the wall and listening to the clock tick was torture. She had to do something until she finally drifted off into that longest night.

Rummaging through an end table's drawer, she discovered an old photo album. No better way to make her exit than by reliving a few old memories. Flipping on a lamp, she began to slowly scan the pages. As she did, the past came alive. For the next five minutes, she relived birthdays, proms, vacations, and parties, and with each of them came the special warm feelings that had been a part of the events. She smiled, up until meeting that broken bottle, it had been a pretty good life.

Slamming the book closed, she tossed it down to the floor and wandered over to her father's desk. There, amid a stack of unopened junk mail, she found a copy of *Fashion and Style*. Leslie studied the face on the cover, carefully searching the image for even the slightest flaw, but she found none. Proudly, she remembered how Carlee had bragged that this was one session where there would be no touch-ups and she had been right. That cover had gone to the printer's, just like the day it was shot. Yes, she once had the perfect face.

Holding the magazine to her chest, she wandered into the living room. After turning on the overhead light, she curled up at the end of the couch to once again take in her best and brightest moment. Hunter Jefferson would have jumped at the chance to take this woman to bed. Tracing her scars with her fingers, she fought back tears. Who could blame him for rejecting her? Leslie certainly wouldn't have wanted to make love to some guy who looked like his face had been assembled by a demented child.

Glancing back to the cover, she shook her head, and for the first time since she had taken the pills, the rush was gone and an overwhelming sense of sadness took root in her heart. Why hadn't she run back into Hunter two years ago? He wouldn't have been doing charity work by taking her out. She would have been a woman that he could not only have cared about, but one that he could have loved—really loved. It wasn't fair, not for him and certainly not for Leslie.

Sitting up, she gently placed the magazine on the coffee table, and as she did, she noted a new issue of *Fashion and Style*. She was shocked. Wendy Wright's face was staring back at her. She was the new cover girl!

Pulling the cover to the light, Leslie frowned. Wendy looked incredible. Speaking directly to the magazine she said, "Boy they must have done a major touch-up job on this picture for her to come out looking like this!"

Opening the magazine she read the short article about the cover girl. It said that Wendy was not just the face of modern style. She was the epitome of beauty. As she turned back to the cover, it hit her. Her funeral! It would take place in the next few days. It would be her last appearance. Jumping up from the couch, she ran back into her father's office. Finding a pen and paper in a drawer, she hurriedly scrawled out, "I want my casket to be closed. Under no circumstances, let anyone see my face."

A great sense of relief flowed through her body as she folded the note, put her parents' names on the outside and placed it on a table in the entry hall. That should take care of it. Her life was in order. The last detail had been covered.

A veil of grogginess was beginning to invade the corners of her mind. She could sense the pills really starting to work their magic. Turning, she steadied herself and began to slowly retrace her steps back to the den.

When these things hit, they hit hard!

The room was suddenly floating. Leslie was so light-headed she could barely balance. Each step down the long hall was a monumental struggle. As she arrived at her final destination she heard something familiar, but it sounded so far away.

What was it? The phone! Who'd call at this time of night?

Driven by habit, she struggled toward the place where the desk phone rested. Yet, even though it was only a few steps away, that journey seemed to take years. Her mind now shrouded in a deep fog, her legs unsteady, she wobbled forward toward her father's desk. In an effort to focus, she began to talk to herself.

"Got to make it to the chair," she whispered as she pushed a foot forward. "I've got to make it . . ." Before she could finish the sentence, her body crashed to the floor.

"So, this is how it is going to end," she sighed.

Her thought pattern had now slowed to a crawl, but there was a part of her that wasn't ready to give up without knowing who was on the other end of that call. She pushed herself to turn over. Resting on her back she stared at the spinning ceiling.

You should have loved me. What was your name? Oh, yeah, Hunter. If you had really loved me, this wouldn't have happened.

Closing her eyes she began to picture her mother trying to explain this event to the neighbors. Flo would come up with some way to put the blame on someone else. She'd probably even try to find someone to sue. Maybe the makers of those wonderful sleeping pills!

An overpowering urge to relax flowed through

her body and she let herself slip into another world, one filled with darkness and without mirrors. She eagerly reached out for the place where time never moved.

50

"Don't kill me. You never gave me a chance to live, and now, just when I have an opportunity to see what kind of potential I had, you're cheating me out of my chance to discover it. You're selfish and lazy, Leslie Rhoads. If it is not easy, not perfect, you don't do it. You give up when there's work involved."

"Who are you?" Leslie's confused mind asked.

"Don't you recognize me?" the voice answered. "I'm the part of you that never lived because you never matured or grew enough to let me live. I was the part that wanted to reach out to people, the part that didn't care if my makeup ran or my hair was out of place. I was the part of you Hunter saw, and I was the part of you that you never saw."

Must be the drugs! They were now playing with her mind. They were even creating voices in her head. Yeah, it was the drugs. Maybe if she just thought about something else, they'd go away.

But the voice came back, even louder and more demanding than before.

"When you looked in the mirror, I was there both before and after the attack, but you didn't know me. I was the depth that you never discovered. I'm the part of you who still wants to live. Save me. Get to your feet and make a call. Get me some help. Don't let me die."

Forcing her eyes open, Leslie struggled to regain at least a partial sense of her surroundings, but the room was spinning too fast and her body was too limp for her to summon any control. So she allowed the dark cloud to once more envelop her, and as it did, she heard it again! From what seemed like a long distance away there was the ringing of the phone. Turning her head toward the sound, she spied the phone wire just two feet to her left. If she could just reach it, she could pull the phone off the desk and end that annoying sound forever.

Focusing all of her energy on just moving her left arm, she inched her hand forward until she was able to touch the cord. Stopping for a moment to concentrate even harder, she wrapped her fingers around it and jerked. She then waited for the phone to fall off the desk and onto the floor. But strangely it didn't.

Turning her face back toward the top of the desk, she became aware of someone standing directly over her. In his hand, he held the still ringing phone. She couldn't see his face, hidden by the room's shadows, but she had no problem hearing his voice.

"Sorry, Sweetheart, but this is one caller that will have to get back with you later—much later."

Setting the phone back on the desk, the man ambled across the room, picked up the empty pill bottle in a gloved hand, studied the label, tossed it back down on the carpet, and walked back to Leslie.

"I appreciate you making this so easy," he laughed.

Even though she could no longer see anything except vague images, and even though her thought pattern had almost completely shut down, Leslie still recognized the voice. This was the man who had attacked her—the man from the car and the alley. The laugh was the same.

A sudden, deep desire to live rushed through her addled mind. She didn't want him to finish what he'd started in that damp alley. She couldn't bear the thought that the last person to see her alive would be the man who made her into a freak.

"I had no idea that you were going to do yourself in," the man said, a sense of merriment in his voice, "but it does save me having to kill you myself. You know, the way you fought in the alley, I assumed you'd have fought harder to live, too. Guess I had you figured wrong. Why didn't you just give in then? Oh, well, doesn't matter much now. At least this proves I was right in not killing you the first time. What I did really made you suffer, didn't it? I drove you to this! That feels so good."

He hovered over her limp form for a moment before asking, "You still with me?"

Blinking three times in an effort to see him more clearly, Leslie nodded her head.

"I think I'll stay here until I'm sure that you're past the point of no return. I mean you need someone with you in these final moments. Besides, I owe you for giving me this incredible high."

Leslie's eyes followed his blurred image as he strolled across the room and settled into her father's favorite chair. Picking up a magazine, he began to look at the pictures, while occasionally glancing over at her. As her breathing became more ragged and shallow, he set the magazine to one side.

The ringing of the phone caused him to jump, but as Leslie showed no reaction to the loud ringing, he relaxed. Getting out of the chair, he slowly crossed the room and bent over bringing his face close to hers. Nodding his head, he walked back to the chair, picked up the copy of *Fashion and Style* magazine he'd been reading and dropped it beside her body. After studying Leslie one more time, he turned, stepping on the middle of the magazine's cover, and slowly walked out of the house. A few seconds later, the noise of an engine broke the nighttime silence.

Would that be the last sound she heard? As Leslie edged even closer to death, the phone rang again. This time she made no move to answer. In fact, she made no move at all!

51

Hunter slammed the phone down. If she wanted to hate him, that was fine. He could live with that. But she at least needed to answer the phone. Letting it ring and ring and ring showed all the maturity of a junior high kid.

Walking back to his couch, he picked up a pillow, punched it a couple of times before tossing it across the room. As it flew it knocked over a framed photo of his late father, but fortunately didn't do any lasting damage.

What a day it had been! It seemed great for a while. It was just what he'd planned. Leslie had gotten out the house, she'd enjoyed the sun and decompressed. But then there was that scene at the cabin. She had changed the plans. She had demanded something he hadn't expected. And he'd likely reacted wrong. He'd likely destroyed her fragile ego. So maybe he did deserve the cold shoulder.

Sitting down he grudgingly decided to give her some space and time. He wouldn't force her hand. It was best to let her call him. After all, what she was seeing in the mirror was probably a lot different than what those around her were seeing. She was likely hypercritical. She didn't note the subtle daily improvements. And Flo probably wasn't helping.

Pulling out his cell, he scanned his directory until he came to a number he'd been given, but never called. It was almost ten. Was it too late? Probably, but he had to talk to someone. He had to explain. He had to get some advice.

Hitting send, he waited for an answer. Unlike the half dozen calls he'd made to Leslie, this time someone picked up.

"Hello."

"Meg, this is Hunter, sorry to bother you so late, but I think I messed up. And you told me if I needed anyone to talk to about Leslie, to call you."

"No problem," came the even reply. "I was doing some laundry. What do you need?"

It took only five minutes to explain what had happened. During that time Hunter did all the talking. As he concluded, he leaned back into the couch and waited for the advice he prayed was coming.

"Doesn't surprise me," Meg said matter-of-factly. "Her whole identity has been predicated on how she looks. That's how she judges every facet of her life."

"So now that I've hurt her," he asked, "what do I do?"

He waited for a response that took so long he wondered if the call had been dropped. "Hunter, don't do anything," she suggested. "Let her think about things for a while. At some point, she'll need to turn to someone and when that happens I'm betting it will be you. And you didn't do anything wrong. In fact, I think you may have been right-on with your response."

"So," his voice was plaintive, "I just wait?"

"For the moment, give her some space, let her see how stifling a life trapped in the same house with her mother is, and she will reach out. I think you'll be the first one she calls."

"OK," Hunter replied. "Thanks for talking to me. I deeply appreciate it."

As he slipped the phone back into his pocket, he nodded grimly. He'd never been good at waiting. He even gave birthday and Christmas presents early. So sitting on his hands and doing nothing would be the toughest test he'd had since when he tried to rehab his knee.

52

Why was the door not locked?

Sitting her two-year-old daughter down on the Rhoadses' front porch, Meg opened the door and yelled out, "Leslie." There was no response.

"Well, Dawn," Meg muttered as she reached down and picked up her toddler, "welcome or not, we're going in."

Carrying the lively bundle in her right arm, she swung the door open and reached for the light switch with her left.

"Les, wake up. You've got company!"

Meg looked into the front rooms. Nothing. She ambled down the hall and was about to hit the stairs and march up to her cousin's room when a voice stopped her.

"Leslie," Dawn cooed.

Looking over to the girl, Meg smiled and nodded. "That's why we're here. We're going to see Leslie. But first we have to find her."

"Leslie," the toddler said, this time pointing to a figure barely visible through the den door.

Meg's eyes followed her daughter's tiny hand to a lifeless form sprawled on the floor.

"My Lord. Leslie, what have you done?"

Sitting her daughter down, Meg whispered, "Stay here."

"Les sick?" Dawn asked.

"Yes," Meg answered. "Now you stay right here and let Mommy help her."

Rushing to her cousin's side, Meg grabbed her wrist. It took a few moments, but she found a very weak pulse. Pulling the cell from her pocket, she hit 9-1-1 and waited.

"This is Meg Richards, I'm a nurse at Springfield Community Hospital. I'm at my aunt's house at 1507 Maple Street and there is a twenty-four-year-old woman barely breathing. I need EMTs and I need the ER ready to receive the woman at the hospital. She is weak and fading quickly."

Meg glanced around the room and spotted the empty pill bottle. Picking it up, she quickly noted the label.

"This is an apparent suicide attempt," Meg barked into the phone. "She's taken an unknown quantity of Zaleplon. Get someone here stat!"

"Mommy."

Meg glanced over to her daughter. "Dawn, go over and sit on the couch. Mommy needs to help Leslie."

As the nurse looked back down at her cousin, she knew why Leslie had done what she'd done.

The rejection she'd experienced that night had hit her even deeper than Meg imagined. So with the why out of the way, the haunting question now was would she live?

53

It was almost five in the afternoon before Leslie began to come out of her deep sleep. When she did, Meg was at her side.

"Welcome back is the term that I've used before when addressing folks who bought the same ticket as you did. It is a welcome I don't take lightly. Hope you don't either."

She patted Leslie on the wrist and softly added, "There has never been a time when I've meant it as much as I do now. I'm glad you're back, kid."

Nodding, Leslie forced a small smile, before embarrassingly starting an apology, "I'm glad, too. Right before I faded off something inside me began to fight a little. I still don't know what it was, but I think I determined I didn't want to die. I think I may have just been trying to show Mom up. You know by using her pills and stuff."

"We'll figure out all the whys later," Meg assured her. "Just you looking at me with those beautiful baby blues is all I care about now."

Leslie shook her head as if trying to push out the fogginess from her mind before she glanced back to her cousin. She then posed a question that would have likely shocked anyone but Meg, "I guess I didn't use enough of them to do myself in?"

"Ah, that would be a negative," Meg shot back. "You took plenty. If you'd been discovered a few minutes later it would have been mission accomplished. As it stood, it was touch and go for a couple of hours. It helped knowing what it was."

The patient nodded. She let her eyes drift to the ceiling as she posed her next query. "Who saved me?"

"I found you," Meg explained. "I came over to check on you after Hunter called me. He told me what had happened. In truth, my motivation was to give you a piece of my mind. But instead I found you on the floor."

"Hunter called you?" Leslie asked. "Why?"

"He didn't know how to handle you, and you wouldn't answer his calls."

"I didn't want to talk to anyone," she answered.

"I think he loves you," Meg said as their eyes met. "I really think he does."

"No, he feels sorry for me. He's just too great a guy to love someone who looks like me."

Shaking her head, Meg shot back, "It is not

your face he loves. It is you. He loves what you are and what you can be."

Leslie's scarred brow tensed up as she formed a scowl and shot back, "What am I? I'm not a model anymore. And if I'm not that, what am I?"

"Are you telling me that as a model, all you were was a face?" Meg questioned. "There has to be more to you than that. At least I always thought there was. Maybe my sister was right about you."

Leslie shook her head. "What did Terri say about me?"

"It doesn't matter," Meg assured her. Patting her cousin's hand, she pushed the conversation in a different direction. "Your mother was here until about an hour ago. I finally convinced her to go home. She needed some rest."

Leslie grinned for the first time since the lake. "Might be tough, I used up all her pills."

Meg smiled and nodded.

"Now, Meg, what was it that Terri always said about me?"

"Sure you want to hear it?"

"Yeah, I do."

Meg leaned back in the chair and studied the woman in the bed. Normally hitting patients with the full force of the truth was not something that was recommended this soon after a suicide attempt. But she knew her cousin well. In this case maybe the unadorned truth was just what was needed to literally wake her up.

"Terri always told me that without your face you wouldn't be anything. Maybe last night proves that you feel the same way."

"I never did like her," Leslie spat. "She always loved to pick on me. I can't remember how many times she pushed me into the dirt when we were little."

"She was and is a character," Meg admitted.

The room grew silent for several minutes. Meg allowed Leslie to mentally roll over what she'd just been told. Finally, when she was sure Terri's assessment had fully sunk in, she reached out to Leslie's chin. Gently lifting her cousin's face until their eyes met, she quietly, but firmly posed the question of the day.

"Are you going to try to do this again?"

Shaking her head, Leslie indicated she wouldn't.

"I won't accept that for an answer," Meg demanded. "You tell me if you are going to try to kill yourself again. I have to hear it from your lips, and you have to make me believe it. Otherwise, you and I are about to become Siamese twins."

"I'm not going to," Leslie answered. "I was stupid. I didn't really know what I wanted, but I know now that checking out is not it."

"So I can trust you?" Meg demanded.

"Yes. You can trust me. Next time I feel like I

did, I'll call you and let you talk some sense into me. But Meg, living with mom, dealing with this etch-a-sketch face, having a man repulsed with the thought of even kissing you, my life is anything but easy."

"I know that, but you are wrong on the last part."

Ignoring the answer, Leslie moaned, "And it's so easy to replace me."

She studied the light shining through the window and bouncing off the far wall, then turned her gaze back to her cousin. Leslie sighed. "The new issue of *Fashion and Style* is out. Another one of Carlee's girls is on the cover. I'm sure Passion Nights has found someone as well. Even with the face I used to have, I was fooling myself. I just wasn't that special."

"Maybe you don't understand the word special," Meg quietly explained. "I know a few folks who still think you're pretty special and that judgment wasn't based on what you see in the mirror."

"You mean like Hunter."

"I can't speak for him," Meg replied, her brown eyes now soft and comforting, "but I know a few others who I can most assuredly speak for."

"Bet it's a short list. You know Carlee hasn't called me once since her hospital visit."

"Not surprising," Meg replied, "I didn't view her as having much depth. Besides, the question is not who you were, the question is what will you become."

"And what is that? What will I become?"

"Well," Meg asked, "do you want to find out?"

"What do you think?" Leslie spat.

"Well, judging from that tone, I'd have to say at least your attitude is still tough. There was fire in that answer. Listen, Leslie, you have got to look deeper inside you—deeper than you've ever looked before. Yes, I'm sorry about what happened to your face, but you'd have had to literally face losing your looks some day. So what happened just accelerated the process. Now you've been freed to see the qualities and talents that make you really special. In a way, your beauty has handicapped you, blinded you, and kept you from becoming the real you."

"I don't understand," Leslie answered.

"You will, as long as you don't pull another stunt like you did last night."

There wasn't time for an answer. Behind Meg the door swished open and a man strolled into the room holding a huge bouquet of flowers.

54

"Hi," Hunter announced his presence, "I hope that you two don't mind another participant in this conversation."

Looking up, Meg waved. "Three's a crowd, so I'm leaving. I'll check with both of you later."

Meg quickly exited the room and closed the door behind her. As it eased shut, Hunter took a seat, leaned over Leslie's bed and softly said, "I thought I'd lost you."

"I guess I owe you a big thank-you," Leslie offered. "Meg said that your call is what angered her enough that she came to visit me."

Putting his finger to her lips, Hunter stopped her. "Les, I love you. It's as simple as that. I called Meg for that reason and that reason only. Now how can I get it through your thick skull?"

Shaking her head, Leslie tried to explain away his feelings. "No, you don't love me, you care for me, and you feel sorry for me, but you don't love me. You couldn't. I know that."

"Then you don't know me because I do love you," Hunter assured her.

"Hunter Jefferson, I know me. Even though I try to avoid mirrors, I see me every day, and I know that if I were you, I couldn't and wouldn't wait for those doctors to put Ms. Humpty Dumpty together again. Not all the pieces are there to complete the job. My face was my life, and without it, I'm a bad dream."

"Wake up, Les," Hunter whispered and then in a much more demanding tone added, "when you wake up, the nightmare will end and you'll discover there is more to life than what you've imagined."

"Get this through your thick head," Leslie barked as she stared deeply into the man's eyes. "I just can't believe you would love this." She pointed to her face and then continued, "Maybe if you give me some time. Maybe then I'll understand why you feel like you do. Right now, I just can't accept it."

"Les . . . "

She raised her hand and cut him off. "Hunter, why don't you try to forget me for a few weeks? Why don't you date someone else? When you do then you can really find an answer to the question that I'm asking. I really believe you'll discover that I'm just another one of your missions. And when you hold someone beautiful, when you kiss her, when you make love to her, you will thank me for yanking the wool from over your eyes."

"You're wrong," Hunter smiled, "there's no wool there."

"Sure there is," she replied.

"No, there can't be. I'm allergic to wool." He flashed a smile. "It's true! I am! But I'll tell you what I'll do. I'll spread myself around, I'll try to find the world's most wonderful and beautiful women and take them out to the finest places, but only if you will still go out with me at least a night or two a week."

"Hunter," Leslie began to argue, but finally just gave in. "Fine. As long as you do find someone else to go out with and they have to be pretty. No, they have to be beautiful, like I used to be."

"OK," he answered, "if you say that I must take out a fox, I will. After all, I must keep you happy, no matter the price I have to pay. You know your cousin Meg is quite a dish."

A tinge of jealousy crept up from Leslie's heart and revealed itself in the flash of her eyes. "Not her. She's off limits."

"But . . ."

"No buts, you can't take out anyone who's related to me. That's just too weird."

Hunter grinned. "OK. Now, how are you feeling?"

"Sleepy."

"Why doesn't that surprise me?" he asked.

"What I did was stupid," she admitted.

"We have all done stupid things," he assured her. "And when we survive them, then we're better people for it. That is, if we decide to learn something. I think that if you haven't, you will."

Those were nice words. They were comforting. For reasons she didn't understand, he had faith in her. Maybe there was something worth saving after all.

55

He was about to present a new possible woman to date when Hunter noted his partner in the conversation had drifted back to sleep. Smiling, he relaxed in the chair, repeated a few prayers of thanks that he still had her, and placed the flowers he'd brought on her bed. He stole over to the wall and flipped off the overhead light. Easing back into the chair, he studied the woman in the bed. Despite the deep scars, he saw a special kind of soft beauty, a kind that the Leslie of old hadn't had. He wondered if she would ever be able to see it, too.

He had planned on just watching as she rested, but as she'd kept him up most of the night pacing in the waiting room, he soon joined her in deep slumber. He'd been sleeping for several hours when Meg's hand on his shoulder woke him.

"Excuse me, Mr. Jefferson, but visiting hours are over. Besides, she'll sleep all night long.

So why don't you go home and come back tomorrow?"

"I probably ought to stay here," Hunter insisted.

"This, my dear man," Meg whispered, "is a hospital, and someone here will look after this sleeping woman. Your job is to go home quietly or I'll have my attorney get an injunction."

"I'm your attorney."

Meg smiled. "Now move."

Running his right hand through Leslie's soft hair, Hunter grudgingly gave up and said good night. Still, in order to make sure he followed her request, Meg walked him to the door.

"You don't even have your uniform on," Hunter observed as she pushed him outside.

"Of course not," she laughed, "this is my day off."

"Well, if you're not on duty," he argued, "how can you order me around?"

"I can do it because I am a woman, and being a nurse doesn't stop with the uniform. On duty or off, that is what we do. Now get some sleep or I'm going to pull my legal business away from you and put it in the hands of someone who takes care of himself."

56

A few hours later, Leslie's room remained silent except for her steady breathing, created by deep restful sleep. Out in the hall, a man slowly mopped the floor. With each large sweep of his mop, he came closer to her door. When he reached it, he wrung out his mop, checked the corridor for activity, and then, seeing no one, pushed the mop and the bucket against the wall. Slowly he eased open the door to the room and just as carefully shut it behind him.

Once in the room, he silently crossed to the patient's bed. Hitting the frame with his knee, he froze for a moment, waiting to see if anyone had heard him. Then, after Leslie didn't move, he edged closer to the head of the bed.

"Who are you and what are you doing in here?" Meg's voice boomed out in the darkness. The man froze as the nurse crossed the room and flipped the light switch. Staring at the startled man, she approached him and in a much softer, but just as firm tone, inquired, "What are doing in this room?"

Backing away from the bed, Jacob shrugged his shoulders and whispered, "I thought it was vacant. I was going to clean it up."

"In the dark?" Meg incredulously asked.

"No," he quietly answered. "You see, last week they told me to clean up a vacant room and when I turned the light on, I woke up a patient. They had given me the wrong number. I was just checking to see if it had happened again. I mean, you know how forgetful and confused Old Man Green can get. It looks like he messed up again."

Jacob hurried out of the room, closely followed by the nurse. Reaching into his pocket he produced a paper, read it, and then handed it to Meg. "You see, Ms. Richards, it says to clean up Room 231."

Looking at the paper, Meg handed it back and said, "Look again, Jacob, the number is 321. You ought to have your eyes checked."

The janitor hit his forehead with the palm of his hand and shook his head. "Oh my, and I thought that Mr. Green was wrong. I hope that I didn't wake up the patient, I mean she must be pretty bad off if you are assigned to spend the night in there."

"No, you didn't wake her up," Meg explained, "and I'm spending the night because she's my cousin, not because she's that sick. Now why don't you get back to work and be a little more careful next time."

"Sure thing, Ms. Richards." Jacob nodded. "I'll make sure that I don't go into a room with someone in it again. You can bet on that."

Meg watched as the man picked up his mop and rolling bucket and hurried quickly down the hall. Shaking her head, she returned to Leslie's room. Within moments, Meg joined Leslie in a deep slumber.

57

"Well, I just saw Aunt Flo in the hall," Meg said as she walked into her cousin's room. "How is she?"

"You know, Mom," Leslie answered, sitting up in bed and trying to straighten her hair. "She tried to convince me I did it by accident. I believe she's decided that I was so tired and hurt, I couldn't count the right number of pills. Anyway, she was here for about an hour, and I discovered that while she was at the convention, she met two senators, a governor, and the mayor."

"Aunt Flo was always a mover and shaker," Meg agreed. "I understand they are going to release you this afternoon."

"Yes," Leslie responded unenthusiastically, "I have the unique pleasure of going home in just a few hours," and added sarcastically, "the fun of television and more television, and when I'm not watching television, listening to Mother or turning a thousand different directions and seeing pictures of myself on every table and wall, and in most of the drawers. The house is almost like a shrine. Has it always been that way?"

A sparkle lit Meg's eyes as she answered, "Always. I would love to know just how much money your mother spent on photographs and new clothes when you were growing up."

"She dropped a great deal," Leslie answered, "and I don't guess I ever really noticed. That was just Mother being Mother! You know, now is the first time it really bothered me, and I don't think it is because of my face as much as it is her reaction to it. I'm not sure that she even knows what I really look like. The first thing she did when she walked in here today was dim the lights. When I made her turn them up, she thought I was crazy."

"Well," Meg broke in, "you've been in the dark for a while. Maybe she thought that you wanted it that way. You have been hiding. What about Hunter?"

"I asked him to date someone else—someone beautiful."

"That shouldn't be too hard for him to do," Meg teased. "If you like, there are at least four nurses in the hospital who would do anything for a crack at him. Do you want me to tell them he's ready for some new blood?"

"Fine," Leslie's answer seemed forced and

bitter. "At least they will have the qualities that can make him happy for the long run." She paused, bit her lip then added, "When I told him to date someone else, he suggested you."

Meg grinned. "He is the kind of man I could fall for—that strong, but sensitive type. I love his wide shoulders and his jaw . . ."

"He's too young for you," Leslie snapped.

"Maybe he is, but there are other nurses who'd stand in line for the chance, and they are his age. Not sure tossing him into the dating pool was such a good idea."

"It's best he find someone who can walk in the sunshine without fear of making others sick to their stomachs."

"You still have a flair for the dramatic," Meg interjected. "Hey, how long will it take you to get dressed, hair, makeup, and clothes?"

"Makeup?" Leslie queried. "That's a big laugh."

"How long?" Meg demanded.

"Half an hour."

"OK, I'll give you an hour, and I'll give you something else. In this bag is a new kind of makeup developed especially for people who have facial scarring. It's not even on the market yet, but Dr. Parks's surgical assistant was able to get the company testing it to send us some."

Leslie took the small sack from Meg, looked inside, and then pulled out a few jars. There were no labels or instructions. Shrugging her shoulders, she searched the nurse's face for some kind of help.

"Well, don't look at me," Meg smiled. "You're the expert."

"Seriously," Leslie sighed, "I wouldn't know where to start."

"Understood," the nurse replied. "Here's what you do. Just get everything but your face fixed up. Victoria Nance, who has a world of experience in this area, will be here in a few moments to tell you what to use and how to use it. By the way, do you have any of your own makeup here?"

Leslie shook her head. "I didn't remember my bag when I left home the other night."

"OK." Meg smiled. "I'll bring some of mine back when I come. You can use it with this stuff. Now get on the move. I've got something to show you in a few minutes."

When Meg came back, Victoria had Leslie sitting in a chair and was putting the last touches of makeup on her face. Pausing for a moment to admire her work, she smiled at Leslie and handed her a mirror.

Slowly bringing it up until she saw her reflection, she studied it for a moment, gently brushing her cheek and forehead, and then looked up at Meg. Smiling, Meg handed her a makeup bag. After taking it, Leslie turned back to Victoria and asked, "What do I do now?"

"Well, for the moment," Victoria explained,

"you're going to have to use your own makeup over these cover-ups and fillers. The key to the application is to mix it until you have matched your skin tone and then apply it to help smooth the face. Don't use too much. No matter how much you use, the scars are still going to be there, but this will make them not nearly as noticeable. It's not a miracle, only a way to build and improve. Given time, after we have done additional surgical work, you will be able to cover more and more."

Meg noticed a bit of a hopeful expression as her cousin glanced back in the mirror. She was far from a cover girl, but she did look better.

"Now," Victoria suggested in a patient tone, "let's apply the rest of the makeup. Do you want me to do it or would you rather give it a try?"

"I'll try," Leslie said. Taking the bag over to the room's large mirror, she began to really fix her face for the first time in weeks. All the other times she'd just caked on layers to try to hide the scars. Now she concentrated on trying to make herself look more natural. While she did, Meg signaled Victoria to follow her out in the hall.

"How did she take it?" Meg inquired.

"A bit skeptical at first, but after I began to put it on and explain what I was doing, she at least gave it a shot. As you can see, the scars are still there and they still show. But it may serve to give her some confidence."

"I want it to do that," Meg agreed, "but I also want it to start her on the road to building a foundation for the rest of her life. She may actually be further from that than she is from accepting her face, and I think that they may be tied together. She needs to feel that she's not so ugly that no one can love her."

"She's not ugly," Victoria smiled. "Once we finish with the surgeries, she will be fine. In fact, I think she will turn heads for all the right reasons."

"That's what we see and we know," Meg agreed, "but you have to understand that Leslie feels that anything short of perfection means she is ugly. We've got to change that mentality. You've gotten us through step one. I have another element that might take us to step two and beyond."

"Understand," Victoria replied, "she is medically and mentally the toughest case we've ever had. Anyway, when she runs out of the makeup, give me a call and I'll get her some more. For the company, she's kind of like a living test subject. They are eager to find out how she does."

As Victoria walked down the hall toward her office, Meg checked her watch. She was already five minutes behind schedule. She needed to pick up the pace. Marching with a purpose, she reentered the room.

"Well, time's up," she announced. "I hope you are ready."

"What am I supposed to be ready for?" Leslie asked as she applied a generous portion of lipstick. "I really need a lot more work."

"That, my dear cousin, is a surprise. Now, follow me, and don't worry if the makeup is not prom ready, you're not going to a dance . . ."

"Wait," Leslie begged as she glanced back into the mirror. "You need to tell me what you think. Be honest."

"What do you think?" Meg asked.

"It's better," she answered while running her finger lightly over the deepest scars. "But my face still looks like a crude piece of modern art."

"Can you show expression?"

Leslie looked deeply into the mirror, twisted her mouth, and raised an eyebrow. "I can at least look confused."

"Good," Meg replied. "You might just have to exhibit that quality in a few moments."

58

Meg led Leslie through the door, past the nurses' station, all the way down the hall, to a flight of stairs. After walking down one floor, the two entered another hall, strolled past another nurses' station and a long corridor of closed doors.

Finally, stopping in front of a children's play-room, Meg looked back to Leslie.

"Take a look and tell me what you see."

Inside there were four kids, who all seemed to be preschool age; one might have been as young as three. There was a trio playing together, and one, a small blonde girl, in a corner by herself. To Leslie they seemed like normal, healthy children. The two boys and the girl, who had teamed up, were charging in and out of a plastic fort-like structure. They were giggling and yapping up a storm. Pointing, Leslie asked, "What is wrong with them? Why are they here?"

"Oh, those three," Meg softly explained. "Two of them have cancer and the other has a very serious disease you've probably never heard of that might leave her blind. They are all here for treatments. If they're lucky, the cancer patients may live. It is going to take a lot of work and prayer to make that happen. Still, odds are pretty good only one of them makes it to being a teenager. Yet, they fight their illness just as hard as they play. And the girl, she is getting experimental treatments that we hope will work, but she is still probably going to go blind before she can ever get a driver's license."

After watching the happy trio for a few more moments, Leslie turned her attention to the small girl in the back of the room. The child was facing the wall, sitting at a small table, and coloring pictures. She seemed totally unaware the other kids were playing so near her. She seemed to be lost in a world of her own.

Her long hair was tied with a pink ribbon. The playsuit she wore was bright and cheerful and matched that ribbon. Little pink socks covered her feet, and her shoes, cast off some time before, were white with pink strings. The entire time Leslie studied her, the girl never looked up from her work.

"What about the other little girl?" Leslie asked. "The one who seems so serious minded. Is she dying?"

Shaking her head, Meg quietly answered, "No, she's not going to die. The better question may be is she ever going to live again?"

Puzzled, Leslie looked at her cousin with an expression that demanded more. Meg didn't notice and she didn't explain. All she said was, "Come on."

"Where?"

"Inside, I want you to meet someone."

Grabbing Meg's arm, Leslie stopped her with both her words and her actions. "Listen, don't hang a guilt trip on me. I'm not dying and I don't need to meet a bunch of poor dying kids in order to discover how lucky I am. I assured you I wasn't going to try to kill myself again. Besides this is a whole different thing. Don't even try to play this game with me."

"It's not a game," Meg shot back. "Not for you and not for these kids. I didn't bring you in here so that you could count your blessings. I brought you in here to help me, in fact all the nurses, and even the doctors, especially Dr. Parks. You at least owe him."

Pushing back toward the middle of the hall, Leslie spat, "What do you mean owe? What can I do? Even with the new makeup I'm a freak!"

"And maybe that is just what I need," Meg's words stabbed the other woman, and she meant them, too. "Listen, we can't do something that we want and need to do, and we're hoping that you might help us. Of course, you don't have to. You have enough problems without ours. At least, that's what you think. But I wish you'd just take a little time to see what I'm talking about."

Leslie was hardly convinced, but she had also learned from more than two decades of dealing with her mother that at times it was easier to go along with someone than try to fight. Besides, once she completed this little mission, she could get her things and check out. So, rather than argue and prolong the agony, she gave in.

She followed closely behind Meg as they made their way into the room. The nurse stopped just after entering, and after getting the youngsters' attention, introduced the playful three, Bobby, Jennifer, and Tom, to Leslie. The children quickly said their hellos, and then launched back into their games. It seemed they looked at their visitor so quickly they didn't even notice her scars.

Meg watched the trio play for a moment, and then announced in a very assertive tone, "OK, you three, time for you to get back to your rooms and get ready for the doctor's visit. Now, hustle." Knowing that it would do no good to grumble, the two boys and girl obediently formed a short line and exited the room. Just before the door closed, Meg loudly announced, "And don't run in the hall."

The room that just moments before had been filled with so much noisy activity was now completely silent except for the sounds of a crayon slowly moving back and forth on a large piece of paper. For a few seconds, Meg just observed the little girl, not disturbing her activity or her thoughts. Finally, when she'd finished coloring Cinderella's dress, she moved to the small table and pulled out a tiny chair. Folding up her full-size body, she took a seat, leaned over and smiled.

Leslie hadn't moved. She felt a little confused and maybe her face actually showed it. Meg hadn't signaled for her to follow, so she still didn't know what was wrong with this girl. As she awkwardly stood there, alone and seemingly very out of place, she wondered what she could do that a hospital full of nurses and doctors couldn't.

"That is a pretty picture," Meg softly told the little girl. She didn't look up, nor did she respond. Undaunted, the nurse continued, "I brought someone I wanted you to meet. You know the lady I told you about, the one on the cover of the magazine? Well, she's here."

"The lady that looks like Cinderella?" the little girl asked.

"Yes," Meg answered. "Would you like for me to bring her over?"

"I guess so," came the timid answer. "Are you sure that she wants to meet me?"

"Of course, she does," Meg answered. Motioning with her head, she signaled for Leslie to come over and sit in the small chair on the other side of the girl.

This was the last straw. Leslie set her jaw and shook her head, turning away from the table and facing the door. She couldn't believe Meg was going to do this to her. She wasn't going to allow a child to make fun of her.

"Leslie," Meg sternly said, "come over here. Now."

She wasn't going to give up. But neither was Leslie. No way, no how! Yet at that moment a large group of people walked down the hall. As they neared the playroom window, their heads turned in Leslie's direction. She couldn't let them see her, not even with the new makeup. Better the child than the adults! Quickly she spun and then grudgingly moved to the table. Yet, even as she pulled out the chair and folded herself into it, Leslie refused to change her angry expression. It didn't matter as the girl never looked up.

"Leslie, I want you to meet Angel," Meg said. "Angel, this is Leslie."

"How do you do?" Angel shyly whispered, still keeping her focus on her drawing.

"Hello," Leslie responded admiring the beautiful blonde hair that hid the little girl's face.

"Angel, Leslie has changed since she had that picture taken," Meg explained. "She had an accident, and her face was hurt very badly. It's going to take her a long time to get it fixed right."

The little girl quit coloring. She sat very still, as if trying to comprehend what she'd just been told. During these moments, the room took on a strange, almost church-like silence. Finally, and very hesitantly, she lifted her face just enough to look at the visitor, then, quickly her eyes darted back to her drawing. They lingered there for a few moments, then the child again raised her head, this time allowing it to come completely up and stared long and hard at Leslie's face.

When Angel raised her head, Leslie had felt so uncomfortable she'd looked toward the wall rather than return the little girl's stare. Still she could feel her small eyes as they moved across her face. Anger began to build, a thick hot flow of blood burned through her body. She couldn't believe Meg, the one person she thought she could trust, was exhibiting her like a freak. Even with the makeup, even with her hair fixed and a nice sweater and slacks, she knew that this child was seeing her as something grotesque and ugly. What was this all about? Why was this so important for this child's ego? Finally, in rage as much as anything, she turned her face back toward the little girl's. Ready to explode with a torrent of harsh words, she was stopped suddenly by something she hadn't expected. As quickly as it had come, her anger departed.

"I am very glad to meet you," Angel shyly began. "I've never met anyone who was important before."

Leslie barely heard the words; she was too mesmerized by the little girl's face. A terrible red scar covered most of the right side, from eye level to the bottom of her jaw. It left the little girl looking like something from a bad dream of a cheap horror show. The side of her face that had been left unmarked showed that she had once been a beautiful child.

Evidently noting Leslie's shocked look, Angel said, "I hope that you're not scared of me. Some people are."

Shaking her head, Leslie finally managed to say, "I'm not scared of you, but I hope that you aren't scared of me."

"I couldn't be," the little girl whispered, "you're like Cinderella. So even if God does hate you, I'm not scared of you."

Puzzled, Leslie leaned closer to Angel. "What do you mean when you say that God hates me?"

"He must, after all. He messed up your face." Her simple logic cut straight to Leslie's heart. "But that's OK, because He hates me, too. Of course, you can see that."

How she needed answers. Searching her mind and sensing it tie to her soul for the first time in years, she fumbled for words. At first none materialized. After all, the little girl echoed Leslie's thoughts and actions. It was not that bottle, it was God who had killed her beauty. He had done this to her. But if that was the case then He had done it to this child as well. She couldn't allow herself to believe that and she didn't want an innocent little girl to think that either.

After almost a minute of uncomfortable silence, Leslie softly explained "He doesn't hate you, and He doesn't hate me. God didn't do this to me, some man that I didn't even know did. I'm sure that God is as upset about it as I am."

Smiling, Angel quietly explained, "My mommy did this to me. She did it to me because I was bad. God made her do this to me because I was bad. That must have been why He made that mean person cut you."

Had either of them been that bad? Surely not!

Once again shaking her head, Leslie took the girl's face in her hands and looked her right in the eyes. "Angel, God doesn't work that way. I don't care where you heard it, but it just doesn't happen the way you think it does. God didn't do this, a man did."

Angel's eyes found Leslie's as she spoke, "That's what people say, but I know better. If I had been a good person, Mommy wouldn't have wanted to hurt me."

A rush of pain pierced Leslie's heart. She fully understood why Angel felt the way she did, but she didn't have a clue as to how to make the little girl see that what happened wasn't her fault. Yes, Leslie was sure that if she hadn't been on the cover of a magazine she wouldn't have been so brutally attacked. But it wasn't because of anything bad she had done that she was hurt—or was it?

When she had been selfish and taken the Buffalo Scotch ad just to further her career, was she paying for that now? Was God getting her for ignoring others' feelings and expectations and only considering her own? But even if that were so, what had Angel done in her short life that could have caused Him to lash out in such fury at her? No, God wouldn't do that. It was unfair for anyone to think that. Yet, even just two nights before when she had tried to take her own life, hadn't she blamed God?

"Angel," Meg explained, "Leslie is getting to go home today. So I need to check her out of her room. It's time for us to leave."

The little girl looked back at Leslie, staring deeply into her eyes. After a few moments studying her face, Angel finally smiled. It was the first time Leslie had seen her express any real emotion. A big gap readily showed at the top of her mouth, a gap caused by losing her two front teeth, and a small sparkle appeared for a moment in her blue eyes. Shaking her head, Angel softly proclaimed, "You have pretty eyes. God couldn't be too mad at you or He wouldn't have given you such pretty eyes."

Staring back at the little girl, Leslie smiled. "No, God's not mad at me." Pausing for a long moment to touch Angel's soft hair, then she asked, "Can I come back and see you sometime?"

"If you want," Angel agreed and quickly went back to drawing her picture.

As Meg and Leslie made the long walk back to her room, the hospital halls were beginning to become crowded with visitors. Many of them stopped and stared at Leslie as they met her, but she didn't notice. Her mind and heart were still back in the playroom.

As they turned the corner leading to Leslie's room, she touched her cousin's arm and asked, "Meg, how did she get hurt?"

Meg didn't answer until they were both in the room and she'd closed the door. "Her mother poured some boiling water on Angel a few weeks ago. It wasn't the first time she had abused her, just the first time she'd been caught. The woman had already had two other children taken away from her for doing similar things. To escape going to prison, a few days ago she signed away all rights to Angel. There are no relatives, so she will be placed in a foster home when we are through with her."

"How much can you do for her?"

"Given time," Meg explained, "a great deal. She has the chance to be beautiful someday. Her prom pictures will be wonderful. So, the problem is not her face, it is her heart. As you can see, she's convinced that she's an ugly person through and through. It's very sad."

"Is that how I am?" Leslie asked, not really wanting to hear the answer.

"Today, you accomplished a miracle," Meg smiled as she spoke.

"What do you mean?"

"That little girl hadn't shown a bit of emotion, not even any signs of pain or hurt or anger, since we brought her in. That has been over three weeks. Today, she smiled. I thank you for that."

The blind leading the blind, that is what this was. Two people who shouldn't have been hurt had been. What kind of world was this? Didn't anyone have a soul anymore?

And there it was, a soul. She'd forgotten about having or needing one. She hadn't prayed since struggling down that dark alley and then it was only for selfish reasons.

She glanced across the room into a mirror. Suddenly, after hearing the story about a girl who had been so badly injured by someone who should have loved her made the image reflected in the glass look far less hideous.

"It's not fair, Meg," Leslie whispered, tears filling her eyes. "It's not fair."

"You or Angel?" Meg asked.

"Both of us," Leslie sobbed. Leaning forward she fell into her cousin's arms. "I hate being ugly."

"You're not," Meg assured her. "The compassion I saw in your eyes as you tried to comfort Angel was beautiful. In fact, I've never seen you look as radiant. Once again, thank you for getting Angel to smile today."

"Thank me?" Leslie responded almost apologetically, pushing herself off Meg's shoulder and wiping the tears from her eyes. "But it is not enough. I mean how can I get through to her enough for her to realize that people can love her without hurting her? She has a whole life ahead of her and if she doesn't open up and learn to trust, she'll miss it all."

"Gosh," Meg quipped, "I wish you would tell that to my cousin. She needs to hear it, too."

"Touché," Leslie replied. "But I'm serious. Everything I'm feeling must be meaningless compared to her. My mother is not the best in the world, but she would never physically hurt me. Her words might sting but . . ." She paused for a moment and then almost pleaded, "Will she go through her whole life feeling like I do? What can we do?"

"On the night stand," Meg pointed as she spoke, "there's a Bible. There are a lot of things in there that will help you if you will read them, but I recommend that you start out with something called the Love Chapter. You will find it in 1 Corinthians 13. I know you've read it before, but I think this is when you need to read it again. You will likely understand it now."

Crossing the room, Leslie opened the book and hurriedly leafed through the New Testament. Finding the passage, she slowly read the words. Stopping at verse 14, she whispered them out loud. "For now we see in a *mirror;* dimly . . .

"Meg," Leslie asked, "do you think that Hunter really could love me?"

"Could you love Angel?" Meg asked.

"Yes, I really believe I could," Leslie assured both Meg and herself. "I think I already do."

"Leslie, I think that it will be far easier for you to love Angel than for her to love herself. I think that Hunter probably feels the same way about you. It's time for you to put away the childish vanities and codes that have ruled your life. It's time to look at the fabric that is underneath. If that fabric has color and beauty then you will know that Hunter could fall in love with you. Of course, that will require taking a chance and creating a new life for yourself. You just told a little girl that God didn't hate you. Then, if you believe that, maybe it's time you asked Him to help you."

Shaking her head, Leslie felt a new strength well up in her soul and a new brightness enter her world. Smiling through tears she whispered, "Let's go for it!"

59

Rosatelli had been in a bad mood for almost a month. No case in Springfield's history had created as much national buzz as the "Model Slashing" and, yet, he had nothing substantial to investigate. The victim couldn't provide any worthwhile clues. The crime scene had been washed clean by heavy spring rains. Crime Stoppers had produced a few wacky calls, but nothing of substance. With pressure coming from the national media as well as the mayor and District Attorney Webb Jones, the police captain was at his wits' end.

As he sat at his desk and stared out a window at the quiet streets of the only town he'd ever lived in, he considered his options. The case was dead. Had it died due to the fact the suspect was a drifter who'd left town or was still hiding somewhere in the shadows? He didn't have a clue, but he was leaning to the former. If that was the case, he'd likely never be caught. That made the captain sick to his stomach.

The FBI profiler they'd borrowed had suggested the victim must have known her assailant. She surmised this due to the violent rage that defined the attack and the manner in which the injuries were inflicted. The attacker had not wanted to kill Leslie Rhoads, but rather teach her some kind of lesson. That education came by destroying what defined her and made her a living. By destroying that, he must have gained a bit of revenge for something he believed the model had done to him. But that trail went cold because Rhoads simply had no enemies. There was no one from her past, from her career, or in her personal life that cared enough about her to carry such hate.

"Captain."

Rosatelli leaned over his desk, pushed a button and spoke into his call box, "Yeah."

"There's a Ms. Leslie Rhoads here to see you."

The cop was shocked. The only times he'd seen her in person was when she had been hospitalized and since then he'd only spoken to her on the phone. He'd been told she wouldn't even go out in public. Yet today she'd made the trip down to see him. Maybe she'd remembered something.

"Send her in," he said. Releasing the button, he got up from his desk and moved toward the office door. He was halfway across the twenty-foot-wide room when she walked in.

"Captain."

"Ms. Rhoads. Please come in. So glad you feel well enough to be out and about. Why don't you take that chair in front of my desk?"

"Thank you," she replied and moved to the suggested spot. As she did, he hurried back behind this desk. When she'd taken her seat, he sat down as well.

Except for the still obvious wounds created by the attack, she looked amazing. Wearing a navy blue suit, the skirt ending just above the knee with an ivory blouse under her jacket, she looked every bit a model. Her hair was perfect with the right side swept around in a peek-a-boo style that not only covered a few of the scars, but added a hint of mystery. She wore blue heels and a single gold chain around her neck. And even with the railroad like red lines that intersected in various points on her face, he was still drawn to those incredible blue eyes. As she crossed one leg over the other and glanced his way, he asked a question that had been burning in his head for more than a month.

"Have you remembered something else?"

She nodded. "Not as much remembered as experienced. Did you hear that I'd taken an overdose of sleeping pills three days ago?"

"I was informed," he replied. "I can understand what drove you to that point, but I'm glad you failed."

"So am I," she assured him. "But there was something strange that happened just before I passed out."

"Really?" He leaned toward her as he waited for the explanation.

"Yeah. I was getting really foggy when someone walked in and talked to me. He told me he was there to finish the job. But when he saw what I'd done, he just watched me drift off. One of my last memories is of him stepping over me and leaving the house."

Rosatelli nodded. "You're sure it wasn't an illusion?"

"No, I've talked to Dr. Cunningham about that and she agrees with me that it was very real. I recognized the voice. In fact, his standing over me made me want to fight death. That visit gave me a reason to live!"

"What did he look like?"

"I wish I could tell you Captain, but it was

dark in the room and I wasn't focusing too well by then. But there is something I can give you."

Rosatelli smiled as he waited for what might be his first break in the case. "What's that?"

"I'm sure he was driving a noisy blue truck that I've been seeing parked across the street from time to time. I've seen it and heard it a few times from my window upstairs in our house. The truck has a distinct exhaust sound, kind of a pat-pat-pat as it picks up speed. The truck I heard leaving that night had that same sound. In other words, I think he's been watching me, maybe waiting for the moment to finish the job. Does that make sense?"

Rosatelli leaned back in his desk chair. The guy was still in town and he was scared Ms. Rhoads knew something. Looking back to his guest, he asked, "What can you tell me about the blue truck?"

"Chevy, I remember the red bowtie on the tailgate, maybe twenty or more years old. Maybe even more. Couldn't see it real well in the dark, but it was not in great shape."

The captain jotted the information down, as he pushed forward another question. "Was it a regular or extended cab?"

"Regular."

"Anything else?"

Leslie shook her head. "Sorry, I really didn't

pay much attention. When I saw it I didn't think it was a big deal."

Rosatelli nodded as he leaned closer to his guest. "What about the guy? Anything else?"

"Yeah, there was one thing. And I hadn't thought of it until now, but he smelled of smoke."

"Cigarette smoke?" he asked.

"Yes," she replied, "it was very strong. In fact, it smelled the same as what I smelled the night the man sneaked into my room at the hospital. I'm sorry I don't have any more for you."

"This is great," he assured her.

Leslie got up from her chair, smiled and walked back toward the door. She was about to exit when his words stopped her.

"Ms. Rhoads, starting today there will be patrolmen making regular drives by your house. You won't see them, they'll be in unmarked cars. If you need us, call 9-1-1 and we will be there in no time."

"Thank you," she replied as she closed his office door.

Rosatelli walked back over to his desk, sat down and smiled. It had been right in front of him all along. He had a suspect and with just a bit of legwork he'd have enough circumstantial evidence to make an arrest soon.

60

Jacob Spence was getting out of the truck he'd been borrowing from his uncle when he saw Captain Brian Rosatelli. Noting the policeman's presence didn't spook him at all. He'd seen him plenty of times and even talked to him on at least a dozen different occasions. Yet, when he took a second look, he noted something very different. The cop had his gun out. The lanky six-foot two-inch maintenance man didn't want any of that action and jumped back in the truck. Pushing the key to the right, he started the old rig and slipped it into drive. His foot didn't reach the accelerator; it was stopped by Rosatelli's forceful voice.

"Turn it off, get out of the truck with your hands over your head, or I'll pull this trigger."

That one strong warning was all it took. Jacob switched the key to the left, pulled the door handle, and slid out of the vehicle.

"Turn around, spread your legs, and put your hands on the hood," the policeman barked.

Jacob followed the order to the letter. While holding the gun with his right, Rosatelli frisked him with the left hand. He was clean.

"Put your hands behind your back," he ordered.

Jacob complied. A second later, he'd been handcuffed.

"Don't move."

The captain observed the now-restrained man for a moment then peered into the cab. It was littered with soft drink cans, fast food sacks, and empty cigarette packages.

"Why you picking on me?" Jacob whined.

Rosatelli didn't answer while he scanned the rest of the vehicle. Grimly nodding, he noted an empty fifth of Buffalo Scotch on the floor. The pieces fit.

"Jacob Spence, I'm arresting you for the brutal assault and attempted murder of Leslie Rhoads."

Turning to face the captain, Jacob shook his head. "I didn't have nothing to do with that. I liked her. I liked her a lot. She was real pretty."

Ignoring the man's protest, Rosatelli recited one of the best-known phrases in the American language, "You know that anything you say could be used against you." He continued through the script until reaching the final word. After once more taking stock of his prisoner, he added, "A patrol car will be here in a few minutes to take you downtown."

"I didn't do nothing wrong," Jacob protested. "I wouldn't hurt anybody."

"Spence, did you used to drive a white sedan?"

"Yeah, an LTD! It was my grandmother's until she died."

"Where is it now?"

"At my house. It's not running."

"Where do you live?"

"2218 West Elm."

Rosatelli pulled out his cell, hit a number and waited. "Hey, this is Brian. I've arrested Spence. Make sure the patrol car is on its way to get him. I need a search warrant for 2218 West Elm, the home, the property, and all the vehicles on that property. Get it ASAP. I need for the CSIs to go over that place with everything they got. We should find something there that ties him to the attack on Leslie Rhoads."

Dropping the phone back into his blue sports jacket, the captain looked back at his captive. He'd been hiding in plain sight, close enough to make contact with his victim. He'd even been stalking her and all it took was the girl remembering one little clue. It was just that easy!

A black and white Impala drove across the parking lot and stopped where Rosatelli was watching Jacob Spence. As the two uniformed policemen got out, the captain grimly said, "He's yours. Take him downtown and have him booked. They're ready for him."

Rosatelli watched Spence loaded into the car and studied the man as he was driven away. He was scared. It showed. He hadn't expected to be caught.

Glancing back into the old truck he saw something peeking from under the driver's side of the seat. Bending over, he took a closer look. It was an issue of *Fashion and Style*. Leslie Rhoads was on the cover and someone had taken a red marker and carefully drawn lines all across the face. As best as Rosatelli could remember, those lines were in the very same place as the scars on the model's face.

61

Carlee was studying a contract she had just worked up for one of her newest models. The gig she was so afraid of losing when Leslie was attacked was once again hers. The girl, Gem McCall, had just been approved as the new image of Passion Nights perfume. And this model had absolutely no qualms about the nudity required in the job.

Her cell interrupted her private celebration. Turning her attention from the contract to the phone, she glanced at the I.D. Finally! Hitting the accept button, she leaned back in her chair and announced, "Is the contract finished? I need to get the media blitz started."

"Not going to be a contract," she was bluntly informed. The man continued, "Not going to be a movie either."

Standing, Carlee looked incredulous as she barked, "What do you mean? This is a can't miss. The story is the perfect combination of sex and violence. And it's real!"

"Haven't you read the news online or watched any TV this afternoon?"

She shook her head. "Been working on a big deal. Haven't had time."

"Well, those hokey cops who you thought couldn't solve anything arrested the guy who cut your model up. He's a janitor at the hospital. He's got no record and he's not very bright. It seems he was a demented fan. At least that's what they're guessing. When she refused his advances, he went all crazy and used the bottle to cut her to shreds."

"But what about that kills the project?" Carlee asked.

"Because the guy who did it is a dud. He's not interesting. Look at his picture online, he's not even scary. There's no lasting shock value."

Carlee hurriedly pulled up the CNN page. Irvin was right, there was nothing haunting about Jacob Spence. He looked like a guy who'd collect beer cans for a hobby. Still, she paused and tried to figure a way to save the deal. She only had one hope—maybe they had the wrong man!

Her eyes turned back to the online story. The more she read, the more she realized she'd never make another dime off Leslie Rhoads.

In Spence's home, police found hundreds of pictures of the fashion model pinned to a bulletin board in the man's room. The police also found several bottles of Buffalo Scotch, the same type of bottle used in the attack on the model. Though Spence has denied any involvement, police assured reporters that they had enough circumstantial evidence to provide motive for the attack. Witnesses have also named him as the man who on at least two occasions entered the victim's hospital room.

Spence, who grew up in Kentucky and was raised by a single mother, had moved to the Springfield area a few months before. Relatives had secured him a position as a janitor at the hospital.

Carlee quit reading the story. They had the guy, and she was left holding the bag. It was like watching the air go out of a balloon. A thousand plans plus a few million dollars were now gone. She'd invested so much time and energy into that model and Leslie was never going to pay off.

Getting up, she crossed the room to a cabinet. Reaching in she pulled out a three-inch-thick file. Grimly she leafed through a few photos of Leslie Rhoads. Closing the folder, she strolled back to her desk and tossed the file into the trashcan. As she sat back in her desk chair, one thought kept running through her mind. It was a thought that would no doubt haunt her for years to come. Why did they have to catch him?

62

"I feel great," Leslie exclaimed as she walked by the nurses' station. "And thanks for asking."

Marsha Kolinek hadn't asked, but quickly returned the visitor's smile, noting that either her facial scars were becoming less visible, or the easy smile and sparkling eyes made it seem that way. Whatever, it was a remarkable transformation. It was as if it had happened overnight.

"I heard the police got the guy," Marsha shot back.

"Yeah," Leslie answered with a smile, "that's what they tell me. Captain Rosatelli told me something I said was the key to closing the case. Still not sure what it was."

"Just glad they got him," the nurse agreed. "I can't believe he worked here. I mean Jacob was strange, but I never figured him as a psycho. By the way, why are you at the hospital?"

"I was down seeing Angel," Leslie explained. "I found this adorable doll over at Coxes and I thought that maybe she'd enjoy playing with it."

"You've been good for her," Marsha's compliment was not given lightly. "You've been here like five hours a day each day this week. Never seen anything like it. She seems to be coming out of that tight shell that has surrounded her since she came in. It's really remarkable. You've accomplished more in four days than we have in a month."

"I've been wondering?" Leslie asked. "Why is she still here in the hospital? She seems healthy. Shouldn't she be released until the time she comes back and they can start working on her face?"

"Yes," Marsha explained, "ideally that's the way it should be. But if we let her go she'll end up in a children's facility, and then, after some evaluation, a foster home. And none of us think that she's ready for that kind of adjustment. Her social worker doesn't even think so. Here, she at least feels safe. And she needs to feel safe more than anything else in the world."

Leslie nodded, leaned over the nurses' station counter and absentmindedly studied a painting on the far wall. She maintained her silence until the nurse interrupted what appeared to be some very deep thoughts.

"Les, what's on your mind?"

"Do you think they'd let me take her home

for a night?" Leslie inquired. "Kind of like a sleepover?"

"You mean Angel?" the nurse asked. "I don't know. But as nothing about this case is normal, I wouldn't rule it out. Carolyn Brooks is her social worker and she's here right now." The nurse pointed down the hall. "She's in Mabel's office going over some records. I know that she's aware of the great strides you've made with her during the last few days. Maybe she would. Wouldn't hurt to check. Mabel's office is halfway down the north wing on the first floor. I'll bet you can catch Carolyn if you run over there right now."

As if on a mission, Leslie marched down the hall, so completely lost in her plans she was unaware that two people had stopped to gasp at her face. She didn't hear the "Bless her heart," but she wouldn't have cared if she did. She had much more important things on her agenda than worrying about her appearance, or how long it would be until the doctors were able to complete the work on her face. When she arrived at her destination, she smoothed her sweater, took a deep breath, considered what she would say, and then knocked on the door. She waited impatiently until she heard a woman cry out, "It's open."

"Excuse me," Leslie sang out as she entered the small ten-by-ten office. "I'm looking for a Ms. Brooks."

"That would be me," a stocky but athletic

woman likely in her forties proclaimed as she stood and smiled. "And you must be Ms. Rhoads."

"How did you know?" Leslie asked then bringing her hand up to her cheek she nodded. "Never mind, I guess it's not hard to pick me out."

There was an awkward silence for a moment before Ms. Brooks chimed in, "Call me Carolyn, and I probably should apologize. I realize now how my words were taken."

"Why apologize?" Leslie laughed.

"Because my response seemed indelicate in light of what has happened to you," came the quick reply. "I really do have tact."

"Tact is overrated," Leslie replied. "I was wondering if I could talk to you about Angel. I have an idea that you might be able to help me with."

"Sit down and join us," Ms. Brooks said, pointing to a chair on the left side of the desk. "Mabel and I have been wanting to talk to you about the miracle you are working." She paused, smiled, and added, "Or should I say that Cinderella is working."

"Yeah," Leslie grinned, "she does call me that about half the time. I'm still not sure the glass slipper fits."

"I'm betting it does," Brooks replied. "By the way, is there a Prince Charming?"

Leslie twisted her lips into a crooked, uneven

smile. At this point, it was the best she could manage. "There just might be one, but I came to ask you something much different."

A few minutes later, Leslie returned to the nurses' station, sporting a lopsided grin that went from the right corner of her mouth to her left cheek. Leaning over the counter she announced as if singing a song, "Guess what?"

"I take it she said yes," Marsha acknowledged the obvious.

"Yes," Leslie beamed, "she gave it her blessing for tomorrow night. That'll be perfect because my folks are going out of town and Angel and I will have the whole place to ourselves. Thanks for the heads-up, Marsha. I'm going to run down and tell Angel. I think this might well be the most unforgettable night of my life."

63

A few hours later, Leslie was sitting in her room going through a big box filled with a host of her old toys. For once, she was pleased that her mother had never shared any of her things with other kids and never threw anything away either. Pulling out a teddy bear, two dolls, a doctor's bag and a coloring book, she set them on the top of her dresser. Shoving the box into the closet, she then bounced across the room and jumped onto her bed. Giggling like a schoolgirl, she grabbed the phone and dialed Hunter's office.

"Hunter Jefferson, please," she asked as the receptionist answered.

"Who may I say is calling?"

"Cinderella," Leslie laughed.

"Who?"

"Cinderella."

"Are you one of his clients?"

"No," Leslie all but giggled. "But if the shoe fits, I might be."

"Just a moment, I'll see if he is in."

A few seconds later, a puzzled attorney broke onto the line and said, "Ah, can I help you? I'm sorry the receptionist didn't actually understand your name."

"Cinderella," Leslie quickly answered.

"Les," Hunter's voice relaxed. "I didn't expect to hear from you, especially after what you said on Sunday."

"Well," Leslie answered with a special energy in her voice, "I just thought I'd call and ask how your dating life was going? After all, I gave you an order."

"Oh, well about that," Hunter stumbled as he looked for the right words. "Vanna White and I have discovered that we have a vowel and a couple of consonants in common."

"She's too old for you," Leslie shot back.

"Well, I also was going to call . . ."

"Yeah," Leslie's reply was short and terse. "Sure you were. Well, do you suppose that you could break away from turning letters with Vanna long enough to take me to Big Al's tonight. I thought that putt-putt or bowling would be fun, too!"

"Tonight?" Hunter answered. "This is kind of short notice, isn't it."

As he spoke, Leslie's heart sank.

"I mean," he continued, "I wouldn't have time to buy a new outfit, do my nails, or have my hair done. You'd see me at my worst. Are you sure you can handle that?"

"Hunter Jefferson," Leslie tried to make her voice sound as assertive as possible, "you be here at seven sharp or you may just have to spend the rest of your life counting your vowels."

"Seven sharp it is," he laughed. "By the way, when you use that tone you sound like Flo."

"Wow," Leslie whispered sarcastically, "that must be even scarier than my scars."

"You said it," he answered, "I didn't."

"Tonight," she laughed as she set down her phone.

Leslie began getting ready at five and by 6:40 she was pacing the front porch.

"Are you sure you want to go out in public?" her mother asked for the sixth time.

"Listen, Mother," Leslie explained, her eyes never leaving the street, "you don't know this, but while you've been at the Garden Club, and whatever other club meetings you go to, I've been out and about all week. I even went into Coxes and bought a doll for a little friend of mine. You know, the girl that is staying here tomorrow night."

"About that," Flo began, "I still don't think it's a good idea to bring a sick child into this house. After all, you're not well yourself. Just how do you plan to take care of her and what if you catch something and pass it on to your father and me?"

"Oh, Mother," Leslie grinned, "I think I'll do pretty well. Give me some credit for growing up. And she isn't that kind of sick. You can't catch anything from her. By the way, what time does church start on Sunday—10:45 or 11:00?"

"Eleven."

"Good, I think I'll go to Sunday school, too. Do they still have a good young singles' department?"

"I guess so," Flo answered, "but you are not planning on . . ."

"Sure am," Leslie smiled as she thought of her grand entrance. "By the way, don't you think my red dress would go best with my scars?"

"What?" Flo coughed, all the color draining from her face.

"Never mind, Mother," Leslie laughed, "it was just a joke." Noting a Jeep rounding a far corner, Leslie turned quickly to her Mother, kissed her on the cheek, and blurted out, "I may be late. So whatever you do, don't wait up." Then, jumping the three steps to the ground, she bounded like a teenager across the yard to the curb. Shaking her head, Flo turned to her husband who was now standing in the doorway. Her words were loud enough they could be heard a block away.

"Johnathon, I think that she's gone crazy. This whole thing has gotten to her in the worst way. There is no way she should be laughing and having fun with everything that has happened to her. I mean I barely sleep when I think about her poor face."

Leslie turned back toward the house and noted a large smile etched across her father's face and a twinkle showed in his eyes. She returned the smile and jumped into the Jeep. Because the windows were down Leslie heard every word he said, "You know, Flo, I think it's time that we had a talk. I'm getting a bit tired of wall-to-wall pictures of beauty pageants. I think it is time we put that largemouth bass I caught four years ago up at Lake North Fork on the wall in the den. And those pink pillows, they need to go."

"What are you talking about?" the shocked woman replied.

Ignoring her, Johnathon continued to speak

loudly enough for anyone within 150 feet to hear. "And this weekend. I've decided that we're not going up to Salem to look at those old restored homes. I want to go float fishing on Spring River. On top of that, I want you to go with me. I'm going to teach you how to take a big old fat worm and put him on a hook. Then, later, I'll let you clean the fish."

"You've got to be joking!"

"No," the man smiled. "Get your purse, we're going downtown and get you some equipment and a fishing license."

"Johnathon, if you think that there is any way that you are going to get me . . ."

"Florence, hush. Get your purse. I'll meet you in the car."

Shocked, wondering if the whole world had been knocked off its axis, the woman meekly did as she was ordered.

As Hunter pulled out of the drive, he glanced over to Leslie. "What was that all about?"

"The beginning to the end of a lot of pent-up frustrations!" She laughed.

64

Though the diner opened in 1978, Big Al's would have been right at home in the 1950s. It was a bright combination of chrome and neon. The main colors were pink, baby blue, red, and black. A Wurlitzer jukebox played 45s in one corner and booths lined three walls of the sixty-by-sixty-foot main dining area. The food was high in fat and low in nutrients, but the taste couldn't be beat. And due to the music, the old pinball machines, and a wait staff that embraced fun, being at Big Al's was like attending the world's best party.

"Well," Leslie said with a smile as she dabbed her mouth with a napkin, "Big Al still knows how to make hamburgers. I never have found one anywhere else that was as good."

Ignoring or not hearing her observation, Hunter said, "You look beautiful tonight."

"Well, I should," she explained almost light-heartedly. "You see, I spent almost three hours putting on this face, it takes some effort and skill to fill in the valleys and dust off the ridges, and when it takes that long and is that much work, someone should notice."

"It's not the face," Hunter interjected, "though

your makeup is great. It's the smile. It's radiant. The most beautiful smile I've ever seen."

"Actually," Leslie laughed, "it droops a little on the right side. But I guess that gives my expression some character. Heaven knows, I've always needed that."

"What happened?" Hunter inquired. "I mean you were so dead set against going out in public, showing the world your imperfections. You didn't even like yourself. Now you're glowing. It is because they arrested that Spence guy?"

"No, the arrest isn't it. I just grew up. I looked into a mirror with grown-up eyes and saw a new person—one that only God, and maybe a little girl, had ever seen before. It was thanks to some childlike vision I discovered that God still loved me, and, in the process, I also discovered that I could still love me, too. You know, everything except love fades away. We lose it all. But real love is as young, vibrant, and bright when you're ninety-nine as it is when you're twenty-five."

"I hadn't really thought about it," Hunter answered. His face still sported a confused expression.

"A few weeks ago," she explained, a whimsical, though severely crooked smile dancing with every word. "I thought I was on top of the world. I believed I had it all. Did you know that I was just a signature away from making a cool million dollars with the promise of a lot more? Well, I was. Then, in one brief moment, everything that put me on top, fell apart. The one thing I had to hold onto in life, died. And my faith crumbled. I had nothing to live for. Or at least that's what I thought."

He shrugged. Reaching across the table, she grabbed his hands in hers and continued. "When I accepted that having a few scars—big as they are—didn't mean that I couldn't still be a beautiful person, my whole perspective changed. What is that old statement, oh yeah, 'Pretty is as pretty does.' Well, I just decided to be pretty. Did you know there is an Angel who thinks I'm Cinderella?"

Hunter shook his head. It was obvious he still couldn't fathom where this incredible attitude had come from.

"Hey," Leslie let go of his hands, leaned across the booth and snapped her fingers in front of the man's eyes, "wake up. I've been filling you in on the secrets of life. People pay big money for this stuff."

"Yeah," he shrugged as he spoke. "Do I have to pay the fee for the information? I hope not because buying the meal is pretty much going to wipe me out."

She laughed before continuing her rapid-fire lecture, "When we were playing the arcade game a few minutes ago, did you notice the kids in the far booth pointing at us?"

Hunter shook his head. "Yeah. I wanted to go give them a piece of my mind."

"Well, I'm glad you didn't," she explained. "It wasn't the way you thought. Like you, at first I thought they were staring at me—you know the circus freak. But then I noticed that your zipper was down. They must have been laughing at you."

After quickly checking his pants, the now-blushing lawyer looked back at his date and argued, "It is not."

"Of course, it's not," Leslie laughed. "They were pointing at me, but that's OK. I can handle that now. I'm not saying that it won't get to me from time to time, but I can take it. Besides, I'm used to being pointed at. When I was beautiful people stared as well and whistled and did a lot of rude things, too. So this pretty much keeps me the center of attention, which is where I've always been. So, I'm at home there!"

Staring at Hunter, she took a deep breath to steady her nerves. The humor had been used to set up something else. Now it was time to get to the heart of the story, the part that would either make or break this night. She had to know something and she sensed it was time to dig for that answer. Employing a serious tone for the first time tonight, she began, "I want to know something. First, thank you for all that you have done for me over the last few weeks."

"Really," he replied, "it was nothing. In fact . . ."

She cut him off with a simple wave of her hand. As he swallowed his last few words, she continued, "I don't even mind if I was a cause for you, because, in truth, I needed to be somebody's cause. But now, I've come to an understanding of God and myself. For the first time in my life, something besides my Mother and her ego is excited about what I am doing."

"You weren't a cause."

Once again she cut him off, this time by leaning across the table and placing her right index finger on his lips. "Yesterday, I went down to the college and registered for classes. I'm all set. In two weeks, I begin school. I'm going to go back and get a degree in social services—if I can make the grades—maybe even psychology. I'm going to try to help people who have been scarred. You see I know that sometimes those scars are so deep that someone who hasn't felt the cutting edge of life, can never see them. I can."

"Leslie," Hunter broke in, "that's great. I'm so proud of you."

Nodding her head, Leslie held up her hand. Then, with only the sounds of the jukebox in the background, she continued, "Hunter, I can now make it without you. I don't need someone to hold my hand any longer. I'm not scared to face the world or for the world to see my face. I wish the scars weren't there, wish this had never happened, but in truth, I kind of like this new quirky smile. I've studied my face in the mirror, my confused expression is a lulu as well."

She took another deep breath and continued saying what she knew had to be said, "If your mission was to help me to the point where I am now, I just want you to know that mission has been accomplished and I appreciate all that you have done."

For a few moments, neither of them said anything. As the silence wore on Leslie let her eyes fall to the table, but Hunter brought them back up to meet his by reaching his hands across the tabletop to a point where they rested on hers.

"Leslie," the man's voice was soft and sincere, "I haven't accomplished all that I set out to accomplish with you. And furthermore, I won't until you love me as much as I love you. You see I want to share more than just a few weeks. I'm not sure a lifetime would even be enough. I hope that you do believe, scars or not, that I love you. And by the way, your mad expression is something to view as well."

Nodding her head, Leslie smiled her crooked smile, jumped up, leaned across the table, wrapped her arms around the man's neck, and planted a huge kiss on his mouth. Not satisfied with just one kiss, she squeezed him harder and kissed him longer.

"Leslie," Hunter pleaded, "please let go. Every-one in the place is looking at us." The woman only shook her head and kissed him again.

"Leslie," Hunter shouted as he pushed her away, "you knocked my Coke over and it's spilling all over my pants."

"Oh," Leslie giggled. "I'm sorry," and then she laid another kiss on him.

Giving up, Hunter wrapped both of his arms around her and practically lifted her across the table. The teenage crowd, who made up a majority of Big Al's customers that night, applauded as the couple continued to both kiss and spill more food and drinks. Soon the whole place was cheering. Suddenly becoming aware of the scene they were creating, Hunter and Leslie released their grips on each other and eased back into their seats. When they did Hunter sat down in a puddle of Coke and ice while Leslie landed on a plateful of catsup-soaked French fries. Blush-ing, they both acknowledged the applause and laughter, then, as casually as they could, paid their bill and left the restaurant.

As they walked to the car, Hunter looked over at his date and said, "I suppose you know that we won't be able to go in there for a while."

Grinning, Leslie answered, "OK, I'll cook for you tomorrow night. By the way, do you have a towel or something in the car?"

"Why?"

"Well," Leslie shrugged, "I'd hate to get catsup all over your seat."

Glancing at the back of her slacks, Hunter laughed and then added, "I think it goes well with your outfit."

"Yeah."

The two laughed and carried on like kids all the way back to the Rhoadses' house, and then, after they had gotten there, sat on the porch swing, counting stars and swapping dreams.

"You know," Leslie sighed resting her head on Hunter's shoulder, "I never really believed in happily-ever-after stories, not even when I was a child. Maybe it was because I didn't see my parents as representing that kind of love. But now, I think there might be something to it."

"Uh-huh," Hunter answered as he kissed a large scar near the top of her forehead.

Leslie pushed her head into his chest and sighed. "I mean, I just assumed you planned a wedding and then tried to keep up appearances thereafter. I really didn't know that life could be so wonderful." Pausing to think about what she'd just said, she decided her words really made no sense. "What I mean by that is that maybe the scars I got in the alley helped erase some scars I've been carrying all my life. Can you under-stand that?"

"Uh-huh," he sighed, finding a spot on her left cheek to kiss.

"Hunter, I want to tell you about this little girl that is at the hospital. She's the reason every-thing has changed. It's not that the police caught Spence, though I'm glad he won't be able to hurt anyone else, but the little girl taught me a big lesson and I hope I can teach her one as well."

"Uh-huh," he answered as she stroked her hair.

"Are you listening?" she demanded.

"You were telling me about this little girl at the hospital."

Pushing out of his arms, Leslie moved to the end of the swing.

"Where you going?" he protested.

"This is going to sound funny coming from me, but for the moment look at my face when I'm talking. I want you to hear every word I say."

"Yes, ma'am." Pushing to the other end of the swing, he stared intently into her eyes.

"Thanks. This girl is just six and her mother poured boiling water on her face. Now think about that. That woman had been abusing the girl for years and she poured the water on her intentionally. Can you imagine that? I mean in my case I didn't know Spence, but she knew, loved, and trusted her mother. Think about someone you loved attacking you in such a way. I mean this kind of thing can scar a person for life! And the scars you can't see are worse than the ones you can!"

"The kids I volunteer to help," he cut in, "the

juveniles that I try to keep out of jail, most of them have been abused. So, as much as I wish what you just told me was shocking, it's not. But it is so sad."

Leslie got him now. She understood why he wanted to work with kids others thought of as street thugs. So, of course, he would understand what she was saying. And maybe it was because of those kids he helped that he didn't really see her scars and they didn't matter to him. Therefore he saw potential that could only be released through acts of giving and love. What a man God had put into her life at just the right moment!

"I should have known you'd understand," Leslie said. "Anyway, this poor child was beautiful before that happened and I think that she can be beautiful again. But the problem is, the doctors can't erase all the negative scars that have been cut into her heart and mind. She's only six, but she thinks she must be the world's worst little girl because of what happened to her. She's convinced what she received was a just punishment. It's so sad. She actually thinks God hates her."

Hunter grimly smiled. "It seems you've gotten to know her pretty well."

"I'm getting to know her. And she trusts me. Tomorrow night, she and I are going to have a slumber party," Leslie explained, her blue eyes aflame with passion. "We are going to play with dolls, color, tell stories, watch television, and say our prayers together. And I want you to come over. Angel and I are going to make supper together, and as we eat, I want you to help convince her that she is as beautiful as you have convinced me that I am. Will you do it?"

"Do I have to put up with your mother?" Hunter asked quietly.

"Oh no, she and my father are going on a trip to see some kind of restored historical town. It has something to do with a festival that Mother thinks Springfield must have in order to be the proper place to live."

"OK." Hunter smiled. "I'll come. What time should I be over?"

"How about 6:30?"

Checking his watch, Hunter flatly said, "Supper in about fifteen hours."

"What?"

"My dear lady, the time is 3:30. We have been sitting out here for four hours. I think it may be time to either pitch a tent or call it a night."

Suddenly a loud crash followed by a scream caused both of them to jump to their feet. "What was that?" Leslie demanded as she pushed close to Hunter's side.

"I don't know," he answered, attempting to figure out from where the noise had come.

The front porch light suddenly erased the

blackness of the night. Seconds later Leslie's father emerged dressed in a flannel shirt, torn pants, rubber boots, carrying a fishing pole and a tackle box. Glancing over toward the swing, he smiled and said, "Morning, kids, decided to get an early start, so we could be on the lake by sun-up."

Just as he finished speaking, Flo grudgingly pushed the screen door open. She was wearing one of her husband's old sweatshirts, baggy jeans, rubber boots, and a rain hat with lures hanging from the brim. Not noticing her daughter or Hunter, she called out, "John, did you pack my makeup bag?"

"No, Flo," the man answered as he placed his pole in her car. "You won't need it. By the way, grab the ice chest—it's by the door—and then hurry up."

"John," she pleaded, "do you really think we should take my Cadillac? Aren't there a lot of dirt roads that we'll have to take?"

"No, dear," he answered, "it rained yesterday. They won't be dirt roads, they'll be more like mud paths. But don't worry, if we get stuck, you have boots on, so pushing shouldn't be too much trouble."

"Hi, Mom!" Leslie's voice startled her mother just as she was trying to adjust the stringer that was hanging from her belt. With a clanking jingle, it fell on the porch's wooden planks.

"Leslie," a shocked Flo answered. "What are you doing out here at this ungodly hour?"

"We've been making out," Leslie teased.

"What?" Flo demanded.

Leslie grinned and asked, "I thought you were going to Salem to look at historic homes. I didn't know you fished."

"Your father thought—" Catching herself, the older woman attempted to adjust her story. "I mean I thought that a fishing tournament might be good for us. You know, the fresh air, the publicity for the lake, that sort of thing. So, I told Johnathon to take me out and show me the ropes."

Laughing, Leslie answered, "I'm beginning to get the idea. When will you be back?"

"Sunday afternoon."

"Oh, Mom."

"Yes, dear."

"I think you forgot your worms," Leslie pointed to a mass of crawling creatures her mother had knocked from a can when she'd dropped the stringer. Staring at them for only a second, Flo raced off the porch into the yard and screamed, "John, you forgot the worms."

"Thank you for reminding me. I haven't closed the trunk yet, so why don't you bring them on down."

Making a terrible face, Flo made her way up the steps, and with a grimace etched onto her face, slowly leaned over and eased her hand toward the mass of living, squirming bait. Turning her head, she swept her manicured, red nails to the porch floor, grabbed the creatures she could find and quickly dumped them in the can. Wiping the coffee grounds and slime from her fingertips onto her shirt, she picked up the can and the ice chest and moved gingerly off the steps to the car. A few moments later the Cadillac pulled out of the driveway and up the street.

"I can't believe that." Leslie smiled.

"Miracles can happen." Hunter grinned.

"I guess they really do." Leslie laughed. "My transformation is not nearly as big as the one I'm seeing in Mom and Dad. I'm liking it, too."

65

Leslie's cell rang as she was leaving to pick up Angel from the hospital. Brian Rosatelli was on the other end of the line.

"What do you need, Captain?"

"Nothing, Ms. Rhoads, just wanted to give you a few updates that weren't in the newspaper stories."

Leslie nodded as she locked the front door and headed to the garage. She would be driving her father's Ford Escape today. "What do I need to know?"

"Not much," came the reply. "We found a couple pieces of your jewelry at Spence's house. A lot of pictures, too. He was much more than a fan; he was a fanatic."

"I'm just glad you got him before he hurt someone else."

"So are we," the Captain agreed, "but if you need anything else, just let me know."

"You know what the best thing about this is?"

"What's that, Ms. Rhoads?"

"I don't have police cars parked on my street twenty-four hours a day and I don't have your people following me everywhere I go. So while you have taken away one person's freedom, you've given mine back to me. Thank you for that."

"You're welcome."

Sliding into the black Escape, she set her phone in one of the drink holders and took a long, deep breath. She was glad the guy had been caught, but she no longer felt the burning desire for revenge. In truth, what should have brought her great joy brought no emotions at all. What happened couldn't be reversed. She would carry those scars for the rest of her life. But the police having the physical evidence to convict Spence allowed her to put away all memories of that night. Now she didn't have to concern herself with trying to dredge up the details of what happened in that alley. If she never remembered the specifics, it no longer mattered. The nightmare was over and it was time to dream again. And thanks to a little girl and a handsome prince, she had something to dream about.

66

"Well, Angel," Leslie asked, "what do you think of my house?"

The six-year-old's eyes were as big as saucers and her face aglow with excitement. She simply didn't know where to look first. Taking a deep breath, she all but shouted, "I love it!"

"Well," Leslie laughed, "it's not Cinderella's castle, but it will do until I find that piece of real estate at a price I can afford."

"Is that your swing set in the backyard?" Angel asked.

Looking out the window to where the girl pointed, Leslie nodded in the affirmative. "That was mine, but Mother didn't let me play on it much."

"Why not?"

"She was afraid I'd fall out of the swing or off the slide and hurt myself. But she's not here right now, so if you want to go out with me and swing, then it is fine."

Smiling, Angel answered, "Maybe later. Right now I'd like to see the toys you were telling me about."

"Let's go up to my room." Leslie pointed to the steps and the two marched forward and then up. A little later, after each of the special toys had been carefully played with, the party moved to the kitchen. As Leslie peeled potatoes and Angel tossed the salad, the little girl began to sing a little tune. Leslie strained to hear the words, but the girl's voice was so soft she couldn't make them out.

"Angel, that was a pretty song. Where did you learn it?"

"Oh, one of the nurses taught it to me," she answered.

"It sounded nice," Leslie nodded as she issued the compliment. "I couldn't hear the words. What's it about?"

In spite of her scarred face, the little one looked like her namesake as she explained, "Nurse Meg said it was about people's hearts and how some people have pretty hearts and others don't. She told me that mine was pretty. I never believed that someone who didn't have a pretty face could have a pretty heart, until I met you."

Smiling, Leslie nodded and sighed. "And I didn't know what beauty was until I met you.

You, you precious little bundle of joy, you showed me what real beauty is." Setting the potatoes to one side, Leslie wiped her hands on her apron, fell to her knees, and hugged the little girl. As she did, involuntary tears fell freely from her eyes and rolled down her scarred face. Composing herself, she whispered into Angel's ear, "So, I guess we both must be beautiful people. Isn't that right?"

Grinning, Angel didn't answer, just began singing her song again. A few minutes later, as they set the table, the little girl paused, glanced out the window into the front yard and asked, "What is Hunter like?"

"Well," Leslie smiled, "he's tall, good-looking, funny, sweet, and gentle."

"Kind of like a prince?"

"I wouldn't tell him that, but he's at least part prince. He may still have some frog in him. You can give me your opinion later."

Just then, the doorbell rang. "Great timing. That's probably him. Angel, why don't you go and answer it?"

Shaking her head, Angel backed toward the kitchen, casting her face to the floor.

"Angel," Leslie whispered, kneeling down in front of the girl, "you don't have to hide or be shy. Look at my face."

Angel raised her eyes to Leslie's. As she did, she lifted her right hand and traced the scars.

"Listen, Angel, if Hunter can love me, he will love you, too. You see he has the gift."

Looking up, the suddenly-puzzled girl inquired, "The gift?"

"Yes, he can see straight through our eyes and into our hearts. He will see your true beauty the second he looks into your big blue eyes. Now, take my hand and let's open the door for him. You should never keep a prince or a frog waiting too long!"

The two walked hand in hand through the dining room and into the entry hall. There, they straightened their dresses before opening the home's big door. Waiting for them, with a bouquet of flowers in each of his hands, was Hunter Jefferson.

"Good evening, ladies," he announced as Leslie opened the door. "My, don't you both look nice this evening." Smiling, he bent over, handed Angel her flowers, and then added, "That is a beautiful dress, my dear."

Shyly blushing, Angel politely mumbled, "Leslie gave it to me."

"Well," Hunter continued, "it was made for you."

The girl smiled and looked toward Leslie. "I don't see any frog."

A confused look crossed Hunter's face. "Frog?"

"Just wait," Leslie grinned, "that part of him will hop out later."

Still confused, he stood to his full height and

gently kissed Leslie. When their lips parted, he handed her the other flowers. A second later he announced, "Excuse me for sounding rude, but I'm starved. What have you got for this hungry man this evening?"

Sweeping past his hostesses, he marched to the dining room table and checked out what was waiting for him. Leslie and Angel headed for the kitchen to put their flowers in water.

"You were right, Leslie," Angel whispered as she placed her flowers in a jar. "He can see a person's heart."

Nodding, Leslie smiled and pointed back toward the dining room. "And he knows how to eat, too. We better get back there or the ham and potatoes will be all gone."

An hour later, while Angel watched an old Shirley Temple DVD, Hunter helped Leslie clear the table and wash the dishes.

"She is something," he said as he put a plate into the dishwasher. "What can they do for her?"

"In the next few years," Leslie began as she rinsed out a glass, "there will be several different kinds of surgeries and those, combined with makeup, should cover all of her scars. Her mouth and eyes were not affected, unlike mine, her facial muscles are rock solid, and so, she can, and I think will, be beautiful."

Leslie handed the glass to Hunter. "I'm not worried about the scars I can see. What concerns me are the ones hidden below the surface. It's tough when someone who is supposed to love you creates such pain. Still, she's young and seems pretty tough. So I believe if she can find someone to love her and help her through the difficult years then when the surgeons erase those scars, she'll be fine."

"I think she has already found someone," Hunter mused.

"I wish," Leslie answered. "But in this state, I just don't qualify. I've got no job, no source of income, no home, not much of anything besides a huge place in my heart."

"Sometimes," Hunter said with a smile, "that's enough." Finishing the last dish, he dried his hands on a towel and took a seat at the table. After Leslie had washed and dried a pan she joined him. As she sat, he reached across and pulled her hands into his.

"This is not the way I'd planned it," he said.

"You mean you didn't think I'd make you help me clean up the kitchen?"

He shook his head. "No, not that! I just always figured I would do what I'm about to do with real flair. This script is good but the setting is all wrong."

"Hunter Jefferson what in the world are talking about?"

"I want you to marry me."

"Do you know what you just said?" Leslie asked.

"That's not the answer that goes with the question," Hunter shot back. "You're supposed to say yes."

"But you didn't ask a question," she pointed out.

"Yes, I did!" he argued.

"No," she giggled, "you said you wanted to marry me. That's a statement."

He paused, laughed, slipped from his chair and fell to one knee. "Ms. Leslie Marie Rhoads, will you do me the profound honor of being my bride?"

"You really want to marry me?"

"I thought that you'd figured that out last night."

"Well, talk is cheap," Leslie answered, "and I've heard some good lines in my life. I just thought you might have been caught up in the moment."

"No," Hunter, still on one knee, said with a smile, "I want you to answer the following question. Do you love me like you have never loved anyone in your whole life?"

Not pausing to think about it, Leslie answered, "Yes. I love you that much and more."

"Then," Hunter said, "I guess you will marry me."

"Right now, if you want," Leslie whispered.

Laughing, Hunter leaned over and softly kissed his bride-to-be. Nodding his head, he said, "I suggest we do it right. I want a church wedding with all the trimmings. Besides, Flo would never forgive us if we don't. This will be the social event of her life."

Caught up in the moment, Leslie failed to notice the ringing cell phone until Hunter finally said, "I guess you'd better get that."

"What?"

"Your cell, it has been ringing for about a minute now."

Nodding, Leslie slowly got up and crossed the room. Picking up the phone from where it set on top of a cabinet, she cleared her throat and answered. A few seconds later she turned toward Hunter and announced, "It's my cousin—Meg. She wants to talk to you."

Hunter smiled and took the phone, putting it on speaker; he kissed Leslie, letting his lips linger on hers just long enough for her to get light-headed. "Meg, what do you need?"

"Hunter, we brought a boy in here tonight—a drug overdose—and he was completely out of it. In trying to find out who he was and whom to call, we discovered a business card in his pocket with your name on it."

"Who's the boy?" Hunter asked as he glanced toward a concerned Leslie.

"No I.D. on him, so we don't know his name. All he had was your card."

"How is he?"

"He'll make it, but it was close. Since we don't know his parents or guardian, I thought you might want to be here when he does come to."

"Yeah, I do." Checking his watch, Hunter made some fast mental computations and added, "I can be there in fifteen minutes. What room is he in?"

"Room 101, just inside the east exit."

"Thanks, Meg, be there soon."

Handing the cell back to Leslie, Hunter shrugged. She shook her head understandingly and followed him to the front door. "Let me know how things are."

"I will," Hunter assured her as he leaned over and kissed her a final time. "I love you and I'll be back later."

"We'll keep the light on," Leslie answered, "and, by the way, I love you, too."

She watched him drive off, closed the door, and joined Angel in the den. Pulling up a chair, she let the girl catch her up on what had happened during the first half of the show, and then she paused the DVD, and the two of them went to the kitchen to pop some popcorn the old-fashioned way on the stove. With the snack and Cokes, they rejoined the movie. By the time the credits rolled, Angel had fallen asleep. Covering her with a blanket, Leslie ejected the disc and flipped through the dial searching for something to keep her awake until Hunter returned.

67

A few miles away, Brian Rosatelli was working late, trying to finish a month-old report. Using the two-finger method of typing, he was spending more time correcting mistakes than he was filling in the blanks on the five-year-old monitor's screen. Even as late as it was, he was grateful when a knock disturbed his frustrating efforts.

"Come in!" he hollered. Looking up, he was greeted by the young, smiling face of Charles Bruner.

"Have I ever told you how much I hate reports?" he asked the patrolman.

Nodding, Charles answered, "That's what brought me up here. I've been doing some paperwork, too. I think I've got something that kind of muddies the waters on one of our cases."

Rosatelli leaned back in his chair and waited for the cop to pitch his thoughts.

"The slasher case," Bruner began. "Are you sure we have the right man?"

Rosatelli nodded. "I think so, but we sure can't pry a confession out of him. Yet the fact one of the earrings that was found in his bedroom seems to have closed the book on it."

Bruner nodded and took a seat in front of his superior's desk. "I think he has to be the guy. A not very bright fan sees a woman he believes he loves and when she refuses him, he turns on her seeking revenge. It just makes sense."

"That's the way I see it," the captain replied. "So what's bugging you about the case? Do you have something against a mystery that is wrapped up too neatly?"

"No," the patrolman answered, "I like them that way."

"There's something on your mind, Chuck, so spit it out."

"OK, the slashing happened on the twenty-eighth, and you and I talked around the first of the month. I think it was the fourth. Well, on that day, I wrote a parking ticket on the car you found at Spence's house. The payment for that ticket came in today. I just posted it on his record."

"So Spence paid the fine," Rosatelli noted as he put his feet on his desk, leaned back, and supported his neck by interlocking the fingers of both hands.

"No," Bruner explained, "he didn't pay the fine. It was a guy named McCloud who paid it."

"So he let a friend borrow a car. I don't see that as a big deal."

"That isn't all," Bruner went on. "I did a little more research, and discovered this guy McCloud had a prior conviction of petty theft and drug

344

possession. Then, when I ran his prints through the files, I found out that McCloud is not his real name. It is Sims. Several years ago, he was the number one suspect in the rape and murder of a young unmarried mother. There wasn't enough evidence, so he was never indicted, but the investigating officer believed him to be the man."

"Interesting," Rosatelli admitted. "But I don't see how it ties to this case."

"I don't know either," Bruner replied, "but after they failed to indict this guy, he left town and moved out west. I just found out that he's wanted in Texas for two different rape charges, theft, and possession of an unlawful substance. This guy is one bad dude."

While the captain said nothing, his mind was turning at a thousand RPMs a second. They might have the man who slashed Leslie Rhoads in jail, but the guy Bruner has discovered might even be more dangerous. The last thing he needed was another story that would frighten the citizens of his town.

Dropping his feet to the floor and his hands to the desktop, Rosatelli looked the patrolman directly in the eye and asked, "Do we have a BOLO on this guy?"

"You bet," the policeman assured his superior. "The second I found he was wanted, I put the word out and contacted the folks in Texas. But everything's turned up dry so far. There's some-thing else, too."

"Well, don't stall around, what is it?"

"I traced the guy a few more years back and discovered he had assumed the name of James Kissom Sims. There is only one James Kissom Sims who ever lived in this country and that man died thirty-five years ago in Rockport, Ohio, when he was five days old."

"So Sims isn't his real name," Rosatelli chimed in.

"No."

"Do you know what it is?"

"Yeah, but only because his fingerprints were on record due to a juvenile arrest two decades ago."

"And," the captain begged, "what is it?"

"J. P. Spence."

"Is he related to Jacob?"

Bruner nodded. "They're brothers."

"Well, violence must run in the family. We've got to get this guy if he's still in town. Send every beat cop a photo to their iPads. Do the same for the county guys and the state patrol."

"Already done."

"Good job, Chuck. Get back to the computer and see if you can find out where this guy might be right now. Use what you've learned to narrow the hunt. Keep me updated on anything you find out."

As Bruner got up and hurried from the office, Rosatelli picked up the desk phone and dialed a number that he'd grown much too familiar with over the past few weeks.

"Hello, this is Nurse Meg Richards."

"Nurse, this is Captain Brian Rosatelli, Springfield police. Do you know if the janitor we arrested for your cousin's attack ever had any visitors?"

"Not that I know of," she answered. "I could ask around. Why do you want to know?"

"He has a brother," the cop explained, "who is wanted in Texas and was evidently in town a month or so ago."

"I haven't seen him."

"Thanks. Ms. Richards, if anyone at the hospital did see a man that resembled Jacob, please let me know. I've got your email, I'll send you one of the guy's old mug shots."

68

After studying the photo on his iPad and then sending it to Meg Richards, Rosatelli hurried down to the county lockup. Ten minutes later, he was sitting in a jail cell with Jacob Spence.

"Jacob," the captain asked as the door locked behind him, "where's your brother?"

The orange-clad prisoner shook his head. "Richard's back in Ohio."

"Not Richard, J.P."

Looking like he'd just seen a ghost, Spence shook his head, violently this time. When he found his voice he whispered, "He's dead."

Leaning against the door's bars, Rosatelli barked, "Not buying it. He paid a parking ticket on your car a few weeks ago. No reports of deaths since then. He's out there, and I'm betting you know where we can find him."

"Don't know," Spence whispered, looking at the floor.

"Don't know where he is or don't know if he's dead?"

Looking back to the cop the prisoner said, "Don't know where he is. Haven't seen him for a couple of weeks."

"So, he was in town then?"

"Yeah, but then he moved his stuff out of my house and left."

"Jacob, did he have a car?"

"Not that I know of. Whenever he needed to go somewhere friends took him or he used mine."

"Who were the friends?"

"Captain, I don't know, I really don't. I only met one of them once. He was a kid."

"Do you remember his name?"

Spence's eyes went back to the floor. He scratched his head before mumbling, "I didn't hurt that model. I loved her. It broke my heart."

Rosatelli's shouts cut him off, "What was his name?"

"Woodson, Stevie Woodson. He was a high school kid. I met him when I first got to town. Stayed away from him though, he's bad news."

"OK, can you give me anything more?"

Spence's sad eyes found the captain's. "I didn't hurt her."

"We have you dead to rights," Rosatelli pointed out. "You even had her jewelry in your house."

"I know," Spence sighed, "but I didn't hurt her."

The captain turned back to the jailer and signaled it was time to leave. Bart McClain walked him out of the jail. When they arrived at the main exit, Rosatelli looked at the jailer and posed a standard question, "You been keeping a close eye on him?"

"Sure, he's kind of a celebrity. In my thirty years working here, we haven't seen many like him."

"Has he had any visitors?"

"Nope, Captain, the only ones who want to see him are members of the press."

Nothing was ever easy. In a perfect world, his brother would have made a habit of checking on Spence, but this wasn't a perfect world. "Bart, has Spence had any special requests?"

"You mean like food and stuff?" the elderly man asked.

"Yeah, more specifically, cigarettes?"

"No, matter of fact I haven't seen him smoke at all. He just sits there and stares at the wall. He's so quiet he gives me the willies."

"Thanks," Rosatelli said as he walked out into the night air. Pulling out his cell, he made a call to Bruner. "Chuck, we need to find a teenager named Stevie Woodson."

Stopping dead in his tracks, an incredulous look frozen on his face, the captain whispered into the phone, "He what?"

69

"What's all the activity?" Hunter asked as he walked in through the ER.

"Hunter, how are you doing?" Rosatelli's greeting was warm. Though separated by a generation, the two men had a long history. Back when he was just a beat cop, the captain had been Hunter's little league coach.

"Fine, Brian, yourself?"

"Good," the officer answered as he shook the attorney's hand.

"Sure am glad you got that guy who attacked Leslie."

Rosatelli nodded. "Strange case. Every time I

think I have it all tied up something else falls into my bag."

"What's that?" Hunter asked.

"Nothing important. Now what was it you wanted to know?"

"What are you doing down here in the ER? Did you bring an injured suspect or something?"

"No, we just need to question a guy about one of his associates. So we're waiting for him to come out of an overdose."

"We must be here for the same reason. Meg Richards called me about a kid who overdosed and had my business card in his pocket. Thought it might be one of the juveniles I've been trying to help."

"Tough job," Rosatelli observed, "but maybe you can save a few from landing a long stretch behind bars."

"Got an I.D. on this kid?" the attorney asked.

"Woodson, Stevie Woodson."

Hunter's jaw dropped. "I thought I had that kid turned around."

"So that's why the surprised look," Rosatelli noted.

"I shouldn't be. The kid needs to be in rehab. He's hooked as bad as anyone I've seen. His home life is terrible and he runs around with a crowd that would scare a terrorist. I don't want to give up on anybody, but this kid might be one we can't save."

Turning to one of the nurses, Rosatelli asked, "Is Nurse Richards here? I'd like to talk to her."

"No, she left just before you got here. She stuck around late tonight to help us out with a drug overdose. When we took care of that and the kid was in stable condition, she ran on home. You know she's a single mom?"

"Yeah, I knew that. Tough break. Between her and her cousin, Leslie Rhoads, that family has had more than its share of tragedies. What about this Woodson kid? Is he awake yet?"

Nurse Nance shook her head. "Not yet. He might come out it in the next few minutes or it could be all night."

"Well," Rosatelli sighed, "guess I'll just camp out here in the waiting room. Come get me when the Woodson kid can talk."

"I might as well join you," Hunter chimed in. "When you finish with Stevie, I want a crack at him. I'm not giving up yet."

As the men made their way down the hall, Rosatelli asked, "Who do you think is going to be in the Super Bowl this year?"

70

Leslie readjusted the blanket that was covering Angel, put on a sweater, and curled up in a chair beside the couch. Flipping through the channels with the remote control, she finally stuck on a station that was carrying a program featuring a South Pacific–looking location. Checking the remote's information button, she discovered this was the same show she'd given up watching a couple of weeks before. What the heck? She'd loved Stephen Collins in *7th Heaven*, maybe *Tales of the Gold Monkey* would be better than its title.

As she followed the action, a scruffy-looking airplane mechanic and his dog were walking along a dock toward a seaplane. Stephen Collins, wearing a Fighting Tiger leather flight jacket, was waiting for them. The leading man waved at the other man and the dog. As he did the short man screamed, "Hey, Jake!"

As quickly as the name had been said, the world around her stopped. Suddenly there were no sounds. She was completely lost in a nightmare and something she had forgotten was now clear and as close to her as her own breath.

Jake was his name. That's what the others had called the man who'd attacked her. And there wasn't just one, it was a gang. They'd been after money and they figured she was rich because she was a model.

Now, suddenly, the trigger being a dog's name, she remembered each word, each action, each movement, and she once again clearly heard the name, "Jake." Surprisingly, she wasn't terrified. There were no cold chills racing down her spine. As she thought about the events, put them in order, and played them over in her head, there was something else she almost remembered, but it was just beyond her reach, lost somewhere in a fog that had been clouding her mind for weeks. Hitting the mute button on her remote control she sat in silence, trying to put together the final pieces of the mystery.

The voice of Jake and the janitor in the hospital —they weren't the same. Jacob couldn't have been the man who attacked her. A chill ran down her spine as she realized the police had the wrong guy.

There was no reason to call 9-1-1, but it was important. What she needed to do was talk to Captain Rosatelli. She had to tell him to keep looking for a man named Jake and the gang of three other guys he led.

Bouncing out of her chair, she ran across the room to her father's desk. Searching through the stacks of paper that covered the top, she looked for a phone book. Failing to find one, she opened every one of the drawers, but came up just as empty. Running to the kitchen, she pulled the one from the kitchen counter and hurried back to the den. There, in a silent room lit only by the flickering images of a television, she scanned the pages, looking for the number of the Springfield Police Department.

555-5034.

As she dialed the number she wondered why she hadn't been able to remember sooner. Why had it taken so long for the images to come back in clear focus?

Sitting down in an overstuffed leather chair, she waited for someone to pick up. As it rang a second time, she fell back into her old habit of talking to herself. "Well, Les, Rosatelli will kill for this bit of information."

The words had no sooner left her mouth than her cell was violently jerked from her hand.

"Maybe he would, maybe he wouldn't," a familiar deep voice behind her announced. "But I'd kill for it."

Jumping out of the chair and whirling around, Leslie found herself staring at a man she knew only as Jake. He held a gun in his right hand.

"Now, little lady," he smiled as he talked, "it's time for us to complete what we started a few months ago."

71

As Leslie faced her attacker for the first time since that night in the alley, she studied his grinning face in the uneven light cast by the television. This moment was much different than she had anticipated it would be. She was relaxed, almost calm, and completely unafraid. And unlike that evening in the dark hospital room, when she could sense him but not see him, a time when panic clouded her judgment and fear ruled her heart, she was almost stoic in her approach to what seemed destined to transpire.

As she waited for Jake to make his move, she thought back to a day some ten years before, a time when she had been forced to sit through a high school assembly and listen to a patriotic speech given by a man who had won a Medal of Honor in World War II. Leslie couldn't remember why he had been so honored, or even the branch of the armed forces in which he had served, but she did recall something he had said. "Courage, the kind that wins medals and saves lives is not inherited, nor is it gained through experience or education, it is simply something born at a moment when certain death seems to be the only possible end to a situation. At that moment, the human spirit, the one that fights for every breath of life, gives up and whatever is left takes over."

A few days before, Leslie would have had nothing left to give. She would have wilted like a flower on a hundred degree day. But not now! This man, whatever his name, was facing a woman who was solid as a rock. She showed no fear because she felt none. As he studied her deeply-scarred face, she grinned her now quirky, cockeyed smile. That look, one he surely wasn't expecting, seem to rattle him. He broke eye contact with her and nervously shifted his weight from one foot to the other.

As the TV's flickering light continued to bounce off his face, Leslie's lips opened into a smile so wide she felt her scar tissue stretching. Planting her feet, she pushed her back straight and placed her hands on her hips. This time there would be no extra hands to hold her down. This time he was going to have to take her on all by himself. This game was being played on her turf and she knew it well.

"You know what I'm going to have to do?" he snarled. His bravado and threat made no impact. She was ready to give back with as much vim and vigor as he dished out.

"I know what you think you have to do," she finally answered, her voice slow and steady. "But I'm not going to make it easy. You tried to take away who I was in that alley, but you didn't. I'm still here. And you know what they say, what doesn't kill you makes you stronger. You wouldn't believe how strong I am."

Studying her for a moment as if he was suddenly unsure what he was dealing with, he shook his head. "You don't have to fake it. I know you're scared. Women like you are always scared."

"Oh no," Leslie smiled, "you scared me once. I won't let you have that kind of pleasure again. You know I realized you must get a charge out of ruining lives and then watching people try to pick up all the pieces. You love to see people suffer. But I'm not suffering, not anymore. If that's what you want, you're not going to get it."

"You can say what you want," he shot back, using his free hand to point to his chest, "but I brought you down. You were so high and mighty before I got a hold of you, and now, well, look at you. I put you in your place!"

"I remember your name," Leslie shot back. "It's Jake. I heard it several times that night—a lifetime ago." She stopped a moment and crossed her arms. "You know, I don't even know your last name. Then again, I guess you never do get to know the last name of your executioner. Just a man in the dark; just a face hidden by the shame! Let me assure you of something—you didn't bring me down, you forced me to look at myself

358

and then rise up. If it ends here, I'm flying high and you're crawling on your belly like the snake you are."

Fidgeting, Jake took a step closer to Leslie. Studying her face, he shook his head.

She knew she was getting to him. His resolve was fading. He couldn't figure out why she was calm and he was a jumbled bundle of nerves.

"How many women?" she asked, her voice even and strong.

"What?"

"How many women have you assaulted? How many have you hurt? Did it give you a sense of power? Did it make you feel like somebody?"

He didn't answer. And as the seconds ticked by, he seemed more and more confused. Maybe it was dawning on him that he wasn't such a big man after all. As she watched him try to figure his next move, she suddenly remembered there was more to this duel that just Jake and her. That realization shook her to her core.

Why tonight? Why now when Angel was here? Suddenly this was more than just a moment when she was standing up for herself, she had another life involved. She had someone else to protect. So this was not just a fight for her life, it was a fight for someone she loved.

Hoping he wouldn't notice, she subtly shifted her eyes from her attacker to Angel. The little girl hadn't woken up. She was still sleeping soundly on the couch. The question was, had he noticed? Leslie had to keep his attention on her. She had to remain the only target. So it was now time for her to really go on the offensive.

"What do you want?" she demanded. "Look me in the eye when you answer!"

His eyes found hers, but he said nothing. Then, as if unsure what to do next, he began to look around the room. She couldn't let that continue. She had to keep his focus on her. Raising her voice another notch she hissed, "What do you want?"

"You," the man's answer seemed far from solid.

"Why?" she shot back, "and if you think you're such a man, look at me when you answer! Or are you scared to really examine your handiwork?"

Pausing for a moment, Jake answered, "Because you can identify me. You're a loose end I should've tied up in the alley."

"But you didn't," Leslie smiled as she answered him, "and because you didn't there will be even more clues now. Someone's bound to hear your gunshot or maybe see your vehicle drive off. If I've noticed your truck, others will have as well. I have very nosy neighbors. And one of them will report it and they'll check on it and then track it to you, and when they do, they'll probably discover that someone you know drives an old white sedan. And look at your hands. You don't have gloves on."

Glancing down, Jake noted his bare hands.

He stared at them briefly before Leslie's voice drew his attention back to her.

"You're sweating, Jake. A big drop just rolled off your forehead and landed on the carpet. That's DNA that you have left here."

Keeping the gun trained on Leslie, he slipped to one knee and tried to wipe the drop with his shirtsleeve. As he did, she smiled while dropping even more bad news his way.

"Let me see, I don't know what door you came in, but you're in the den now, so you probably touched a wall or two, maybe a table, and who knows what else. You can't even remember now, can you?"

He looked back into the face that he might have, until a few minutes ago, viewed as his masterpiece. Now it was becoming his nightmare.

"Think about it, Jake, you got sloppy. You probably have gloves in your truck, don't you? You meant to wear them but fear pushed the details you needed to remember out of your mind. Let me see, your fingerprints are going to be everywhere. Can you remember all the places to wipe down before you leave? Can you retrace every step?"

As he glanced over his shoulder toward the front hall, she realized the tables had been turned. He might have had the gun, but this time she had the power.

"You know, Jake," her voice caused his head to

turn so their eyes met again. "You're right, you should have killed me, because now you have a big mess created by your little game of who has the power. You started that game in that alley, and try as you might, you aren't going to be able to find all the pieces needed to keep you from losing this game. One of the things you forgot, one of the things you missed, will catch you. And you know it. You're as sure of it as you are your own name. The clock's ticking, the game is almost over. That has got to be scary."

"Shut up," Jake suddenly screamed.

Leslie took advantage of the moment to look back across to the couch. As her gaze crossed the room, Angel moved. Jake's outburst must have awakened her and she was now slowly sitting up, rubbing her eyes, and attempting to shake the sleep from her head. Afraid that Jake might see the little girl, Leslie moved slowly, step-by-step in the opposite direction, toward the hallway door, thus diverting the man's attention from the den.

"Where are you going?" Jake demanded, pointing the gun at the woman's midsection.

"You're not going to shoot me," Leslie answered. Through sheer will and the need to protect Angel, she managed to keep her voice calm and steady. "If you did, the whole neighborhood would wake up. Listen, I opened all the windows tonight. Can't you hear all the sounds of outside coming into the room? That bark is the Thomases' dog Bart. You hear the TV, it belongs to the Meyers. So what we are doing and saying in here can be heard out there, too. Someone might be listening right now. If they are, they are likely calling the cops too."

Jake tilted his head toward the front of the house. As he did, Leslie kept up her verbal assault on his courage.

"You can hear the wind blowing through the trees can't you? Listen, there's a car driving down the street."

As she continued to inch out of the room, he followed her with his eyes and feet. "You see, Jake. Noise travels really well at night. I'll bet you every house in this neighborhood has its windows open, too. And I think I told you I have busybody neighbors. When they hear anything, they make it their business. So, if you want to put a noose around your neck, go ahead and pull the trigger."

Leslie watched as Jake nervously considered her words. Even in the dim light, she thought she could see large beads of sweat on his brow and she distinctly heard his breathing quicken.

"Jake," she was now almost flirting, "I don't believe you have really taken a good look at your work. Now, don't shoot me, not yet anyway, but I'm going to step over here into the dining room and you just follow me. I'm not going to

363

touch anything other than a wall switch. I think that you ought to see what you did in real light. I mean if you enjoyed bringing me down, then maybe this memory will help you make it through those long nights in prison."

Confidently walking across the hall, Leslie quickly crossed into the dining room, flipped an overhead light switch, and carefully stepped to the center of the room. Jake followed. He must have sensed he had lost control, but did he know how to gain it back? Stopping just inside the threshold, he stared at Leslie's face.

"Is it what you expected?" Leslie asked as she pointed to her face. "I think that this one," she singled out a long, thick ragged scar that ran up from her cheek and across her nose, "is the one that represents your best work. Of course, there are two or three others that are special, too. It was a good job. But as you can see, with enough surgery and some makeup, I'll be able to cover it up in time. Speaking of time, what will they give you for killing me? Maybe sixty years? Due to the violent act of cutting me up and then coming back to finish me off, I don't think I'd count on parole. Maybe if you just walked out of here and gave yourself up society would be through with you about the same time that the surgeons finish with me."

"I'm not going to prison, lady," Jake grunted. "They'll have to kill me first."

"So you're going to be the tough guy." Leslie knew her words were now digging into the man's biggest fears, so she pushed harder. "But let's think about it. Suppose you do die in a hail of bullets—kind of like Jimmy Cagney in *White Heat* or Warren Beatty in *Bonnie and Clyde*. In reality, what and who died? I mean what have you got that is worth dying for? A few dollars maybe? The thrill of cutting me up? If you're dead, those don't count. What about some friends? I'll bet you the thugs who helped you that night will forget about you in a real hurry." Noting he was still staring at her face, she smiled for a moment then almost whispered, "Do you have a mother, Jake? What's it going to do to her to see her boy gunned down by the cops? I'll bet she'd rather know you're alive in prison."

"Leave her out of this," Jake shouted. "She didn't do nothing to you. I did!"

"What are you going to do now, Jake? How are you going to kill me? There's nobody here to help you and no one to share the blame. You were in my hospital room one night and couldn't do it. What makes you think that you can do it now?"

Shifting his weight and rocking back and forth, the man took an unsteady step forward. Wavering, as if he was dizzy, he rebalanced himself, and watched in amazement as Leslie took a small step toward him. Less than five feet separated the two.

"I had you figured wrong," Leslie told the man. "I just assumed that you were cool, sure, and lacked the element that could feel guilt. Look at you, sweat is dripping off your forehead, that's more DNA you're leaving behind, and you've got wet circles the size of softballs under your arms. When someone challenges, you cower under their glare. You don't like this scene, do you? You really don't have the stomach for it."

She was sure her words had brought the man down to size—both in her eyes and his. She could see the doubt written on his face and the shaking in his hands. If she could just push a little harder, he might bolt out to his truck without doing anything. Or maybe if she could stall for a few more minutes, Hunter would come back.

As she observed Jake attempt to regain his composure, Leslie noticed a movement in the hall behind him. Checking a clock on the buffet, her heart momentarily soared. Hunter's back! She had bought the time she needed.

72

It wasn't Hunter!

"What's going on?" a confused Angel asked as she tried to run past Jake. He encircled her with his left arm before she got through the entry to the dining room. Too shocked to cry, the little girl's fear showed in her eyes as she looked to Leslie for an answer and protection.

"Don't hurt her," Leslie ordered.

Smiling for the first time since Leslie had stood up to him, Jake drew Angel closer, tightening his grip as he laughed. "You may not care about yourself, but what about this one?" Confident and cocky, he knew that he was once again in control. "I'll bet you care enough about your little friend here to make this a whole lot easier on all of us."

As she watched helplessly, Leslie felt a new kind of fear snake through her body. Her legs instantly became rubbery, her heart weak and face flushed. In a matter of seconds, sweat popped out of her pores and drenched her clothes. Now it appeared that because she was who she was, and because she stood between this man and a prison cell, Angel would be hurt, too.

"What could you want with her?" Leslie argued, her voice not nearly as strong as it had been just minutes before. "I'm the one you want. Remember, I'm the one that was the unfinished piece of business. Let her go and settle this thing with me."

Leslie figured that her words would hang in the air for a moment and then just drift away, almost unnoticed. And she was right. Jake was well aware that while Leslie's face was no longer a trump card, her obvious affection for this little girl was. Not only had this given him his strength back, it had also nurtured a plan.

"You know, sister," he bragged, "you've got something to you after all. You're smart. I mean, everything you said about the fingerprints and the noise, that's right on target. I wasn't thinking. I came in here so intent on doing such a quick job I never even stopped to consider how I was going to cover my tracks. And you see, I've always been good at that. Besides, I don't think Mama would want me getting killed by the cops or shipped out to prison. So, I'll just take care of this my way and avoid both. Now let's go into the kitchen."

After taking a quick look at Angel, trying to comfort her with her eyes, Leslie slowly backed toward the swinging door that led to her mother's large and often-remodeled kitchen. Following closely behind was the frightened little girl being pushed by a now demonic-appearing Jake. When the three of them were in the kitchen, he took a quick look around and smiled.

"So you had popcorn tonight?" he asked Leslie.

"Yes."

"Get some unpopped corn out," he ordered, still squeezing Angel.

Walking over to a pantry, Leslie pulled out a large bag of white popcorn for the second time tonight. Holding it up so that Jake could see it, she set it on the table.

"Get a large pan, a couple of bowls, a salt shaker, and cooking oil," he demanded. "We are going to make some corn the old-fashioned way."

Nodding, Leslie returned to the pantry, pulled out a gallon bottle of corn oil, then walked across the kitchen to the cabinet. Picking out two plastic bowls, she gathered them in her arms and returned to the table. After taking inventory, she turned, pulled a large metal pan from where it hung over a chopping block and laid it beside the other items.

Studying it for a moment, Jake grinned and added what must have been the final ingredient for his recipe. "I want you to get two big aprons. I want them to be nice ones—ones like you see those housewives wearing in old TV commercials."

Opening a drawer beside the stove, Leslie picked through a stack of dishtowels and aprons until she found two that fit Jake's needs. She unfolded them, letting him see the fancy lace and embroidery work and then waited for his next order.

"Put 'em on! One on you, the other one on the little girl."

Tying the larger of the two floor-length aprons around her waist, Leslie then signaled for Angel to come over to her. Releasing his grip, Jake shoved the child across the room and into Leslie's arms.

"I'm sorry, honey," Leslie whispered as she wrapped the apron around her small body. "I was hoping he wouldn't find you. I only wish that you'd stayed in the den." A tear forced itself from her left eye and slid down her cheek as Leslie drew Angel to her and sighed, "Oh, why didn't you just stay asleep?"

"Don't worry," Angel whispered, "it'll be OK. We're good and God will take care of us. You told me that, remember?"

Suddenly Leslie hated herself for ever trying to convince this child that faith and love were things that kept people from feeling pain. The last week was now nothing much more than a lie. It was a lot of promises, a lot of hopes, but no payoffs. As she held the child she shook her head and cried, "It's not fair."

"Shut up!" Jake's voice thundered from across the room. "You, little girl, sit down at the table.

370

And you, turn on the big burner of the stove and get that pot."

After Angel was seated, Leslie grabbed the pot and turned the electric burner up to full heat. As she did, he smiled.

Picking the almost full gallon bottle of oil from the table, he opened it and poured it all over Angel's apron. Moving over to Leslie, he splashed it all over her as well. Grinning, he then swirled the remainder of the liquid across the floor by the stove, dropping the empty plastic bottle in the middle of the mess he'd created.

"You," he pointed at Angel, "come here." Getting up from her chair, Angel obediently crossed the five steps to a point between Jake and Leslie. "OK, now put your arms around her waist, and squeeze hard. Whatever you do, don't let go."

Jake studied his work one more time, and as he continued to point the gun at Leslie, he laughed.

"It will look like nothing more than an accident," he explained. "Another house fire! It happens all the time. There will be no investigation, no search for fingerprints or DNA, and no gunshots for anyone to hear. I'll be clear and you'll be dead."

"I understand killing me," Leslie pleaded, "but she didn't do anything."

"She saw me," he barked. "That's enough."

Satisfied, he reached into his pocket and pulled

out a package of matches. He opened that box and pulled one out. Then he carefully closed it.

Leslie watched with a morbid fascination as he took the match and slowly brought it down against the side of the box. She was both relieved and shocked when the small stick of wood sparked, but didn't light. She watched as Jake reopened the matchbox and pulled out another match. As he tried again to get a light, this match broke.

Maybe Angel was right. Maybe God was working to save them.

Jake cursed as he again looked inside the box but it was empty. Throwing it down, he uttered another oath and reached into his pocket. This time he came up empty. Looking on the stove, he spied a cup filled with big kitchen matches. Moving quickly past Leslie and Angel, he reached out to grab the cup. This was the opening she needed!

Pushing the little girl toward the dining room, Leslie spun toward the stove. Jake had just managed to hook the match cup's handle with his finger when she picked up the now red-hot pan and slammed it across his wrist. His skin sizzled like frying bacon as she pushed down with the pan.

Screaming in pain, Jake stumbled as he tried to lash out at the woman and then slipped on the oil-covered floor. When Leslie raced toward the dining room door, Jake's elbow came down on the range's now empty heating element, burning his arm as it caught his shirtsleeve on fire. Pushing away from the stove with his gun, he momentarily gained his balance, but when he tried to make a move toward Leslie, he lost his footing on the oil-slick floor and fell down hard. As he did, the smoldering sleeve of his shirt, now resting in a small sea of corn oil, ignited the liquid that covered both him and the floor.

Pushing Angel through the door, Leslie turned back just in time to see the flames erupt. Reaching behind her back, she swiftly untied the apron, tossed it on the table and kicked her shoes across the room. Running around the flames and the screaming man, she opened a closet door, grabbed a fire extinguisher, and aimed it at Jake. Pulling the trigger, she filled the room with a white chemical spray. Less than a minute after it started, the fire was out.

Setting the extinguisher to the side, Leslie yanked the gun from the unconscious man's hand and ran out of the room. Finding Angel in the hall, she bent over and kissed the little girl on the forehead.

"I told you God would protect us," the little girl whispered as the two hugged.

"You were right," Leslie softly answered. "Now, can you be a big girl for me?"

Angel nodded.

"OK, I need to make a telephone call. You go

out the front door and wait on the porch. Don't go anywhere but the porch. You promise?"

"Yes."

She pushed the child toward the front door. After she'd made it to the porch, Leslie turned back toward the den. Grabbing the phone, she called 9-1-1, asking for both an ambulance and the police. Racing back through the dining room, she sized up the situation. The smoke was clearing and Jake's badly-burned body was now obviously visible. Leslie stared at him for a moment before boldly walking over to the spot where he had fallen. The closer she got the more her senses were filled with the pungent odor of burned flesh. Yet as she studied the man at her feet, he was still breathing.

What a waste. Like all people who relied solely on themselves, this man had been brought down to size. But his fall had brought her no joy.

Bowing her head she prayed loud enough for him to hear, "Dear Lord, help me be enough like You to help him."

"God, I hurt," he moaned.

Nodding her head, Leslie stared into her attacker's eyes. He was now a very pitiful creature. The fire had severely burned his upper body, including most his face. If he managed to live, he was going to be badly scarred. And with the amount of skin that had been destroyed, Leslie doubted he would last much longer. While the smell of burned flesh turned her stomach, the knowledge she was probably watching a man die, even if it was the man who scarred her for life, made her even sicker.

Looking at him, Leslie whispered, "Those who sow the wind, reap the whirlwind."

Five minutes had passed, help would surely arrive very soon, and with that help her long weeks of terror were finally ending. Looking back at Jake, she again leaned forward and whispered, "I've called for help. Someone should be here very soon. I know you must be in pain, but try to relax. It won't be much longer."

Suddenly, a puzzled look replaced the pain in his eyes. He didn't seem to understand compassion or maybe his life had been so void of love that he didn't recognize it. Either way it was so very sad.

Hearing a siren, Leslie jumped up and ran outside just in time to see a police car and rescue unit roll up, closely followed by Hunter's Jeep. Rosatelli was the first person to get to Leslie.

"What happened?" the captain demanded.

"You had the wrong guy," she explained. "The guy who attacked me came back and this time tried to kill me. His plan backfired, literally. He's in the kitchen and has been badly burned."

Leading the paramedics into the house, the captain left Leslie outside. Looking across the porch, she opened her arms and Angel raced across the wooden planks to her. Not far behind her was Hunter.

"Are you all right?" he asked.

Nodding her head, Leslie sank to her knees and hugged Angel even harder. Smiling, the little girl whispered, "I told you it would be all right."

"You sure did, honey."

A few seconds later, Rosatelli ambled out the front door. Scratching his head, he offered a far from official assessment of the situation. "I don't know if there is real justice, not here on earth anyway, but maybe there's a price that some people pay that amounts to a living hell for their crimes. The boys in there tell me that Spence might make it, barring infection. And if he does, he's burned so badly, he'll be a man without a face. All things considered, it seems like God's extracted a fair judgment."

Moments later, paramedics rushed a stretcher carrying Jake Spence to the waiting vehicle. As they drove off, Leslie picked up Angel in her arms and turned to Rosatelli. "No, Captain, what happened to him did not come about by God's hand, but rather by his own. He chose his own pain and his own downfall, and yet even now, after he's lost his face, freedom, and misplaced pride, he still has time to choose a better life and a better tomorrow."

She took a deep breath before continuing, "My scars were only skin deep, his go clear to his soul.

They are rooted there. He has probably always felt ugly. But God can heal those deeply-seated scars too."

Pushing a strand of blonde hair away from Angel's face, Leslie turned her attention back to the ambulance. "Every tragedy is either a turning point or the end. Jake is now on the cutting edge of life and I pray that he doesn't sever the ties of hope. I'm sure grateful that I found someone— make that two someones—who wouldn't let me."

Feeling Hunter's strong hands on her shoulders, even as Angel wrapped her arms tightly around Leslie's neck, she fell back into his arms. Never had Leslie Rhoads felt so secure or so needed.

73

"I didn't expect to see you today," Marsha noted as Meg walked through the employees' entrance of Springfield Community Hospital.

"Well, you notice I'm not exactly in uniform," she laughed while pointing to the red suit. "This is just one of my best outfits and I wouldn't waste it on you all."

"And pretty it is and so are you," the on-duty nurse agreed. "Now, why are you here? I thought the bridal shower was today."

"It is," Meg replied, setting her purse down on the counter, "but I forgot to take my present home last night. Left it at my station. So, I had to drive ten minutes out of my way to get it. You are coming to the wedding, aren't you?"

"Wouldn't miss it," Marsha answered. "You know, it doesn't seem possible that it's been almost a year since it happened."

"A lot has happened in those fifty-two weeks," Meg added. "Jake and his brother are locked up for a long time, they found and convicted the other gang members, and the Woodson kid is getting the help he needs too. Once he gets clean and finishes his short stretch in prison, maybe he can get his life back on the right track."

"If it hadn't been for Leslie," Marsha noted, "that boy would have gotten a much longer sentence. I don't know how she could ask the courts to forgive a kid who helped hold her down during the attack."

"Forgiveness is not easy," Meg agreed, "but somehow out of this tragic experience Leslie has made such a wonderful turnaround. Now she is going to be a bride one day, and through the miracle of love and the state courts, a mother the next. It is amazing that her pain brought hope to a hopeless child."

Marsha nodded. "I'm so glad the adoption worked out so easily. Angel couldn't have found a better mother and father for that matter. But I still can't believe Leslie, you know, doesn't lash out. She was so beautiful before this happened."

"Maybe more beautiful now," Meg said.

Meg slipped down the hall to the nurses' station, pulled her wrapped present from under the counter, and returned to Marsha. Waving, she started to leave only to be stopped by another voice belonging to Molli Cassle.

"I saw your cousin yesterday," the nurse announced as ran up and hugged Meg. "Seeing her reminded me of the shower and, of course, that reminded me of shopping. And you know how I love to shop. Can you give this to her?"

"Sure," Meg answered, "just set it on top of mine."

"Meg?" Molli's tone indicated a question was coming.

"Yes?"

"Did Leslie have another round of surgery? I couldn't believe how great she looked. I mean, I figured Parks must have done the third round while I was on vacation and no one told me. I mean, the scars are still there, but they don't jump out now. In fact, when I ran into her at the mall she was radiant."

Smiling, Meg shook her head. "No, Molli, Leslie's been too busy going to school and getting ready for the wedding to schedule it. But you're right, she does look good. I think her secret's coming from the inside and blossoming out or maybe she just isn't someone who can be scarred too deeply. Whatever it is, I know she's happy. I'm sure she is right with herself and God, and I feel she is immersed in that special kind of love few folks know. I think, my dear nurses, and heaven knows I'm not belittling our profession, but the greatest gift of healing can't be found in a hospital."

Grinning, Molli asked, "By the way, what did you get her for a wedding present? You know her better than anyone, so you probably got the perfect gift. You've got to tell us, what is it?"

Smiling, Meg answered, "A glass slipper."

"What?" Molli was stunned.

"A glass slipper." Meg giggled. As she walked toward the door, she added, "After all, could anything be more perfect for Cinderella?"

Discussion Questions

1. Leslie did not consider the opportunity to star in the perfume ad for very long before deciding to accept the offer. Who do you believe was the person most responsible for her sacrificing her principles to take the job: her agent, her mother, or Leslie herself? Why?

2. How much did Leslie's magazine cover shot have to do with what transpired in the alley? Would things have turned out differently if she had not been perceived as a famous and wealthy celebrity?

3. We don't find out what Meg told Leslie's parents when she called to let them know about the attack and Leslie's injuries. What would you have said if you had to deliver that news? What could you have told them that could have cushioned their shock?

4. Carlee, Leslie's agent, has a much different reaction to the full nature of Leslie's injuries than anyone else. Is Carlee's reaction a normal one for a woman in her profession? Do you

believe, as Carlee stated early in the book, that in the business world people are nothing more than products? And does it have to be that way for a business to make profits? Why?

5. Why do you believe that Hunter Jefferson was initially interested in reconnecting with Leslie? Was he more driven by a need for friendship, an old crush, or pity?

6. What does Hunter bring into Leslie's life that her parents do not?

7. Why is Meg so important in helping Leslie come to grips with the reality of a life without physical beauty?

8. Angel takes one look at Leslie and says, "So even if God hates you, I'm not scared of you." How common is that kind of thinking in Christian circles? Have you thought that God must hate you? Do bad things happen to people because God makes them happen? Why doesn't He stop the pain and suffering?

9. Leslie closes the curtains and hides in the dark because of her injuries. What are some other reasons people pull out of the real world and hide behind closed doors?

10. Who is more responsible for Leslie coming to grips with her condition and deciding to give life another shot? Hunter or Angel?

11. What do you see as Leslie's mother's biggest flaw? And how has the dynamic of her marriage allowed it to fester and grow?

12. Why do you believe that Leslie suddenly found the courage to face Jake?

13. What was the symbolism of Leslie feeling the need to protect Angel from Jake?

14. Was the price Jake paid at the end of the story enough? Was it fitting?

Want to learn more about author Ace Collins? Be sure to visit Ace online!

www.acecollins.com